Keeper of Coin

The Carty Sisters Series

Mary Kay Tuberty

Mantle Rock Publishing
www.MantleRockPublishing.com

2015© Mary Kay Tuberty

Published by Mantle Rock Publishing
2879 Palma Road
Benton, KY 42025
www.mantlerockpublishing.com

Printed in the United States of America

ISBN 978-0-9961734-5-2 Print Book
ISBN 978-0-9961734-6-9 Ebook

Cover by Diane Turpin, DianeTurpinDesigns.com

Published in association with Jim Hart of Hartline Literary
Agency, Pittsburg, PA

for Larry

The Keeper of Coin story grew out of a combination of family lore, the author's imagination, and the letters Anne Carty received from her family in Blackwater, Ireland. The letters are included in the tale just as they were written some one hundred and fifty years ago.
Mary Kay Tuberty

Acknowledgements

I owe supreme gratitude to:
My Carty and Duff cousins, nephews, and nieces, scattered throughout the world, with whom I share these amazing, courageous ancestors.

The folks of Blackwater, Ireland, whose culture and traditions make up such a strong part of our heritage.

My brothers and sisters: Susan and Jerry Spann, Betty and Tom Pisoni, Tom Duff, Pat and Janet Duff, Ellen and Stan Poniewaz, Mike and Joyce Duff.

My family: Larry, Dave and Mary Jo, Dan and Nancy, Jim and Kitty, Laura and Scott, Julie and Tom, and Jessica, Chris, Alex, Kyle, Nicole, Jack and Gaby.

My Friday afternoon consultants: Joe and Jerri Rabe.

Special thanks to:

Jim Hart; Hartline Literary.

Kathy Cretsinger and Diane Turpin; Mantle Rock Publishing.

Praise Be To God!

Chapter One

If no sailing vessels are coming to Victoria or San Francisco, she might come by steamer to New York and thence by steamer to San Francisco via Panama or Nicaragua. I expect this last route will be the most expensive and dangerous, but of these matters you must make enquiry and determine for yourself.

If she comes by New York, caution her to buy her ticket for California from the agents of the steamer and no one else, or she will be swindled. The runners are in the habit of selling bogus tickets and thus defrauding the passengers.

(Surviving scrap of a letter sent from James Carty, St. Helena, Oregon to John Carty, Blackwater, Ireland, Envelope postmarked November 17, 1858.)

Blackwater, County Wexford, Ireland, December, 1858

"It's settled then. Anne will go out in the spring." John Carty leaned toward the candle that flickered on the table and shifted the letter before him, rereading its contents.

7

"Ah, no, Father, it cannot be me. Julia is the oldest. She is so brave." The soup ladle slipped from Anne's hand and clattered along the worn plank floor. She had never addressed her father in such a harsh tone.

She retrieved the soup spoon from the floor, and walked back to the table to face him directly. Far from taking offense at her response, he appeared to be ignoring her words altogether. Brushing his thick, graying hair from his eyes, he continued reading his letter.

Her mother, Nell, suffered no such restraint. Shaking out the cloth resting on her lap, she gave it a brisk snap. "Go on with you, now. You're all of sixteen. A grown girl. You'll be with Uncle James in Oregon." She tossed the material into her sewing basket, and turned to Anne, her dark, blue eyes blazing. "There is no need for fretting."

Anne felt the sting of her rebuke glance across her cheeks, as if it were a physical blow.

Still, her mother went on. "Your father endeavored to prepare you children. He permitted you to attend school and taught you proper speech habits."

Ah, there was no hope for it. Anne sighed. The harangue could go on for hours, and nothing would be settled.

"And while most will teach only the lads, he saw fit to instruct you girls in bookkeeping and such."

"Yes, ma'am." She made a great show of wiping the spoon clean with a kitchen rag. If she could distract her mother's attention, she could make another appeal to Father. But no, the scolding went on.

"You joined in the talk of going out to America with as much spirit as any of the young people in Blackwater. Departure dates, travel partners, relatives already there, passage money were explored, discussed, and reviewed at every opportunity."

"I never intended to go."

Surely, she never meant to travel to America on her own. Had she not confided to Julia her hopes that, when the time came, their younger sister Kate would be old enough to go in her stead?

"Faith, child, we allowed you to tend old Mrs. Bishop and save your meager earnings, even with the funds needed here." Her mother's voice rose. Her fragile body rocked slightly. "Now, you say you do not wish to go? God help us!"

When she paused for a breath, Anne seized the moment and pushed on with her challenge to her father's astounding proclamation that she would leave Blackwater.

"Surely, you do not mean to send me." Once again, the impudence of her words made her cringe, but she persisted. "Julia longs to go to America."

All movement in the room stopped. The rain pounding against the outside walls of the cottage was the only sound that could be heard. Attempting to collect herself, Anne stood still for a moment, watching water stream down along the small front windows.

Her family had gathered around the battered, wooden table that filled half the cottage and made do as both dining room and parlor. Father sat at the head, with Mother on his right, baby Maggie to his left, and the little ones spread out at the far end.

With Father continuing to read his letter and giving no response to her pleas, a feeling of hopelessness surged through Anne. She returned to her station near the hearth where Julia and Kate waited. The three eldest Carty girls, each slight of stature, with abundant brown hair and distinctive blue eyes, arranged bowls and utensils, preparing to serve the evening meal.

"Let us begin with Jimmy." Her heart pounding, her attention distracted, Anne led them over to their young brother, who reclined a little apart from the rest in an ancient chair her father had padded for him with pieces from old quilts.

"How are you feeling?" Managing a smile for the dear child, she placed a tray across the arms of his chair. With Julia holding the unwieldy tureen, she ladled soup into his bowl, and Kate poured his tea.

"I'm fine." He grinned up at them, and they moved on to the table.

When everyone had been served, Julia and Kate slipped into their places beside their mother. Anne gathered Maggie in her arms and sat next to her father, balancing the baby on her knee. Her gaze moved along the far end of the table. Even the little ones seemed to grasp the importance of the letter Father held and sense the tension in the air. No tiny arms jostled the table, no giggles escaped, and no stern looks were needed from their big sister this evening.

After a brief prayer of thanksgiving, the family settled in to eat the thin broth. The younger children did not enjoy the cabbage soup, but Anne had learned to tolerate it. If she managed to ignore the sharp scent such as the one now filling the entire cottage and the tanginess of the initial taste, a sweet, satisfying reward would come with the second sip. There would be no time for lingering over tastes and sips tonight, however. She had taken only her first spoonful, when Father pushed his letter aside.

"How much have you saved, Julia?"

"Near five pounds, sir." Julia pressed her lips together and lowered her eyes.

"Anne?"

"You know, Father. Twelve pounds, in my cracker tin on the shelf."

"I planned all along you and Julia would go to America together." He retrieved a bank voucher folded inside the letter and held it up for their inspection. "This note Uncle James sent will not be enough for two fares."

"With Anne in America, will our Maggie have her own chair?" Young Michael spoke out from the children's end of the table.

"Hush, son." Father's voice sounded stern, but Anne noticed his brief smile. Her own tension subsided some, and for a fleeting moment, even Julia's face appeared to relax a bit. Then, Father spoke again.

"You will go, Anne. I will inquire after possible travel companions and make the arrangements." He turned toward her older sister. "Julia will continue to save her coins and join you next year."

Julia's distress and the depth of her disappointment were etched across her face. Always ready to climb higher, run faster, push a little beyond, she was the adventurous one. Yet, Anne must concede the wisdom of her father's decision. Her dear sister, whom she loved above anyone on earth, could act impulsively at times.

She tried another approach. "How can I leave the children?"

"They will miss you, it's certain, but there is naught I can do." Her father threw up his hands. Desperation clouded his usually clear, blue eyes. "I must call upon Julia and Kate to extend their already great efforts and take your place with them. Our situation is dire. These children will not survive if they remain here.

"You must go out to America, seek employment, and save every penny to help me transport them out of this misery."

The likelihood that Anne could remain in her beloved, familiar home appeared to be slipping away. She felt as if a heavy weight had been placed across her shoulders, the burden pushing her down. Defeat hovered all about her. "I prayed we could harvest sufficient food."

"Even if we could feed everyone, little medicine is available. We cannot depend on Aunt Mary's cures to ease Jimmy's labored breathing. If he grows weaker, or illness strikes the others—" Father looked toward little Jimmy, now dozing in his chair, and the slight shake of his head wrenched Anne's heart.

And yet, she was not ready to leave her home and family, sail to an unfamiliar land, and live among strangers. The idea of it, now sinking deeper into her awareness, made her tremble. Then too, she could not imagine being apart from the little ones. The babies had been her particular charge since birth, and she held a special love for each one. These thoughts of the children caused a new and different stirring within her. Could she deprive her brothers and sisters of a chance for a decent life?

Still another truth entered her mind and heart. She would surely not be able to deny anything her father asked of her. She turned back to him, and—

Kate, who had been seated directly across the table from Anne, now lurched forward. She had been following the conversation, her expression severe. Anne watched in horror as, leaning on one elbow, she tilted toward Father, coming within inches of his face. "Sean Flynn's father says 'tis the fault of the dirty Brits."

Her mother glared at the girl. "Mind your tongue, miss."

Kate rose from her chair and stomped away from the table, her heels pounding on each rung as she climbed the ladder to the sleeping loft. Though she raised her arm to shield her face, every inch of the tiny cottage was in clear view from the table and Anne needed only to raise her eyes to see Kate's expression. She observed the disdainful look that crossed her sister's face moments before she threw herself down on the nearest straw pallet.

The exchange did not distract her father's attention. It seemed nothing would divert him from carrying out his mission. He reached for Anne's hand. "Do you understand the sacrifices I am demanding of you? I am asking you to set aside your own dreams and make a home for the children in America. I must have your promise, my dear. Their fate now rests with you."

Silence fell over the room once again. All eyes turned to Anne.

She brushed her fingers through Maggie's silky hair, and then wrapped her in a strong hug. After placing a kiss on the baby's soft cheek, she jumped up from her chair and handed her over to her father. Moving to the hearth, she lifted a heavy dish pan from the shelf and hung it on a hook above the fire. Julia rushed to help. She held the pan steady, while Anne poured well water from the bucket they had drawn earlier in the day.

Retrieving the cake of soap and small knife hidden behind the hearth, she began shaving slivers into the water. She worked vigorously, her hands moving in pace with each new thought, a mound of soap flakes accumulating across the top of the water. Father expressed faith in her abilities, but was she capable of accomplishing this daunting task now placed before her? She did not share his strong confidence.

What Uncle James had written of his life in Oregon concerned climate, crops, and cattle. His letters described the vast forests and the growing lumber industry. He made scant mention of his home or other buildings or dwellings nearby. No details had been forthcoming about positions suitable for a young girl, or costs of anything. How could she acquire enough money to establish a home for her five sisters and two brothers? The entire idea was beyond her comprehension.

Her attention diverted, the knife slipped and nicked her finger.

Julia stepped closer, and taking the soap and knife from her hands, she placed them back on the shelf. When she turned toward her again, Anne surrendered her injured finger to her sister's ministrations. As Julia placed the hem of her apron on the cut and pressed down, she whispered in her ear.

"Will you go?"

"I suppose I must."

"What about James Duff?" Julia asked. "I saw you talking with him after church. Is he sweet on you?"

"He was just being friendly." Anne felt a blush rise from her neck to her cheeks. "He has already returned to school in Dublin. I'll likely never see him again.

"If only, you were going with me." Anne sighed. "Do I have any choice in the matter, at all?"

"Pray for guidance."

This same sister she had just minutes ago dismissed as being flighty had set aside her own grave disappointment to offer her solace and counsel. Anne leaned close to Julia, accepting the comfort she offered. Her turmoil eased for a brief interval, long enough for her to recognize the wisdom of her sister's words.

She, who always meant to do things on her own, must turn to her Father in heaven for help.

Anne bowed her head. Willing her mind and body to be quiet, she prayed silently. *Father, help me accomplish this impossible mission.* A long, soft sigh escaped her, and then she continued. *I place my trust in You.*

Her days as a hard-working daughter of the house had come to an end. She turned back to the table, where her father sat waiting. Managing a weak smile, she placed her hand in his and bowed to his wishes.

"I understand, Father. I will go."

Chapter Two

St. Louis, Missouri, U.S.A., June, 1859

"Is it you then, Anne? Anne Carty?"

Anne leaned out across the ferry's rail and searched the sparse crowd. They had pulled abreast of the landing, so close she could almost touch people lined along the edge of the cobbled riverfront.

A tall, broad-shouldered gentleman, who stood off to the side, raised his arm in greeting, catching her attention. Beside him, a short, round-faced woman waved a handkerchief and once again called out her name.

Anne turned to Edward Donahoo and his sister, Grace, her travel companions. "The tall gentleman resembles old Mr. Dempsey back home, does he not? They must be his nephew and niece."

"Ah, faith. No one will be meeting us," Grace said. "We will be left here to wander the streets alone, catching our death. And, there's an end to it." Grace stamped her feet, shaking dust and grime from her shoes and the hem of her cloak. "I cannot go on much longer, that's the truth." She lowered her head, brushing at her tears with her fingertips.

"There, there, my dear. Do not fret." Edward reached out and patted his sister's arm. "See now, the folks out on the wharf are signaling us again. It is the Dempseys, I'm sure." He joined Anne in returning their waves. "We are blessed to have someone from our homeland here to meet us. Haven't they already offered you a place to stay? And now, they've come to conduct you to their home. They must be fine people."

As Anne extended her arm in greeting once again, the ferry rocked. A great splash of water rose above the wooden slats that formed the sides of the vessel and provided their sole protection from the elements. Anne held her valise high and attempted to lift her skirts. It was no use. She watched, help-less, as the foul Mississippi River water rushed toward them, flooding the deck and adding a new layer of mud to her shoes and clothing.

Several men hurried from the wharf to tie the ferry to the dock. The tears and the muck receded from her attention as the vessel continued to bump against the pier. People all around her slipped and stumbled. Mothers gathered their children close. Men hastened to retrieve the bags and belongings roll-ing all about.

Anne spied a corner of a bench that jutted out beneath a wall of crates and baggage. Choosing to suffer soaking feet and skirts in favor of a place to rest and a firm grasp of a trunk handle, she sat down.

"Come Grace, sit here with me a moment and rest." When the girl shook her head, Anne eased herself back, settling against a crate. A spot at the base of her neck had begun to ache, and she took a moment to collect herself. When had she last tasted food?

Early yesterday morning, while hurrying for the train, they had paused a moment to purchase a loaf of bread. Once they were settled in their seats and Edward removed the wrapping, they discovered the bread crust covered with mold. When he broke the loaf open, she and Grace looked on in horror, as tiny, fluttering insects swarmed all about. She had tasted only small bites of street vendor's wares from then on.

For a few moments, things all around her appeared calm. Anne relaxed, thinking the ferry had been secured. A strong thump interrupted her respite. And then another shook the entire ferry. After a moment, the vessel shuddered and banged into the dock once again.

"Oh my word, we will all be thrown into the river and drown." Grace stumbled and nearly unseated Anne. "I will never see my Will again." Tears streamed from the girl's sad eyes and soaked her pale cheeks. She made no attempt to cover them now.

Anne moved to the edge of the bench and pulled the poor, wretched girl down beside her. "Come dear, we will brace ourselves against this turmoil."

Her father had chosen the Donahoos as her travel partners, believing she would be more secure with Grace as a companion and her brother Edward a protector. Protection perhaps, she mused, but little comfort could be gleaned from Grace's company. Hadn't the poor creature girl cried throughout the crossing and along the dreadful train ride from New York City, because she had been forced to leave her betrothed William Stapleton behind?

"My father," she had explained to Anne on more than one occasion, "provided the means for my journey, but he made one provision. He insisted I travel in the company of my brother and leave Will to journey to America on his own.

"It will take him a full year to save passage money." Grace had muttered the same complaints, over and over. "Will is a world away. I'll never set eyes on him again."

Anne felt sympathetic at the outset. Grace, two years her senior, was Julia's dear friend, after all. But day after day of her whimpering, which droned on with the endless rocking of the ship, tried her patience. She, too, had begun to wish for Mr. Stapleton's swift arrival.

Grace now fixed her eyes on her shoes. With her wispy, brown hair blown against her pale face and her frail body engulfed in an ill-fitting coat, she appeared too delicate to have survived the arduous trip.

Anne attempted to direct the girl's attention elsewhere. "Let us look out over St. Louis, your new home."

"I wish you were to stay here as well. Whatever will I do on my own, with Edward gone on to the seminary and you off to Oregon?"

"I will be with you at the Dempseys' home, until I establish contact with my uncle."

Anne leaned her head back, but there were no more opportunities for rest. They were jolted about by more shakes and thuds, as the ferry continued to pitch.

An eerie, creaking noise erupted above their heads. Anne looked to the wall of trunks behind them. Unsettled by the bumping and crashing against the wharf, the containers began to shift. Edward reacted quickly, pulling the girls to safety. Then, he jumped on the bench and braced the crates with his arms. Several men rushed forward to lend their help, rearranging the boxes and carriers until the stack appeared steady again.

While the men were working on the crates, the rocking and banging stopped. The ferry now stood firmly moored against the dock. As the crew pulled back the cumbersome, wooden gate, a hush of anticipation fell over the crowd.

"Move along! Hurry on!" The men shouted and cajoled, urging the passengers to proceed ashore.

Anne and Grace headed toward the ramp with Edward right behind them. Without any notice, Anne's knees grew weak. She reached out and grasped the railing for support.

"Are you unwell?" Edward took a firm grip of her arm.

"I felt only a mild tremor. It is naught but weariness."

While they waited for the ferry to be tied down, the crowd on the riverfront had continued to grow. Anne stepped forward with the Donahoos now, looking out over a steady stream of people approaching from all directions. To her dismay, the Dempseys had become lost in the throng. With Grace's cries occupying Edward's attention, Anne searched the mass of faces before her. At last, she discovered them again.

"I am Anne—"

As she extended her arm in a wave, the people in the crowd appeared to jump every which way. Their voices rose to a great pitch. Anne struggled to compose herself. She tried to ignore the ache at the back of her neck, now grown to a powerful thudding sensation, and persisted in her effort to gain the Dempseys' notice. She pushed aside the numbness creeping through her body. Summoning every remaining ounce of her strength, she called out to them once more.

"Mr. Dempsey! Miss Demp—" Everything went black.

When she recovered her senses, she found herself stretched out on the ground. Above her loomed the faces of Edward and Grace and the two people she presumed to be the Dempseys. They were gathered around in an apparent attempt to shield her from the noisy, jostling crowd.

"Praise be, she has fallen into a stupor." Grace held a handkerchief out to Anne, and then pulled back and pressed it to her own eyes to halt another rush of tears.

"What will I do for you, Anne?" Edward's face loomed before her. His strong features grew large and distorted, and then bobbed away from her, then drifted back.

While Anne attempted to raise herself to a sitting position, the small lady eased Edward aside. "I am Mary Dempsey, Miss Carty. This is my brother, Walter." She knelt on the ground beside her. "Are you able to stand, my dear? We must move you out of this desperate throng."

"Yes...please help me up...I have strength enough." Again, she struggled to rise. Walter Dempsey offered his arm, but her legs would not support her. Spots danced before her eyes and the entire riverfront scene blurred. When she slumped to the ground again, Walter bent, lifted her into his arms, and urged the little group forward.

They made their way through the crowd, Anne finding her face so close to Walter's she could measure the sweep of his eyelashes. She blinked her eyes shut, still a little confused. After a few seconds, curiosity won out over discomfiture. She raised her eyelids a bit and cast a glance off to the side. If she eased her head a little to the left and made no quick movements, her eyesight cleared. Walter held her high off the ground, but she could see his sister beside them, hurrying to keep up with his great strides. She could not see the Donahoos, but she could hear them conversing right behind her. Grace sniffled and whimpered, and Edward continued to soothe her.

They must have made an unusual party, but no one gave them notice. An assortment of trunks, crates, and carriers were being thrown down in rows along the wharf. People called out, searching for friends or loved ones. In the midst of the melee, hawkers moved through the mass of people. Strong spicy scents Anne did not recognize and heavy greasy smells, perhaps pork or some type of sausage, drifted toward her, all blending together as the peddlers pushed past, selling their wares.

They left the riverfront and entered a wide avenue filled with horses and mules pulling carriages and wagons of every size and description. They followed the stream of pedestrians, keeping to the side of the road to avoid being trampled. Her eyes met Walter's, and again she looked down. He must imagine me feeble, and Mary must be dismayed to find what sorry boarders she has acquired, one in a constant fit of tears, the other unable to stand on her own feet. She grimaced with the shame of it. She had never considered herself delicate. Hadn't she often begun her day's chores at home with a meager cup of tea and a crust of bread shared with her sisters? Sure, she had never fainted in her life before. Why had her strength failed her now?

"We'll have you home in no time." Mary looked up at Anne and smiled. "'Tis not far."

Anne nodded and tried to return the smile. Though her limbs remained a bit numb, her headache had lessened and her vision cleared. With the sharpening of her senses came the awareness of Walter's hands on her person and the brush of their bodies with each step he took. A flush of new embarrassment swelled within her. She wished for the blackness to come again, but she would receive no such reprieve.

Even in her weakened state, she could not help but observe the Dempseys' fine appearance. Walter and his sister wore simple, well-made clothing. Mary's light-weight dress looked fresh and clean, and his starched shirt had been scrubbed to a brilliant white—*oh my word, my muddy shoes and the wet hem of my skirt must even now be soiling it.* Clothes notwithstanding, Walter and Mary looked healthy and robust. They presented a sharp contrast against the hollow cheeks, pale complexions, and threadbare attire of her little traveling party. The Dempseys must have prospered here in America.

Walter's pace changed as they entered a narrower road and now climbed a slight hill. After progressing a short way, they stopped before an imposing stone and brick church. Anne looked up at the enormous cross stretched from the rooftop toward the drifting clouds and marveled at its beauty. She pulled her attention back to her companions, as Edward extended his hand to Walter and then Mary and thanked them for providing shelter for his sister. Turning from the Dempseys, he shifted his attention to her.

"Goodbye, Anne. I pray you will soon be restored to health."

"I offer my thanks to you, Edward, for all you have done for me. I could never begin to convey my gratitude for the kindness you extended and the security your presence offered during our long difficult journey." To her dismay, her voice sounded weak and foolish. She realized her present awkward position, held high off the ground in Walter Dempsey's arms, provided little opportunity for a serious word with him. Still, she felt her obligation keenly, and she tried once more to express her appreciation. "I—"

Edward, however, was otherwise occupied. Walter had gained his attention, pointing out the rectory where he would be staying.

Grace's whimpers increased, and Edward turned his full consideration to his sister. "Farewell, for now, my girl. Please do not weep. Anne and the Dempseys will care for you, and I will come to you as soon as I am able."

Edward patted Grace's shoulder and repeated his promise of frequent visits, but she continued to sob. When he dropped her arm and headed off, Anne imagined she heard a sigh of relief escape from him. In the next instant, she was overcome with shame. She had been the impatient one, while Edward had extended fine care to Grace. She renewed her resolve to find an opportunity to state her appreciation to him properly.

They had come to a standstill on the street, and Edward was moving away, disappearing quickly from their sight. Wishing to have her feet firmly planted on the ground again, Anne took advantage of their pause. She cleared her throat and attempted to sound firm.

"I believe I will be able to stand now."

Walter nodded, and with great care, lowered her to the ground. He placed his arm at her waist for support, while she took a few tentative steps.

At the same time, his sister relieved the weeping Grace Donahoo of her reticule. "Now, my dear, there will be no need for tears. We'll care for you." Mary took a firm hold of Grace's arm, and they began to move again.

After climbing what seemed an endless hill, they rounded a sharp corner. Mary pointed toward a brick building standing before them, so vast it encompassed an entire lane. "Here we are, then."

At last, they had arrived.

A sign, extended across the top of the square shop window and narrow front door, proclaimed the establishment to be *Dempsey's Bakery*. The size of the place amazed Anne. They had passed many tall buildings in New York City, but she never imagined her stay in St. Louis would be in such an imposing place.

They crossed the road, and Walter pushed open the door and ushered them all through the high narrow entry. Once inside, Anne found a warm cheerful shop occupying a small area at the front of the building. The scent of freshly baked bread filled the air, but she had little time to savor the aroma. Her attention was captured by the group of women crowded into the room. To her surprise, she discovered they were immigrants from Ireland themselves, all come to greet Grace and her.

While Mary Dempsey made the introductions, the women surrounded the two newcomers and plied them with questions.

A tiny woman took hold of her arm. "Aye, ya poor girl, you have come at last. It is a frightful, long journey, is it not?"

"Yes—"

Before Anne could finish, another woman, wearing a faded blue dress nearly covered by a woolen shawl, pushed her way through the group and interrupted her answer. "And, what towns did you pass through on your way to Cork?" Tears filled her eyes, as she spoke. "My home is in Macroom. Have you family living near there?"

"No, I—"

"What will you tell us of the sad conditions of our homeland? And our lovely hillsides, are they green as ever they were?"

The strong blue eyes bore into Anne's soul, bringing an image of her mother before her. She hugged her arms to her person to sooth the onslaught of pain that came, unbidden and unexpected, with the talk of Ireland and the reminder of her dear ones there. It would not do to be discourteous, though. The poor woman sought a connection with someone who held a recent touch of home. Anne knew her anguish.

She answered the woman's questions as best she could. Then, noticing Grace edging herself out of the crowd, she pushed away her own distress and moved slowly through the group, speaking with each of the women, attempting to answer their questions and satisfy their need to hear about home. Then, Mary called for everyone's attention, interrupting their talk.

"God provided this beautiful summer day, don't you know, and their trunks had already been delivered." Mary looked all around the room, warming to her story. "Walter and I made the foolish decision to forsake the carriage and walk to the riverfront—"

While Mary talked, Anne felt the heat of the crowded room close in around her. The women standing nearby, the bakery walls, the doorways and shelves commenced to swirl about. She made her way toward the center of the shop and leaned against the counter. Her attempt to steady herself did not go unnoticed, though. Mary broke off her storytelling and rushed to her aid.

"Come now, let us settle you in." She separated Anne and Grace from the women and guided them toward the stairway. "Sure, I can see you need rest. And, a cup of strong broth will build your strength."

As Anne took hold of the sturdy, wooden banister and lifted one shoe toward the first step, her knees trembled. Then, the entire stairway moved—

"Summon the doctor." Anne heard Walter call out directions as darkness crept around her once again. She felt his strong grip, as he knelt down to rescue her.

Chapter Three

St. Helen, Oregon
5*th* August, 1859
Miss Anne Carty

My Dear Niece,
 I have a letter from your Father dated
Blackwater, June 14*t,h* 1859, informing me you
started in company with a young woman of your
acquaintance for Saint Louis, and he was to re-
mit you money to pay your expense out here. I
have also a letter from Mr. Fortune conveying
the pleasing intelligence of your safe arrival at
Saint Louis and stating you would remain there
until you heard from me, all of which is satisfactory.
 I anticipate that ere this reaches Saint
Louis, you will have received from your father
funds enough to pursue your journey. To guard
against any contingency which might arise and
to hasten your arrival, I have made arrangements to send by Wells Fargo & Co. Express,
one hundred dollars to be paid to you in Saint
Louis.
 It is my earnest request that you will start
by way of New Orleans and Nicaragua to San

Francisco, from which place the steamer leaves semi-monthly for this point, and place yourself under the protection of a gentleman with a family coming to San Francisco. This appears to be the best route you can come as it will consume less time than via Panama, and you will be less subjected to sea sickness. Of course, you will be somewhat guided by the advice of Mr. Fortune who has a better means of knowing the least expensive and most pleasant way to come. Of the money I send you, I desire you to use all necessary toward paying your expenses and refund any sums Mr. Fortune may have advanced you.

If however, you already have ample funds for those purposes, I desire you to deposit the $100 with Wells Fargo & Co. in Saint Louis and take a certificate of deposit which you can bring out with you.

I cannot close this letter, my dear niece, without expressing my earnest desire to have you with me as soon as may be and the hope that you will have a safe journey out.

Please present my regards to Mr. Fortune and tell him he has placed me under many obligations by his kindness towards you. With best love I remain, your affectionate uncle,
James Carty

October, 1859

Anne rose from her bed at 5:00a.m., dressed, and prepared for her day of work in Dempsey's Bakery. She recited Psalm 7 with the undergarments and stockings. She began Psalm 8, *"O Lord, our Lord, how glorious..."* as she pulled her thin, gray dress over her head and fastened the row of tiny buttons. She continued on through Psalm 9, while she tied a starched bakery apron at her waist.

The routine brought to mind early morning contests with her sisters back home—Julia always finished first—and her mother's fierce scowl, and the writing out of the *Ten Commandments* she assigned if she caught them at their game.

Taking no time for a candle, Anne worked by the dim light that slipped through the small windows across from the bed. She hastened to straighten the quilt and return her few possessions to order. She smoothed the cover of the second bed and dusted the wardrobe, the writing table, and her trunk. Taking a moment, she inhaled the freshness of the tiny, attic room scrubbed fresh and clean, from ceiling to windows to walls and wooden floors, just a few days before. Mother would approve.

Her eyes roamed the cozy room. Things had changed rapidly in the first weeks after her arrival. She regained her strength, and she had begun to help out in the bakery when the shop girl departed abruptly.

"We would like to offer you the position," Mary Dempsey had said.

"Of course, I need the work," Anne said, "but you do realize I will only remain here until I receive word from my Uncle James?"

"We will be happy to have you for as long as you wish to stay." Mary's assurances had settled the matter.

The attic room, designated for the shop girl had come to her. Until a new roommate arrived, Anne was on her own. Reflecting on her good fortune, she hid the dust cloth beneath the bed and gave the room one last look. Reaching across to the desktop, she retrieved her uncle's letter, already worn from many readings. Pushing the folded sheets into her apron pocket, she headed for the stairway.

She flew down the first flight of stairs, pausing for a breath in the shadowy second floor hallway. Toward the front of the house were two doors, one to Walter's bedroom and the other to his sister Mary's room. At the rear, another, wider door, set into a low archway, led to a larger room where the other Dempsey girls stayed.

At times, this room housed as many as eight young women from Ireland. Four resided there at present. Cara, the senior member of the group, helped Mary with meals and cleaning. Ellen and Kitty were employed at a nearby garment factory. The fourth girl, her old friend, Grace Donahoo, now worked at the St. Vincent's Mission. Anne prayed the pleasant company of the other girls would raise Grace's spirits. As week after week passed, her tears had slowed. Grace's gray eyes remained sad, though, and her long, thin face never lightened with a smile. Anne wondered if she would ever be able to cast off the gloom.

"Sure you are in good time." Mary Dempsey called out a greeting as Anne hurried through the doorway to the bakery shop. "Come have a cuppa before we begin our long day." The short, brown curls escaping from beneath Mary's cap were damp, and her round face appeared flushed, but she welcomed Anne with a grand smile.

"I thank you kindly, Mary." She accepted the tea and a thick, golden biscuit from Mary's tray. "The rolls smell wonderful." Pausing to enjoy her first sip and her first bite, she listened to the early morning sounds of the bakery. Walter and his workers, busy in the oven room in the back of the building, banged doors and dropped trays on counters. Snatches of the men's conversation, along with the enticing aroma of their baked goods, drifted out to the shop.

Without warning, a picture of home slipped into her mind—an image of her sisters beginning their long work day with no more than sips of weak tea and bits of bread to sustain them. Her earlier good spirits plummeted. She attempted to push the desperate vision away and halt the comparison that rushed in behind it.

Her longing for home had developed into a sharp pain she tried to bury deep within her being and hold at bay throughout her days and nights. Drawing herself up, she determined she would not allow herself to indulge in this melancholy. She could not spare the time. Mary Dempsey and her brother Walter had treated her with kindness and generosity, inviting her to stay in their home and offering her a position. She may not have survived without their care, and she intended to repay them in the best manner available to her: with dedication and hard work. Taking a deep breath, she willed the sadness away.

Mary noticed her hesitation, Anne knew, but she continued on, pretending nothing was amiss. "Do not have a care, Mary. I will be fine. It is only that, at times, my family's difficult lives matched against my situation in this bright, cozy bakery cause a tear to escape despite my attempt to suppress it."

"Sure, that's good to know. Let us finish our tea, and then you must tell me about your dear mam and your sisters as we prepare the shop for opening."

They went right to work, transferring goods left from the day before to a narrow wooden table at the adjacent wall, where they would be sold at half-price. They scrubbed each bare table and shelf, as they emptied it.

She had just finished telling Mary a story about winning a footrace against Julia—"After the race, the two of us searched for hair ribbons, to smooth back our hair and avoid a scolding from our mother."—when she realized suddenly that she was feeling better.

As if by prearranged signal, Walter and his helpers began bringing their freshly-baked goods from the oven room. The men were dressed all in white, with long aprons wrapped at their waists. Their arms balanced trays high in the air, the miniature parade lacking precision yet brimming with enthusiasm and good humor.

Anne and Mary worked to keep pace, removing rolls and biscuits from the trays, placing them on the long, narrow counter in the center of the store, and loading the bread in bins along the back wall.

They stacked iced cakes and pastries in the shop window, delicacies Anne had learned the bakery prepared for hotels and other business customers. The Irish immigrants of the neighborhood, clinging to familiar touches of home, preferred the simple soda bread and biscuits to such fancy fare.

When the counter and shelves were filled, the men returned to the oven room.

Mary collected the last of the empty trays and turned her attention to Anne. "I'll move on back to my work table now. Since you wrap and make change with the skill of a Dempsey, there's no need for me to linger. It's back to my accounts I must go—"

Voices raised in an intense conversation spilled forth from the dining room, causing Anne and Mary to look to each other in alarm. A moment later, Mr. Dermot Fortune appeared in the doorway.

She had encountered Fortune on but few occasions, the first being at church on the Sunday after her arrival in the city. Her severe initial impression of him—tall and thin, long, stringy, black hair and beard, and cold sinister eyes—had been reinforced each time she met him since, the present moment included. With only his head and shoulders visible, he appeared to dangle sideways from the door frame like a marionette. The menacing look in his eyes sent a chill along Anne's spine.

"I say there, Miss Carty, have you received further funds from your father or uncle?"

"No sir, I have not." Her first customer of the day had arrived, and while she wrapped the young woman's bread, she looked away from him for a moment. She counted out change, extended a brief thank you, and then turned back to Mr. Fortune, but he had disappeared.

"Please wait, sir." She called out to him in the strongest voice she could muster. "I must speak with you."

She turned to Mary. "May I try to overtake him? I must know if he has secured my passage to Oregon."

"Of course, child, run after him. Wait, I'll come too. Will I not be of service, if I stand on his boots while you speak with him?"

They rushed through the dining room, oven room, and out into the back passage, but their efforts proved futile. He had vanished.

"I am outraged." Mary took several deep breaths, as they retraced their steps and returned to the shop. "Such a display of poor manners. Why has your family entrusted your funds to such a person?"

"I am not certain. Somehow, they believe Mr. Fortune has tended to my needs since I arrived in St. Louis. They consider themselves indebted to him for his kindness."

"He must fill his letters to his family in Blackwater with tales of his good deeds." Mary's breathing had returned to normal and her words came freely now, but disdain filled her voice. "Sure, he did not show an abundance of helpfulness when he learned of your impending arrival. He came here to convince Walter—he does not deign to speak directly to me, you see—that we should fetch you at the ferry."

"What a blessing for me."

"Well, we had already learned of your coming from our aunt and uncle in Blackwater and we planned to meet you. We needed no persuasion from the likes of Dermot Fortune." Mary unfolded a white cloth and began to move baked goods aside and apply a brisk rub to the already spotless glass countertop.

"His want of concern is the least of it. I worry his business dealings are not the best. While working out here in the shop, I've heard reports casting an unfavorable shadow over his integrity. You must convey our reservations about Mr. Fortune to your parents and implore them to post no further funds to him."

Walter entered the shop from the oven room, his sturdy frame filling the doorway, his solid appearance and steady manner a marked contrast to Mr. Fortune's leaning and weaving. He removed his baker's hat and wiped his hands with his apron.

"I apologize for Fortune's behavior, Anne. He lacks manners, it's sure. He did leave a message for you. The fare to Oregon has increased and the funds you received from your uncle will not be sufficient to take you out west." Walter shook his head, and he and Mary exchanged glances before he turned back to Anne.

"I am sorry I cannot tell you more. I demanded Fortune stay and discuss this matter of passage with you. I offered to take your place out here while he did, but he insisted he must rush off."

Anne stepped back from the counter, stunned. Willing herself to remain calm, she looked from Walter to Mary. "He possesses information that could alter my entire life, and he would not spare even a moment to discuss it with me. Whatever will I do now?"

"You will hold your position here and remain a part of our family until you are prepared to leave," Mary said. "In the short time you have been here, you have become an asset to Dempsey's."

"I had no idea I would remain in St. Louis for so long" Anne felt the need for reassurance. She could not hold back her words. "Are you certain my indefinite stay is agreeable?"

"'Tis a comfort to have you with us, and I mean every word of it. Haven't Walter and I said many times already, how pleased we are with the fine assistance you have given us?

"Have no care," Mary said. "While you gather the needed funds, you will have some time here for proper meals and a good rest. Then, you will be bursting with impatience to go on. I'm sure of it."

Walter added his encouragement. "We will do all we can to help you, Anne. Meanwhile, you must not place any more of your savings under Fortune's control." Walter shifted his feet, looking uncomfortable. "I hesitate to put myself forward, but in this instance, I believe I must. I do not trust Fortune."

"I agree with you. It is just that I hesitate to go against my father's wishes. I will write to Father immediately and explain what you are proposing. I thought I would be on my way to Oregon by now. I did not realize there would be such weighty decisions to make.

"In truth, I am more than a little reluctant to set out." She favored the Dempseys with the strongest smile she could muster. How warm and kind they were, and how comfortable the life they provided for her here at the bakery had become. On the other hand, she barely remembered Uncle James, and she dreaded the uncertainty of what her life with him would hold. Still, Father had directed her to travel to Oregon and she intended to follow his instructions. At the same time, she appreciated the good fortune of a delay. Her smile continued to grow.

❀ ❀ ❀

Anne worked alone in the shop throughout most of the day. The steady stream of customers wanting her attention allowed few idle moments for contemplation.

At the first momentary lull, she slipped Uncle James' recent letter from her pocket and began to unfold it. A sudden rush of wind rattled the window and the door, delaying her reading and announcing the arrival of her favorite customer.

Mrs. Delia Flynn, a tiny, cheerful, and energetic lady, placed her shopping basket on the counter. "Two bread, please, and I'll thank you for it."

Anne removed the smooth, white cloths Mrs. Flynn carried in her basket, unfolded them, and began to wrap the choicest of the loaves for her.

"Now tell me, my dear, how are you faring? I met Walter outside and he told me of your visit from Mr. Fortune. Has that great eejit upset you?"

"The matter of going on to Oregon crossed my mind a time or two today, I cannot deny it," Anne said. "After Mr. Fortune left this morning, Walter checked with the steamer agents, and what he said is true, the passage has increased. Walter also intends to inquire about prices and schedules of wagon trains, but—"

"She's much better than on the day she arrived here." Mary returned to the shop, in time to hear a part of their conversation, but only enough to misunderstand it.

"We were not speaking of my falling ill on the riverfront, Mary," Anne said. "Mrs. Flynn is concerned I am distressed over my visit from Mr. Fortune. She worries I have taken leave of my senses, is all."

"Ah, go on with you. I said no such thing." Mrs. Flynn laughed with her.

Mary, bent on her tale, would not be distracted by their frivolity. When she appeared ready to continue with the story of her collapse on the riverfront, Anne tried again to change the course of the conversation.

"The pitiful state of my health that day will distress Mrs. Flynn, Mary. We do not want to burden her with the sorry tale again."

Anne was relieved, when Mary relented a little and moved to the more pleasant part of the story. "Ah now, in the end all was well. In a weeks' time, our Anne regained her strength and begged to be allowed to walk about, eat with the other girls, and do some work."

"I could not bear the idleness."

"But still," Mrs. Flynn reached out and patted her cheek, "you are a bit pale."

"My dears, I appreciate your concern," Anne favored each of her new friends with a tiny curtsy, "but I assure you, there is no cause for worry. I am strong and vigorous as ever I have been."

"Well, at least for now, I will agree that you appear healthy and untroubled." Mrs. Flynn nodded, as she pulled a book from under her arm.

"I've near forgotten my purpose in coming today. I am here to offer you *Pride and Prejudice,* my favorite story in the entire world."

"Oh thank you." Anne accepted the book and couldn't resist looking through it, brushing her fingers across the pages. "I have read many fine accounts of the works of Jane Austen."

Mrs. Flynn grinned up at Anne. "I am surrounded by fine people at home, saints each one to abide my foolishness, but there's not a reader in the bunch. Before I discovered Mary

Dempsey to be a great reader, it had been years since I enjoyed the friendship of someone who shares my love for books. Now that you have come to join our group, perhaps we could discuss this story after you and Mary have an opportunity to enjoy it?"

"Of course, we will review it." Anne handed the book to Mary, as Mrs. Flynn took up her basket and headed for the door.

"Thank you again for this grand treat," Anne said.

"We will begin reading right away." Mary tucked the book in her apron pocket. "Then, we'll settle in around the teapot and have a grand chin wag over Miss Austen's story."

Chapter Four

Blackwater
22ⁿᵈ September, 1859

My dear child,
*   We hasten to acknowledge receipt of your*
welcome letter. We are rejoiced at your recovery
from ill health and beg you to return our thanks
to those friends who sheltered and attended to
your wants in the hour of need. Present our
thanks to Mr. Fortune, to Walter Dempsey and
sister, to Miss Donahoo and brother and all we
can do is pray for their welfare. We are sorry
to hear of the uncertainty of your departure for
Oregon. The voyage will be expensive from St.
Louis and I wish we could be of help to you. It
is kind of your Uncle James to send you mon-
ey toward your passage and we hope, my dear,
when you do reach him you will do all in your
power to repay him.
*   Before leaving St. Louis, write to us and*
let us know what route you will travel. Is it all a
sea voyage or across the Isthmus of Panama or
an overland journey?
*   My dear child, I am happy to inform you*
your mother's health is good. Kate is at your

Uncle Martin's. He and family and Aunt Mary
are well and send their love to you. Julia is at
home. We all thank God in the enjoyment of
good health. John Donahoo and family are in
good health. James Dempsey and family are
well. We had a drought here this summer in
consequence of which the potato and barley
crops are short.
  Your mother, sisters, and brothers and I
join in sending our love,
    John Carty

When evening came and closing time approached, Anne
began to cover the few items remaining on the counters and
shelves. Before she finished, Mary appeared with two bulky
wicker baskets. "You begin with the day-old goods, Anne," she
said." I will add fresh bread to the top." When the baskets had
been filled, Mary stood back and allowed Anne to fasten the
lids.

Anne put on her cloak and took up her burden. "I'll hurry
right back," she called to Mary, as she hurried out the door,
headed for the church mission.

Along the first two blocks, the brick sidewalk provided
sure footing. Anne passed narrow row houses, oil lamps blink-
ing a greeting from their windows. She walked by storefronts
situated at almost every corner, some already darkened for the
evening.

At O'Toole's Dry Goods Shop, she turned into Park Street,
a busy thoroughfare brightened by the recent installation of gas
lamps. With rows of factory buildings lining the edge of the
road here, their great, shadowy masses looming above her, she
decided the additional lights were a true gift from God.

The sidewalks ended at the next corner, and the pathway
became uneven. Her pace slowed. Walter had expressed out-

rage over the city's use of his hard won tax money for this new street paving process called Macadam. He claimed heavy traffic cracked the inferior limestone surface and turned it to dust. With a strong rain the streets became rivers of mud. Anne smiled to herself, recalling him teasing Mary with the foolish rhyme chanted throughout the city these days:

"Macadam, Macadam, these city streets ain't worth a da—!"

"It is ma-`cad-um. The fools don't even know correct pronunciation." Mary would mutter her displeasure each time she heard the silly ditty.

The mud followed the path of the road, sloping down toward the Mississippi River. The closer Anne came to the mission, the more treacherous the walk became. Agreeing with Walter's opinion of the pavement quality, she gripped her baskets and trudged on.

At last she came upon her destination. The St. Vincent de Paul Mission, housed in the basement of the church, offered aid and comfort to needy immigrants, newly arrived in the city. After climbing down several deep, stone steps to the entrance, Anne pushed open the heavy door, and entered a spacious, yet cozy and cheerful, room.

"*Dia duit!* Good evening!" she said to the first young man she encountered. Since they all tried to set aside the old expressions and adapt to the manner of speech of their adopted country, she seldom spoke the ancient Irish. The comfort of a familiar Irish greeting, though, would warm the poor traveler's heart after a long, frightful journey.

"What fine children." She spoke to a young woman holding two babies in her arms. Their tiny shifts, peeking out beneath grimy blankets, were no more than rags. She patted another small boy and pulled out her handkerchief to wipe his runny nose. She set her baskets down to hug a little girl, who looked so like her baby sister, Maggie.

"Here's our Miss Carty, come with her grand treats." Bridget Rice, one of the mission's faithful volunteers, called out to her from behind an immense oven in the kitchen alcove. "Come and warm yourself. 'Tis a chilly night."

Bridget, also from Blackwater, had been in America for many years. Anne held but a slight memory of the Rice family living at the end of their lane back home, but she and Bridget had become great friends since her own arrival in St. Louis. They chatted and laughed now, while they sliced the bread Mary donated and arranged the baked goods on trays.

"It's grand to see you, Anne." Reverend Dennis Daly, who operated the mission in cooperation with the Irish Immigrant Society, emerged from his office. "The aroma of Mary's bread drew me right out of my chair. Tell her we appreciate her gift. We thank you, too, my dear. These fine goods are a blessing tonight."

"I will relay your message to Mary, Father." She gathered her empty baskets and prepared to return to the bakery. "Goodnight, to you all."

"Aye, you are here in good time." Walter called out a greeting, as she stepped into the bakery. "Mary's fine dinner is near to ready."

Anne closed the door behind her and hung up her cloak. She passed through the shop and entered the dining room, a spacious open area separating the bakery from the oven room.

"Good evening." She nodded to Walter and his two young helpers, William and Eddie, who sat on either side of him at the table.

Grace, who had left the mission ahead of Anne, came up beside her and reached forward to set two steaming bowls of vegetables on the table. Anne shook her head. No matter how early she arrived at the mission each evening, or how short her stay there, Grace always managed to slip out ahead of her. She would have enjoyed company on her walk home, but Grace seemed to entertain no wish for conversation, and most every night they each climbed the hill to Dempsey's alone.

The bakery door opened and closed once again. "Here are our Ellen and Kitty, relieved I am certain, to be shed of that impossible, noisy factory." Mary placed a deep round bowl, heaped with potatoes, on the table.

Anne noticed the glow on each girl's face as they moved into the room and caught sight of the plentiful meal before them.

"Come," Mary said, "let us offer our thanksgiving and eat while the food is warm."

After Walter bowed his head and led them in a brief prayer, they began passing the heaping platters and serving themselves. When everyone's plate had been filled, Anne took up her fork and began to eat, listening, while Mary inquired after the well-being of each one at the table.

"Tell us of your day at Simpson's," she said to Ellen and Kitty. "I have never been talented at sewing. Working in our folks' shop near all of my life, I never had an opportunity to learn. Didn't I always wish I had?"

"We only do piece work, the same pieces again and again, hour after hour." The flickering light from the candles on the table reflected on Ellen's bright red hair as she spoke and also illuminated the particles of lint it was impossible to avoid in the garment factory. "We are seldom allowed to admire a finished piece. There is no satisfaction to it at all, Mary, no feeling of accomplishment, no sense of a task completed.

"The finest moment of our day comes after we have been dismissed and we make our way home," Ellen said. "Yet, many immigrant girls fare much worse. Do you not agree, Kitty, we are fortunate to have a position?" Kitty's dark eyes looked solemn and her thick braids bobbed, as she nodded.

Hearing Ellen's words, Anne breathed a sigh of relief and offered a short prayer of thanksgiving. If not for the Dempseys awarding her a position, and of course Uncle James awaiting her arrival in Oregon, she would be working in the garment factory alongside Ellen and Kitty.

"And, what of your day, little Grace?" Walter said. "It is fine work you do at the mission, and new stories must arise by the moment."

Anne admired Walter's attempt to draw her friend out, but Grace's reply, tonight as every night past, consisted of few words. "No sir. It is just endless cleaning."

❀ ❀ ❀

When they had all enjoyed Mary's delicious desert, Anne and the other girls tidied up, while Mary retired to her room. By eight o'clock, her chores completed, Anne climbed the stairs to the attic. She untied the sash of her apron, slipped it over her head, and then removed a folded sheet and another envelope from the pocket stitched into the seam on the right side.

After Mrs. Flynn's afternoon visit, Walter had come in from the post office with a letter for her from home. She placed it in her pocket with Uncle James' letter, and during the few quiet moments in the shop, drew it out and read a paragraph or two, each word an ounce of gold to her.

Alone in her room now, she set Uncle James' worn, tattered letter on the desk. Holding the envelope that bore the Blackwater postmark in both hands, she rubbed the paper against her cheek and inhaled deeply, wishing to draw forth the scent of home. Since her arrival in St. Louis, she had received only one other communication from her family, though in the letters she sent them every week she begged everyone to write. Father, Mother, Julia, Kate, have you forgotten all about me?

She had been anticipating this moment, when she could sit quietly on her own and take pleasure in each word written in her Father's hand. She began with a sense of expectation and hope. As she read the sad message the letter contained, her heart filled with sadness over the hardships the folks back home were experiencing.

"If only I could help them," she said aloud to the empty room. A sigh escaped, as she folded the letter and placed it carefully under her pillow.

Wishing to push away her melancholy, she reached for Mrs. Flynn's book. Mary insisted Anne must have it first, and she settled in for a pleasant hour of reading. The romantic tale captivated her and held the loneliness away. Since no new roommate had arrived and she would disturb no one, she felt tempted to continue a few more minutes, read a few more lines. All too soon, though, the time came to put out the candle and pray for each member of her family.

She had finished her prayers and nestled in bed, when memories from her life in Blackwater returned: sounds of the children's chatter and the feel of their constant clutches at her arms and clothing; images of her mother, bent to her sewing, but persisting with her instructions to the children: "say your prayers, keep your hands clean." She pictured her father, laughing while he checked their school work or reviewed the bookkeeping tasks he assigned to the older ones. She missed them so. How she longed to have them all here with her.

She spent a few moments thinking about James Duff. She wondered if he was still at school. He had likely moved on, found new companions, she decided. It was no matter. Another sigh escaped. She had made a promise to her father, and she was not free to pursue a life of her own.

While it may take years to fulfill her father's demand to bring all of the children to America, she resolved she must, at least, bring Julia out. Whether she remained in St. Louis or made her way to Oregon, the companionship and support of her dear sister would sustain her. Before drifting off to sleep, she tried to picture Julia here in the attic room, resting in the empty bed beside her. The ache she had pushed back throughout the day now pounded at her insides. Burying her face in her pillow, she allowed her tears to escape.

Chapter Five

Blackwater
24th August, 1860

My Dearly Beloved Child,
    *I received your kind and affectionate letter
of the 28th and your check for £4. It gave your
mother, brothers and sisters and me great consolation to learn you are now in the enjoyment
of good health as this leaves us all, thanks be to
God for His mercy.*
    *My dear child, your cousin Edward Carty
wrote a letter home just a few days before yours
came to hand in which he stated that he was
with his Uncle James. He states his uncle is rich
and he gave him 360 acres of land together with
16 cows and 20 sheep. He seems reconciled to
being settled for life and has mentioned in his
letter to be prepared to let his brother and sister
go out to him as soon as he would send money to defray their expenses which would not be
longer than next spring.*
    *He also said Anne Carty was not arrived
yet although his uncle sent her one hundred
dollars to defray her expenses to him and he*

daily expected her. His letter was dated the 16th of June last. My beloved child, I have written your uncle as you directed and stated to him the cause of your delay that the fare was raised so high what he sent you would have no chance of bringing you and less than 270 dollars would not bring you to him. I also stated you were most anxious to go to him and you were in a good position and earning all you could to put along with what he sent you. My beloved child, should your uncle send you money, it would be your mother's wishes and mine you would go, but we do not insist you do so. No my dear child, we leave you to your own judgment and we recommend you to go to your clergy and be directed by him and pray fervently to God to direct you to the best.

Mag often speaks of you and I know I need not ask that if you are to send a present to little Maggie you will not forget your Aunt Mary also as you know old maids grow childish.

Give our respects to Mr. Fortune and let him know his brother & family are well. Give our respects to Walter Dempsey and his sister. We never can forget their kindness.

With regard to your uncle's money which you spoke of sending to us, it would be our wish you secure it and not send it till you know whether your uncle would send any more to you. If your uncle answers my letter, I will be the better judge and will write you.

John Carty

P.S. Give our respects to Edward and Grace Donahoo. William Kelly requests to be remembered to you and Grace Donahoo but my fingers are getting cramped, I am so long scrib-

*bling this, not being used to writing. I hope this
will go safe to you.*

September, 1860

Anne settled into a comfortable routine, tending the shop each day, delivering day-old goods to the mission in the evening, helping with the Saturday laundry chores, and attending church on Sunday. She worked hard to fill her time, wishing to ease her loneliness and allay her worries over her family. The months passed swiftly. Checking through Mary's wall calendar the evening before, she realized she had been in America for well over a year. Even with the passage of time, the longing and concern for her family had not diminished. *If Julia were here* became a silent cry that invaded her mind and heart each hour of the day.

"I've been noticing your worried expression." Mary interrupted Anne's reflections, as they stood in the dining room, packing bread and pastries for Walter's deliveries. "Are you troubled? Sure, I do not wish to pry. It is only my concern for you."

"The same worry I have held since I came here. My uncle assumes Father will send me funds. At the same time, Father believes that, in addition to the check he already sent, Uncle James will forward further money to me. Here I am, though, with drafts from neither." She stacked the cartons on the table for Eddie to carry out to the wagon, giving each box an extra shove.

"I promised my father I would make a home for the children in America. Now, over a year has passed, and—"

"But, it will take some time." Mary interrupted her. "You send money home each month, I know you do. You pay for your board here. Sure, I wish we did not have to take it from you. You cannot expect your savings to grow overnight. And there are so many children. How many, now?"

"Five sisters and two brothers. Ah, you are right, the task appears impossible. You and Walter are generous employers and I save every possible penny, but I have made little progress."

"And, is your father also expecting you to send fare money for all the children? 'Tis an awesome task for a young girl."

"It does appear to be more than I can do by myself. I cannot accumulate enough to take myself to Uncle James, or bring even one sister out.

"My sister Julia so longs to come. Even though she is two years older, Father sent me in her stead, thinking I possessed the greater proficiency for saving money. As it turns out, Julia could have done every bit as well.

"Forgive me for prattling on so. I assure you, my speech is finished and my complaints are at an end." Anne folded her arms across her apron front, and sighed. For so long, she had kept her own counsel. Now that she unburdened herself, a measure of relief settled over her.

"There's no need to worry so." Mary took Anne's hand. "Do you not extend the best effort both in the bakery and with putting your money by? And faithful keeper of coin that you are, you will see, your funds will commence to grow. And then won't those Carty children, one-by-one, begin to arrive in America?

"Walter will leave soon for his rounds," Mary said, when they finished packing the cartons. "He has invited you to accompany him on this pleasant morning. St. Louis is a fine city, but with the exceptions of church on Sunday and evening walks to the mission, you've explored little of it. No arguments, young lady. This idea of Walter's is a grand one, and you must go. Off with you, now."

Anne still could not drive away the memory of her arrival in the city and her collapse right out on a public road. The picture of Walter carrying her almost the entire way from the riverfront to the bakery made her blush, even now. She also suspected that, though Mary attributed the plan to Walter, the outing could be a sisterly attempt at matchmaking.

The clear, crisp morning and the idea of an excursion out of doors overcame Anne's reluctance, though. She ran to fetch her shawl and handbag.

Anne supposed the jovial, talkative Walter was accustomed to making his deliveries on his own. He said not a word when he handed her up to the wagon seat and they pulled away from the bakery. Every few blocks, he stopped the horse, carried boxes to their destination, and then resumed the drive without any conversation at all.

She did not allow the silence to distress her. Instead, she eased deeper into her seat, relaxed her mind of its cares, and gazed out over a part of the city she had not seen before. She wished to capture the images of people, buildings, even the magnificent, cloudless sky, and describe it all for her family when she wrote to them.

At Carondelet Boulevard, Walter turned the wagon to the south. Perhaps it was the new direction or the lovely breeze blowing right up into their faces that changed his demeanor. For whatever reason, the brisk businessman sitting erect and proper beside her disappeared and the jovial baker she had come to know in her days at Dempsey's returned. He began to point out landmarks and businesses, relate a little of their history, and explain the architectural styles of the grander places. He proved an excellent guide.

"The work on the Arsenal here is near to completion." He gestured toward the imposing stone building. "Just beyond, you will see the expansions to the military compound at Jefferson Barracks—the heightened activity a sure sign war is on the way. Aye, it is a sad business."

This threat of war had, until now, been a newspaper story to Anne. Walter's putting it into words, and the multitude of workers across the road, and the frenzy of their pounding hammers and thudding shovels now made the conflict a possibility she did not wish to accept. A tinge of concern crept in, disturbing her tranquility. She must pay close attention in the future, when Walter discussed the country's growing unrest.

He diverted her thoughts from the war threat a few moments later, as he turned the wagon to the left. "Here we are in a fine German neighborhood." He kept his attention on his horse and wagon as they entered a long street, where small, neat houses lined the road on both sides.

Anne observed tiny porches across the front of most places, shiny windows everywhere, and narrow, white walkways extending from each door out to the road. A variety of cooking scents drifted toward her, a distinct vinegary smell, and some others she couldn't discern, unusual to her, but pleasant all the same.

Walter found his voice again. "Our next stop is Gus Mueller's bakery. I often visit shops in the French, Polish, and other neighborhoods, areas as isolated from the rest of the city as the Irish ones are. It sometimes proves difficult to overcome the restraint of the local bread makers, but Gus accepted my overtures of friendship from the first. He practices the language with me while we discuss methods, and suppliers, and equipment. Sure, we have become great pals."

A German bakery. Anne raised her hand to shade her eyes and also to hide the startled expression she could not hold back, but Walter had already observed her reaction.

"You have a bit of concern?" At the end of the long block, he pulled his wagon alongside a square building many times the size of the others. "What caused this trepidation in you?"

Anne told him a brief version of one of her Uncle Patrick's stories of his time as a carpenter's apprentice in Germany. Like many of his tales, it centered on the stern, miserly people he resided with while he was there.

Walter nodded. Perhaps he had heard these same stories? "When you come to know Gus and Tilda and find what warm, gracious people they are, you will discover how mistaken that notion is."

"You are far more experienced in these matters. I will bow to your judgment and refrain from hasty conclusions." How wrong she had been about Walter's meaning. Anne straightened her shoulders and prepared herself to meet her first German-born neighbors in her new country.

When they entered the shop, they were greeted by a short, sturdy woman, a smile spread across her face and warmth shinning from her wide, blue eyes.

"Welcome. Welcome." She moved out from behind the counter, beaming at Anne and Walter.

"Good morning, Tilda," Walter said. "I've brought you our Miss Anne Carty."

"I am pleased to meet you, Mrs. Mueller." Anne made a slight curtsy.

The woman reached out to touch her hand. "Please call me Tilda." She bestowed another grand smile and a bow upon Anne. The thick brown braid wrapped around her head bounced with each nod. With much ceremony, she led them back to the oven room in search of Gus.

They found him on his knees in front of a massive oven, tools spread all about him on the floor. "Walter has told us many fine things about you, Miss Carty," he said.

Gus was a slim man, and nimble, Anne noted, when he pulled himself up from the floor. His short, thick hair was the fairest she had ever seen. He spoke with deliberation, but his words were distinct, with only a trace of his native accent.

"Thank you for your kind welcome, Mr. Mueller. I must say your command of the language astounds me. Even though I came to America with the knowledge of English, I found a vast difference in everyone's manner of speech here. I cannot imagine the difficulty you experienced. You and Tilda have done a grand job of it."

"Aye, I agree," Walter said. "Gus and Tilda are quite proficient." The Muellers' faces glowed with appreciation at their praise.

"You must inspect our oven room and Tilda's fine, busy shop," Gus said, leading them toward the front of the building. He introduced her to the shop girl, Anne's counterpart, but Agnes was occupied with a customer. Anne waved her arm to acknowledge her understanding that the girl could take only time enough for a nod in their direction.

They walked through the entire place, and Anne could not help but compare it to the operation at Dempsey's—Walter and Mary baking most of the night, and delivering, ordering, planning, handling accounts, and keeping their equipment clean and well-maintained in the daytime. As was true of the Dempseys, she observed the Muellers' easy-going, friendly manner with workers and customers.

In a corner of the baking room, she noticed one great difference in the two places. She watched a young worker add a heavy cream mixture to the pastries. At another table, she edged a bit closer to inhale the wonderful aroma of the jellied filling a young man was placing on top of each roll on a wide wooden tray. Both delicacies were so unlike Dempsey's delicious but simpler fare.

By the time they left the Muellers, the sun had gained in intensity. A strong breeze moved through the trees, sending leaves of rich gold and orange fluttering in all directions. The brisk morning had developed into an altogether grand day.

At the market, they made the purchases on Mary's list, and at the bank, Anne deposited her savings. Since she had received no response from her father regarding Mr. Fortune's questionable reputation or his control of her savings, she continued to deposit her money in the account.

Though he said nothing, just knowing that Walter disapproved of her placing additional funds under Fortune's control made her shift in her seat. She massaged the tightness at the back of her neck and avoided his gaze. She wished fervently that her father would inform her of his wishes in the matter. When the wagon pulled away from the bank and they began to drive along the riverfront, she relaxed in her seat once again, her tension already beginning to ease.

"You missed most of these sights the day you arrived." Walters' eyes now held a teasing glint, the unspoken subject of Mr. Fortune seeming forgotten.

Anne laughed. Was she becoming comfortable in Walter's company, at last? His comments about the riverfront did ring true, though. While she recalled a little of the noise and the crowds that day, she held no memory of the ships of every size along the waterfront, or the businesses, factories, and stores they now passed.

Walter drove to an area north of the city, where he stopped for deliveries.

"I didn't realize you traveled this far to deliver goods," Anne said.

"The Regent Inn and Good Shepherd Hospital are two of my newest customers," he said as he supervised the unloading, which required assistance from several workers.

The city's prosperous business neighborhoods halted at the next turn. On Second Street, a desperate scene stretched out before them. Rows of filthy shacks lined block after city block. In some, windows were broken or missing altogether. In others, parts of walls or doors were torn away. Anne noticed boards nailed at haphazard angles, holes gaping at frequent intervals, some stuffed with rags or newspapers, others left untended. Piles of rubbish stood outside of the doors, and in some places, garbage trailed out into the road.

"Oh my word!" Anne grimaced at the stench that hovered around the place and reached in her pocket for a handkerchief. "There are many such places back home, but I never dreamed I would encounter the like here in America."

"They are called shanties," Walter said. "It is a disgrace so many of our poor families are forced to live in these tumble-down hutches.

"A short time after our arrival in St. Louis," he said, "we rescued our own Cara from one of these same dreadful places. Mary and I had been spending a day working with Father Daly at St. Vincent's. That afternoon, he introduced us to Cara, telling us of the fine work she did at the mission while she also cared for her invalid sister, Sally. He described the terrible condition of the row house where the young women lived and asked if we could take them in as our first boarders.

"Here we were, living in this cavernous factory building. Our furniture consisted of our own two beds and the long table I had built for the baking room where we also ate our meals. Still, Mary and I agreed we must do what we could to help Cara. We borrowed a horse from a neighbor and hitched it to an old cart I had rescued from a scrap heap and patched together. Then, we took Cara home to collect her sister and their things.

"You see the filth and disrepair outside of these buildings," Walter slowed the wagon as he told the story, "on our closer inspection, conditions proved far worse. We made our way through the maze of hallways. Climbing the stairs, we encountered garbage, and waste, and every form of varmint.

"Inside, was a different story altogether. You know how our Cara will clean a place? Well, she had done her work. While their little room held not one piece of furniture, it had been swept and scrubbed to perfection. Their scant possessions were piled in a corner in a neat stack.

"Her sister, Sally, lay huddled on the floor, wrapped in a blanket. We lost no time in carrying her out and loading their things in the wagon. We took her home and summoned the doctor, but his efforts proved futile. Naught could be done to save Sally, and she died a few days later.

"Cara came to work in the bakery then, and she has been with us over ten years. She's a wonderful girl, Cara is. She thanks us still for the help we extended in her sister's final days. We assure her again and again no thanks are needed and we are the fortunate ones to have her grand assistance."

"I quite agree," Anne said. "Cara is a fine person, and I am deeply sorry to hear she lost her sister. I am happy, though, that she no longer lives in such a place." Feelings of guilt tugged at Anne's mind and heart. She admitted to her relief when Walter urged his horse along. Still, she could not censure these poor folks. Without the help of the Dempseys, she could be living in this frightful place herself.

On the drive back to the bakery, Walter began telling her a little of the last days he and Mary spent in Ireland and of their early times in the city. "When our father and mother died of cholera in 1848, we made the decision to escape the desperate conditions of our homeland. We sold their place in Enniscorthy and set out.

"Arriving in St. Louis the next year, we discovered a terrible fire had ravaged the riverfront and the downtown area. With the profits from the sale of the shop back home, we purchased our bakery building from the city, one of the many damaged warehouses abandoned by its owner. For the next ten years, we worked to restore the place and expand our business."

He moved to another subject altogether. "I'm sure you noticed we serve no drinks at Dempsey's?"

"I'm not accustomed to having wine with my dinner." Anne laughed a little at the thought. "Back home, we were lucky to have a cup of tea on most days."

"Still, Mary must have told you I have taken the pledge?"

When Anne shook her head, Walter continued. "Before he died, my father called me to him, and demanded I pledge never to take a drink. I was but a lad, not mature enough to understand just how long the word *never* meant. But, my father was a fine man and I loved him dearly, and so, I gave him my word. Though at times I have been tempted, I have not relented. I do not suppose the sacrifice will kill me."

"I must say, Walter, it does not appear to be a grave deprivation. Of course, I am speaking from a girl's perspective. I have never sampled wine or beer. I must admit, though, I have learned to enjoy coffee, and I had never tasted that beverage until I came to Dempsey's. I suppose I am useless to give an opinion where the drink is concerned. It is one of the many things about which I have little or no knowledge.

"As you know, I do have firsthand experience with the weight of a pledge made to one's father. Before I left Ireland, my father sought my promise to bring my brothers and sisters to America before I pursued a life of my own. I was sixteen at the time. My days were filled with studies and chores. I had no goals. A home and family of my own were only dreams to me.

While I wished to please my father, I soon learned how long such a promise could take to fulfill. With our lofty pledges, we do have something in common, do we not?"

Anne and Walter had time for only a short laugh together. They were drawing near to Dempsey's and her grand excursion had come to a close.

Back at the shop, Anne experienced difficulty in settling down to her work. Filled with the excitement of her morning adventure, her thoughts danced and spun. While they served customers, she recounted to Mary all she had stored in her memory. "The many tall buildings, and the factories and businesses amazed me. The marvelous architecture of the Cathedral and the Courthouse, with this morning's bright sunshine radiating off of their white stone surfaces, proved the most impressive sights.

"I am happy I trusted your judgment and rode out with Walter. It was a delightful morning, and since there were just the two of us, we were forced—in truth, I was forced—to lose my awkwardness and converse with him. He was kind and pleasant, and by the time we were on our way home, we spoke together like old friends."

For now, she decided the safest thing would be to ignore the mischievous little grin Mary bestowed on her. It would, perhaps, be a wise idea to mention the name of James Duff a time or two in Mary's presence; even though there was a great likelihood she would never see Mr. Duff again.

Chapter Six

October 7, 1860
Blackwater

My Dearly Beloved Child,

I received your welcome letter of the 1st on the 20th and we were delighted to learn you were in the enjoyment of good health as this leaves us at home in the enjoyment of the like blessing thanks to God for his goodness. My Dear Child, the constant wet all summer and even up to the present moment has caused a loss on the corn crop and green crops such as turnips and cabbages. Those disappointments together with your mothers' illness which I told you of in my last letter has left me disturbed and to augment my difficulties I was obliged to pay a year's rent for both my holdings which leaves me bare.

You mentioned you would send me a present against Christmas. I think very hard to trouble you or to take your hard earnings but the potato crop failed this year like all green crops. If you would send me what you could perhaps it would be the last application I would have an occasion to make and I might yet be able to reimburse you.

My Dear Child, I have had no letter from your uncle nor did Uncle William get one. I have no hopes he will ever again write. I might be mistaken, but I am of the opinion your cousin Edward has put him from corresponding with either you or I.

My dear child, as to your brother Jimmy, he is just the way he was when you left, and as to Lizzie she is not the size of Kate, but small as she is, she threatens to go to you for a new coat. You are now aware of how I am circumstanced and I dread I will be obliged to sell the cow if it is not in your power to help me and if I part her I never will get her equal again.

John Carty

October, 1860

Saturdays brought an alteration in Anne's usual routine at Dempsey's. Walter had negotiated with the owner of the laundry in the next block for an exchange of services. Under the arrangement, bakery linens and tablecloths, along with sheets and towels from the living quarters, were laundered in return for a generous supply of baked goods for the owners' family. Anne's part in the bargain came on Saturday morning. When the bakery's early morning rush slowed, Mary took over in the shop, and Anne helped Cara with the personal laundry.

Since Grace, Ellen, and Kitty, and of course Walter and Mary, worked until mid-afternoon each Saturday, Anne and Cara labored together scrubbing, wringing, and hanging out the laundry for them all. The other girls were so grateful for this kindness they repaid them by borrowing Cara's flat iron and pressing blouses and dresses for the laundresses.

The Saturday after her outing with Walter, Anne discovered she and Cara had been blessed with another glorious fall day for their laundry chores. The sun shone brightly and the breezes skipped between the buildings and trees and teased the girls' hair from their caps. The crisp air also dried the garments a few minutes after they hung them on the line. In no time at all, Anne and Cara were pulling the first round of clean things from the line and hanging a second load of wet clothing.

"With these strong rays of sunshine, our dreaded laundry task will be finished in no time," Cara said.

"I do not mind it," Anne said. "The laundry chore is hard work, but nothing different from what I did back home in Blackwater. In fact, I welcome this change in my routine in the bakery. As a girl who spent a great part of my life working in the fields, it feels grand to escape the confinement of the small shop. The freedom to move about in the fresh air raises my spirits so, I believe I may just begin to skip and dance with the joy of it.

With the work moving swiftly, Anne felt her restlessness growing. "Our laundry chore is almost done," she said to Cara. "Could we not take some time now to indulge in a bit of exercise? At home, my sisters and I could run the six miles to Enniscorthy without even making a stop."

"Yeh, until a few years ago, I could run ten miles without even a thought." Cara turned to Anne with a grin. "Do ya think we could do it still?"

"If we ran the three blocks to the park, followed the path around its perimeter, and ran back, the laundry would all be dry when we return."

"I dunno. I should not be bounding off." Cara's expression reflected some concern.

"Come, Cara. Please. I never have an opportunity to stretch out my legs. Are you fast enough to beat me? What if I challenge you?"

The word challenge had no sooner left Anne's mouth, than Cara took off running. She proved an able opponent. They had gone a full block and Anne had not managed to catch up with her. By the time they reached the park, followed along its outside edge, and then turned back toward the bakery, they were side by side. From then on, it was an all-out race, Anne sprinting with all her might, Cara keeping pace. Few people were on the street so early on a Saturday morning, but Anne did notice a glance or two directed their way.

They reached the yard, Anne a slight step ahead, both girls panting and laughing. Pushing their hair back into their caps and wiping their flushed faces, they moved right back to their work. They pulled the last of the laundry from the line, still smiling and giggling as they went. After lifting the heavy laundry baskets and carrying them inside, they went about folding and sorting, laughing together, their breaths coming in short spurts.

Even with the time off for their race, the girls finished their laundry chore earlier than usual. Anne returned to the shop in time to help Mary prepare for the early afternoon closing. Before she even stopped to think, she had related the whole of their adventure to her.

Mary approved. "It is grand you were able to indulge in such good exercise. I am amazed our Cara is capable of running such a good race. I wonder what other talents she is withholding from us."

They continued working until the leftover goods were all moved to the side table and the empty shelves were scrubbed clean. With the bakery readied for closing, Anne leaned against the counter, resting. A moment later, Walter entered the bakery and handed her an envelope.

At last, a letter from home.

She had just opened the envelope, when she realized Mary was repeating the story of the race to Walter. They were both laughing, and Anne joined in with them, though she did worry Walter would tease Cara over the escapade. She must apologize to her running partner for spilling the secret.

"Good afternoon." Grace Donahoo came through the door, returning from her work at the mission. She spoke so quietly, Anne could not be sure of her words. She could only guess Grace had spoken her usual greeting.

Walter pulled a letter from his pocket for Grace, and she thanked him with the briefest of smiles. With no further word to anyone, she tore open the envelope and began to read as she climbed the steps to her room. Grace's sudden, agonized scream filled the tiny shop.

Memories of the morning's race with Cara flown from her mind, Anne rushed to the stairway with Walter and Mary right behind her. They found Grace in a swoon, prostrate on the stairs, her face pressed against a rough, wooden step, her limbs stretched out at odd angles. When Walter struggled to grasp the girl's limp body, Anne and Mary held up her arms and legs and helped him carry her to her bed.

When she rallied enough to speak, Grace related the letter's fateful message. "William Stapleton will not come here. There will be no marriage." After uttering only these few words, Grace became incoherent, thrashing and rolling from side to side on the bed.

Walter rushed out to fetch the doctor, mumbling as he went, about foolish, untrustworthy lads. Anne and Mary tried to settle Grace with cool cloths pressed to her forehead and soft words and entreaties for calm, but to no avail.

Anne attempted to retrieve the letter from Grace to ascertain if there was any more to the message. Any hopes held out? Any undying love offered? Grace grasped the paper with a tight grip, though, and would not relinquish it.

Dr. Gallagher arrived a short time later. Anne escorted him to the second floor and sat beside the bed while he examined Grace with great care and gentleness.

"What brought this on?" he asked.

After Anne explained to him what she knew of the story, he ran his fingers through his thick, white hair and removed his glasses. "I'll leave this mixture for her. Use it sparingly." His grim countenance emphasized his final words. "The powder will offer a temporary solution. In my opinion, the passage of time alone will ease her pain. God help the poor child. Pray for her, and I'll add my prayers to your own, I promise you."

Anne sat with Grace for a time, but after a few long sighs, interrupted at intervals by tears, the poor girl succumbed to the sedative and drifted into sleep.

After church the next morning and a silent walk home, Grace climbed to the second floor and passed the rest of the day in her room. She refused to eat. She spoke with no one, brushing aside all attempts at consolation. Each time Anne stopped by to visit with her, she found Grace seated on the same straight chair pushed back in the darkest corner of the room. Her eyes remained red-rimmed and swollen, her head bowed down, and her shoulders slumped.

Toward evening, Anne again tried to comfort her. "Do you wish to speak of it?" She received no response. "Shall I write to your father for you?" Still, there was no answer. Her heart ached for Grace. Whatever could she do to help her poor friend? Sitting beside the girl, she searched for an answer. She hesitated to leave her alone. In desperation, she tried once more. "Can I do for you at all, dear?"

"No thank you." At last, Grace spoke, her voice so low and her speech so soft Anne leaned in close to make out her words. "I appreciate your concern, but there's nothing for it. I will need time to think this through on my own."

Anne respected her wishes and left her to her grief. Later, while reading through her letters from home, she realized they often mentioned Mr. Stapleton. She wondered if she should continue to share them with Grace, as had been her custom. She decided she would hold back any letters that might cause her friend anguish. From that evening forward, she followed Grace's lead in their conversations, and the two never discussed the affair or William Stapleton again.

Mary broached the subject with Anne one morning a few days later. "Grace is a melancholy child. She has good reason, I grant you, with her dreams of marriage dashed, her brother moved on to the seminary at Perryville, and an ocean separating her from her family in Ireland. I wish I could help her, true enough."

"I, too, would like to do something, perform some miracle." Anne brushed crumbs from the countertop into her hand and carried them to the fireplace. She stirred the flame with the poker, before she spoke again. "She seems determined to be sad. You are far more patient than I. At times, I have the temptation to shake her."

"Did you know this Stapleton fellow? What manner of man would abuse a girl, as he has done to our Grace?"

"I did not know him well. He was older than all of us. He lived away from home much of the time, at school, or work, or somewhere. Julia and I did wonder at their unusual form of courtship, Will off in Dublin or Cork and Grace in Blackwater.

"He seems to be spending time at home now. My parents write of speaking with him. They all appear friendly, more so than he and his family ever were when I lived at home. The entire business is beyond me."

"Do you suppose Grace could have known Mr. Stapleton would not come, even before she left Ireland? She did cry more when she arrived here, you remember, than she does even now."

"Could I ever forget how she wept all the way from Blackwater to St. Louis? Oh, perhaps you are right. Deep in her heart, she must have known Will Stapleton's devotion did not match hers."

"As Dr. Gallagher suggested, I am praying for the child. Sure, I do not know what more to do." Mary shook her head slowly, from side to side.

"You know, Grace and my sister Julia have always been great friends," Anne said. "I hold out the hope that, once I gather the funds to send for Julia, she may exert some influence over her.

"Ah, Mary, I cannot wait until you meet Julia. She is nothing like Grace Donahoo, or even like me. She is spirited and merry, and she possesses an enthusiastic outlook about everything. I pray she will be here before too long."

Chapter Seven

My Dear Child,

We were sorry for Grace Donahoo's disappointment. It appears heaven did not intend that young man for her husband. I should not be surprised if she was in great grief after so affectionate a young man, but I can say she has the good look to have the favour of kind young men here as well as in St. Louis.

Nell Carty

P.S. Please let Grace Donahoo know her friend Mr. Stapleton removed from Blackwater to Featherton and the night before he went he got married to Kitty Read and went away next morning. He has since removed to Duncannon and never came to this place since. His wife remains at home. It was a private, solitary wedding. N.C.

My Dear Sister,

In compliance with your request I take up my pen to give you a sample of my handwriting. I hope God will spare me till I see and embrace you when with God's blessing we never will be

*separated again. Adieu, my dear sister for the
present and remain yours,*
    Julia

December, 1860

On a bitter, cold Sunday afternoon, a few weeks after the sad incident with Grace, Anne decided on a solitary walk. The other girls attempted to sway her from her plan, suggesting a ride in the carriage with Eddie, a lesson in embroidery from Ellen, and all sorts of other activities. She remained steadfast. She had difficult matters she must mull through on her own. She would examine her choices carefully and come to a conclusion. She bundled herself against the wind and chill and set out.

She paced back and forth along the path between the bakery and St. Vincent's, and while she moved along, she reviewed the whole of her situation. For a year and a half, she had been employed at Dempsey's Bakery, living in their pleasant, third floor attic room. Compared to the sad state of her family back home, her life in St. Louis, if not grand, was comfortable. Yet, she suffered great anxiety. She must make a momentous decision, one she felt ill equipped to dispatch.

Should she remain in St. Louis and send the funds home for Julia's passage? Should she pour her efforts into saving money enough in the next year to go on to Oregon? Since she received Uncle James's first letter, soon after her arrival in St. Louis, no further word had come from him, a matter that caused her grave concern. Why had he not responded to her letters? From her father's recent communications, she gathered he too despaired of ever hearing from Uncle James. As she walked, she asked herself these same questions over and over.

The hour grew late. The afternoon's meager rays of sunlight had long since disappeared. Still, she had reached no conclusions. She decided the cold air stiffening her fingers and seeping beneath her cloak had dulled her mind along with her chilled body. Since she could no longer concentrate on the problems at hand, she returned at last to Dempsey's, as uncertain as when she had left.

In the attic room that night, Anne tossed and rolled in her bed. Just when she despaired of getting any rest at all, she did finally drift into a disturbed, restless sleep, dreaming of her home in Blackwater. In one dream, she strolled along the road to the center of town with her sisters. In another, she worked over ledgers with her father late into the night. After each vision, she awoke with a start, her agitation still with her.

At last, the skies began to lighten. At the moment when she anticipated the dawn would break through, the conclusion she had so long prayed she would reach became evident. Excitement and joy surged through her. A shivering sensation moved all the way to her toes. Filled with energy now, she anticipated the start of the fresh, new day. She would discuss her plan with Mary and Walter. Once she secured their approval, she could move forward.

As soon as she entered the shop, Mary greeted Anne with her own scheme. "Few will brave the cold and damp to purchase goods this morning. Here's our time to give the place a proper scrub."

Though weary from her restless night, Anne felt invigorated by the decision she had just made, and she directed her energy toward doing Mary's bidding. With a great flurry, they gathered warm water, soap, rags, and brushes. Cara worked in the dining room, while Anne and Mary began in the shop.

Anne cleaned with enthusiasm, her thoughts filled with her newly-formed plan. This time alone with Mary, their arms immersed in soapy water, would provide an opportunity to confide her ideas to her dear friend.

"I reached a decision that has rendered me a bit unstrung." Her voice rose a bit, as she began to speak. "I am sure it would calm me, if I could share it with you."

"Wouldn't you best be telling me then? Whatever is it?"

"You already know of my concerns. Should I proceed on to Oregon, or wait for Julia to arrive? Yesterday, I pondered the situation all afternoon, and then I could not sleep last night with the worry."

"You poor dear, and here I am making you work so." Mary shook her head, concern showing in her eyes.

"Oh, that is of no mind. The sleepless night proved worthwhile, and the cleaning is helping calm me some." Anne pushed trays and bins aside, moving with vigor.

"Early this morning, a truth entered into my heart and mind, a reality I have avoided all these many months. Sometime in that gray hour, I came to the understanding that I am now on my own.

"In these past months, I lived in accordance with what I assumed Father and Mother would wish me to think, or do, or say. While, in fact, the wise counsel of my parents is lost to me now. Unless they had been to America, they could not imagine my circumstances or advise me on how to proceed. Ah, this sounds frightful, disloyal, an insult to their intelligence." Anne shook her head. Her words brought sadness into her heart, but she straightened her shoulders and pushed on with the telling of her plan.

"The vast distance from New York to St. Louis and the long way I still must go to reach Oregon were incomprehensible to me before I left home. We all studied the routes from Cork to New York, New York to St. Louis, and St. Louis on out west. I knew how many miles it was, but until I observed for myself the wide meadows, the great rushing rivers and streams, and vast mountains and forests, I could not envision it. These distances would no doubt astound the folks in Blackwater.

"We knew the topography and climate, and the particular areas of danger or difficulties. But until you set out and experience the long journey for yourself, that knowledge is maps and charts alone. No one could prepare you for the hardships involved. Until you experience it for yourself, you could never really understand the toll that traveling such a great distance will extract from a person.

"It is also foolish to think my parents will help with money," Anne said. "They have no funds. In fact, they now depend on me to send them something each month.

"And so, I resolved to remove money from my savings and send it to Father for Julia's passage. I must apply to the formidable Mr. Fortune. Uncle James arranged that I may deposit money into my account, but Fortune's signature is required for a withdrawal. The idea of approaching him makes me tremble." Anne faced Mary, attempting a look of confidence and bravery. "Now that I am such an adult, I will not allow him to present an obstacle.

"I am also concerned that, once Julia does come, we will not have sufficient funds to transport us both to Oregon. And so, I devised a plan to replace her passage money and add to the account.

"I will speak to Ellen and Kitty about obtaining a sewing position with their employer. I could work in my room at night, once my duties have been discharged here in the shop. Of course, I will proceed, only if you consent and Ellen and Kitty agree to carry the goods to and from their factory for me.

"Once Julia arrives, we will both work to accumulate enough for our passage to Oregon. Or, we may decide to repay Uncle James, send for my sister Kate, and remain in St. Louis.

"Well, Mary, have I overwhelmed you with all of this? It has taken me all these months to accept the fact that this responsibility rests with me and I must make the decisions. After all this time of worry, the answer came to me with surprising ease. Somewhere in the breaking dawn, as I tossed and rolled about in my bed, I developed this entire plan. Now I will stand quiet, while you tell me your thoughts."

"Have I not observed your struggle with this problem, day after day? Have I not seen the worried look you try to conceal?" Mary took Anne's hands in her own and patted her fingers, smoothing out the reddened skin as she spoke. "Matters of this import, in particular those that concern others, are difficult to conclude. You are a fine, intelligent girl, and I am pleased you have worked it all out. 'Tis the right decision, I am sure of it. Won't your parents be proud of you?"

A customer entered the shop, and Anne rushed to help her. The woman, unaware she had interrupted a most important conversation, unwound her wide rain coat and placed it on the rack beside the door. Anne concentrated on holding her feet still and keeping her fingers from drumming on the countertop, while the woman set her umbrella in the corner, and after a long, slow deliberation, chose one small loaf of bread. Anne moved quickly, wrapping it, placing it in the woman's satchel, accepting payment, and thanking her. The moment the door closed behind her, she hurried back to her scrub bucket and brush.

Mary had not forgotten their conversation. She was waiting for her return. "It will be grand to have your sister here. With our families left behind in Ireland, we must depend on our friends, but no one takes the place of kin. Together, you and Julia will establish a home, as Walter and I have done.

"Your dear one will be our guest until she finds employment, sleeping in the attic room with you and sharing our dinner. I am sure you will wish to obtain a position for her at once, though, and begin saving for passage for your next sister. I will inquire of everyone I know on Julia's behalf."

"The matter of a position for Julia does concern me," Anne said. "I obtained a sample of her handwriting and passed it on to Father Daly and Father Burns. They each promised to approach their businessmen friends in hopes of finding her a clerk or shop girl position."

"We should not delay then. I will speak with Walter, when he returns from his rounds. I know he will want to help you in your dealings with Mr. Fortune.

"Your sister must come soon. All we hear these days is talk of war. The newspapers are filled with it. Though the city has been kept from strife thus far, restrictions could soon be

placed on travel." Mary turned away, as the side door just beyond the dining room banged shut.

"Ah, here's Walter now. I will speak with him right away."
All thoughts of soap and brushes seemed pushed from Mary's
mind when she bustled off. "Walter..."

After a few moments, Mary rushed back through the doorway with Walter right behind her. "Before you speak with Mr.
Fortune, we wish to discuss this whole matter with you." Mary
pulled Anne over to the two straight-backed chairs placed together inside the archway leading to the dining room. They
both sat, while Walter leaned against the wall, his hand on the
back of Mary's chair.

"A few weeks back, you told us of the bookkeeping training you received from your father. Since then, we have been
working out a plan to involve you with the accounts for the
bakery." Mary turned to Walter, and after he nodded, she went
on. "I will instruct you on our procedures, and it is our hope
you will take over this chore for me. Once that task is removed
from my hands, William and Eddie will teach me to mix batter
and manage the ovens. With this arrangement, Walter will have
more time for the operation of his business."

"Our business, Mary," Walter said. "We would be nothing
without you. Sure, that's the truth."

He turned to Anne. "Please do take some of this burden
from Mary. We waited to determine the seriousness of the war
threat before approaching you. Now, the conflict appears un-
avoidable and we must move forward with our plans.

"We will find help for you in the shop, and of course, increase your wages. Ah, we have not yet discussed an amount,
have we, Mary?" Walter turned to his sister, and when she gave
a slight shake of her head, he addressed Anne again. "It will be
more than you would earn with nighttime sewing. Do not think
about nonsense such as that."

The idea of her work changing from bread and biscuits and
buckets of soapy water to ledgers and sums, with no nighttime
sewing, made Anne chuckle. Walter continued on, though, and

not wishing to interrupt him with her frivolity, she covered her mouth.

"Aye, won't we experience many changes here? I have already purchased the warehouse behind us and developed a scheme to renovate the additional building and connect the two." Energy and excitement spilled from Walter's voice. "We will need the space, as earlier this week, we received a military contract. If the war comes to pass, our orders will double."

Anne shook her head. The talk of a coming war deflated her hopeful spirits. Mary took her arm, nodding in understanding, but Walter's eyes flashed, his thoughts likely filled with his new assignment and the arrangements he must make. He went right on talking.

"For the next four Saturday nights, William, Eddie, and I will train with the bakers at Jefferson Barracks. In a matter of weeks, we will begin to supply bread for the camps and medical facilities being established around the city. So you can see, I will need Mary in the oven room and your work with the accounts will be of great assistance to us."

"Thank you for placing your trust in me," Anne said. "This war venture appears an enormous task. I will work hard to master your bookkeeping process. I pray my work will help you." In truth, this war talk frightened her. With all of her good intentions, she had still paid scant attention to the newspaper reports. The conflict seemed impossible to avoid and had now invaded the operation of the bakery.

"I am relieved and grateful to be spared endless nights of sewing, and though she does not yet realize it, Julia will want to extend her own thanks." The idea made Anne laugh, and this time, Walter and Mary joined in. Anne had once confided to them that sewing with their mother at night was a bane to all the girls except Kate and the one thing she did not miss about home.

"It may not be necessary to hire another girl, though. I may be able to complete the account work when no customers are in the shop."

"Already trying to hold down expenses," Mary said. "That's our girl."

❀ ❀ ❀

Anne and Walter located Mr. Fortune's office on the second floor of the bank building on Fifteenth Street. A small, spare sign attached to the door read "D. Fortune, Attorney."

When they entered, Fortune was seated behind a long, impressive desk, the rich dark wood shined to a fine glow. Anne noticed it held neither ledger, inkwell, nor paper. A wooden chair at the side wall completed the room's furnishings. Walter walked over to the chair and sat down.

Anne approached the desk. Fortune did not look up or acknowledge her presence, but continued to scrutinize the folder in his hand. Undeterred, she drew her shoulders to their full height, took in a deep breath, and spoke out.

"Good afternoon, Mr. Fortune. I wish to withdraw money from my account and send for my sister."

It seemed a full minute passed before he lifted his gaze toward her, and when he did, his head moved slowly from side to side. His eyes looked sad. "It would be a serious mistake to remove such a large portion of your savings from the account, Miss Carty."

Walter's chair scraped against the wooden floor. With a determined, heavy step, he came to stand beside Anne. In a deliberate motion, he placed his hand on her shoulder. "Mind what the girl says, Fortune."

Strengthened by Walter's words and the pressure of his hand on her shoulder, Anne again addressed Mr. Fortune. "I have made my decision, sir. I intend to remove funds enough for Julia's passage."

The man ignored her words entirely, instead turning his attention to Walter. Anne began to tremble. After months of consideration and prayer that she would make the right decision, this foolish man presumed she was acting with no prudent thought at all.

Walter had not forsaken her. While Fortune made the mistake of continuing to apply to him for agreement, Walter's grave expression and the resolute shake of his head must have finally convinced the man his cause was done. He rose from his chair, his demeanor transformed.

"Of course, Miss Carty, I am here to serve you." He bowed, bent, and smiled, all at once. Still, he avoided her eyes and Walter's, as without further delay, he accompanied them downstairs to the bank and signed the necessary document.

When they parted company with Mr. Fortune, Anne let go of her anger over his rudeness. More important matters were waiting.

She and Walter hurried across the street to the post office. With an envelope and a note to her Father already prepared, the message and the bank draft were in route to Blackwater in a matter of a few minutes.

As they walked along toward Dempsey's, Anne tried to express her appreciation to Walter. "Without your support, I would not have possessed the strength to insist Fortune complete the transaction."

"You would have been capable of standing up to him. You are a determined girl. The manner in which you conducted yourself impressed me."

"Thank you." Walter's praise sent a warm blush creeping along her neck, but she ignored the sensation. There was more she must say.

"I removed all of the funds in the account except the money Uncle James sent to Mr. Fortune for my passage to Oregon. I have written to my father and Uncle James, asking them both to advise me on how to proceed."

"You know, I do not wish to interfere," Walter said, "but I advise you to remove the balance of that money from Fortune's grasp. I urge you to do so as soon as possible."

"I will do it, I promise you."

"Well, you have accomplished a considerable task, for today. You've earned a rest, before I badger you again about

Fortune and your funds." They had reached the bakery now, and Walter smiled down at her, as he opened the shop door and moved aside to allow her to enter.

Anne could not hold back her own smile. The money for Julia's passage had been sent on its way to Ireland, and her sister would soon make her way to America. Her mission had been completed.

That evening, as she prepared to retire, she took Walter's advice and allowed her worries over Mr. Fortune, Uncle James, and her savings to slip from her mind. For just this evening, she decided, she would turn her thoughts, instead, to the pleasant anticipation of Julia's coming.

How long would it be before her sister, now so far away, would be sitting on the bed beside her in the attic room? How many months would pass before she had the pleasure of a sisterly talk with the person she felt closest to in the entire world? Joy flooded into her heart at the thought of the happiness Julia's arrival in St. Louis would bring her.

Chapter Eight

February, 1861

Anne shivered and gathered her shawl around her shoulders. Sitting at the desk Walter had installed at the back wall of the shop, she worked on accounts. While figuring, and copying sums, she listened for the shop bell that would signal the arrival of a customer. Outside the window, the sodden trees drooped and swayed, until she expected their limbs would crash down at any moment. The dismal weather, combined with the endless talk of war now prevalent throughout the city, had cast a pall over the entire group at Dempsey's.

She lowered her head. Even her most determined efforts could not ward off the spells of melancholy that crept over her on occasion. Somehow, she must immerse herself in this work and keep to her task.

She had mastered the bakery's simple bookkeeping procedures, and soon she would be qualified to assume what Mary called her monthly reconcile. The work proved time-consuming. On many evenings, she carried the ledgers to the attic room and worked on them far into the night.

"Good afternoon, Anne." Mrs. Flynn entered the shop, interrupting her reverie. Like the folks at Dempsey's, her dear friend and reading partner had become dispirited by the weather and the outbreak of war. Her face looked drawn and her shoulders slumped, as she unwound her rain-soaked wrap.

Once she removed the shawl, Anne noticed the bright pink ribbon that circled her neck and hung down below her waist, almost to her knees. Following Anne's gaze, Mrs. Flynn began to explain. "It is my pin holder. While sewing, I remove any unnecessary pins from the cloth and push them in the ribbon."

"I did not realize you sewed."

"Very little. My dear mother taught my Janey so well she has become an expert seamstress. There is no need for me to stick my fingers at all. In truth, I only wear the ribbon because I enjoy the bright color."

Mrs. Flynn rubbed her hands together. "Brrr! Colder even than yesterday." She approached the counter, and Anne took her basket. "My usual bread, please." One topic seemed to fill her thoughts these days, and Mrs. Flynn moved quickly to discussing it: the war and all things related to the war.

"I pray your sister will arrive soon. Have you any word? There's talk the trains have become unsafe."

Anne selected two plump loaves and began to wrap them. Considering Mrs. Flynn's question, she did not respond immediately. Her hesitation brought an expression of even more intense concern to the dear lady's face.

"Ah now, bless me, where are my senses? I should not have said such a thing. I would not wish to cause you undue distress."

"It is no mind. I am already worried about Julia. I have heard the stories of raids on the trains, and I have been concerned about her for a while now.

"About a month ago, John Dunne, a young man from Ballincooly, stopped at the bakery with a message from Father. John told me Julia had begun preparations for her departure. Then last week, Mary received a letter from her aunt in Blackwater, and across the bottom of the last page, Julia had written 'I will soon be in America.'" She could not help but smile, a little. Her sister was coming. She felt confident it would be soon, but she would not rest easy until Julia arrived at Dempsey's, safe and well.

She pulled her thoughts from Julia and turned back to her bakery duties. "Would you like some biscuits?"

"No thank you, dear." Mrs. Flynn leaned in, so close Anne could feel the chill from her red cheeks. "Sure, there is no end er life in America been a foolish dream? We could have stayed in Ireland and starved."

She placed two coins in Anne's hand, patted her arm, and turned toward the door. "Ah, pay me no mind, my dear. I promise I will cheer myself before I come in again."

❀ ❀ ❀

Two days later, Anne awakened to a light so bright she found it difficult to adjust her eyes. She pushed aside the layers of burlap Mary helped her hang across her windows to hold out the wind. The sight of the marvelous, glistening white city made her gasp.

In her first winter in St. Louis, there had been snow and freezing rain. During one storm, ice formed on tree limbs, rooftops, and on every step, veranda, and patch of pavement the moisture could reach, halting the movement of the city for a time.

A remarkable scene, as beautiful as a museum painting, was spread out before her now. Snow blanketed the rooftops and sidewalks. Soft, damp hunks encompassed tree limbs, as though layered on like thick fluffy icing. The city had turned to white, and Anne `     `   `could not make out the church steeple a few blocks away.

In the afternoon, the snowfall eased, and by the time Anne closed the shop, it had stopped. She had begun to fill the baskets with day-old goods, when Mary brought out an additional covered hamper.

"Weather like this will bring out the needy." As she spoke, Mary filled the third basket with fresh bread. "Sure, cold, hungry folks will crowd into the mission, and we must provide something to soothe their insides. Shall I accompany you and help with this great load?"

Anne shook her head. "Your meal is already simmering on the hearth. Besides, you have developed the sniffles like the others. Don't you be fretting. I will manage."

"You must wear my heavy work boots and take this warm shawl." Mary helped Anne pull on the hefty boots and then wind the long, woolen wrap around her own thin cloak. "Ah, there you go. Now, proceed with care. We will hold supper until you return."

After only a few paces, Anne realized she had been mistaken about her heavy load. Uncomfortable with the bulky clothes and burdened with three cumbersome baskets, it became difficult to maintain her balance as she trudged along the frozen streets. She had crossed the last intersection and headed for the church, when her foot slipped and the baskets began to sway. Reaching out, attempting to keep the lids fastened and prevent the bread from spilling, she fell hard on the pavement.

While she struggled to rise with what grace her snow outfit would allow, she heard heavy footsteps approach.

"Hold on. I'm coming." A familiar-sounding voice called to her. In another moment, strong arms lifted her and set her on her feet. "I'm James Duff. Right yourself, and I'll see to your baskets."

"James?" The impact of the fall and the shock of being rescued by someone from her old, distant life rendered Anne a bit dazed. Sure enough, though, head and face almost covered with a wide-brimmed hat and broad shoulders all but hidden beneath a thick overcoat, here before her stood James Duff from Blackwater.

"It is Anne, James. Anne Carty."

"Lord bless me! I would never have recognized you buried under all that wool. And here I was, on my way to Dempsey's to find you." He brushed snow from the shoulders of her cloak and shawl. "Are you experiencing any pain?"

"I am not hurt."

"Well, your baskets are secured again." He held up one grimy loaf for her inspection. "This one landed in the mud. I'll tend to it. Are you headed for the church, then?"

"Yes, but—" She stopped a moment and shook her head, trying to push aside her surprise and confusion. "It cannot really be you...James Duff...come from home? Come from Blackwater? Oh, it is too much to comprehend.

"I am confused. Are you recently arrived? You were in Dublin when I left home." Anne's questions tumbled out. "Have you seen my family, talked with them?"

"I have. Take my arm, now, and let us hasten you inside and settle you before a warm fire. I will deliver your goods, and then tell you the full story."

James escorted her upstairs to the church rectory and guided her to a soft armchair. He recounted the details of her accident for Father Burns, requested tea from Kathleen, the housekeeper, and carried the baked goods down to the mission. As Kathleen was placing a mug in Anne's hand, James hurried back, concern for her well-being showing in his eyes.

When she had consumed two cups of tea, she assured Father Burns and Kathleen that she bore no ill effects from the fall. Over their protests, she rose from the chair and retrieved her cloak and shawl.

"I will see Anne safely home," James said. His promise seemed to satisfy the concerned priest and housekeeper. After she had extended a final few words of thanks for their care, and bid them good evening, they set out for Dempsey's.

The deep snow drifts slowed their walk and provided time for Anne and James to talk. He began right away with the story of his journey. "I reached New York City in November. I worked in the railroad yards, or wherever I could hire on along the way, to earn train fare. After spending Christmas alone in Chicago, I started out again, arriving in St. Louis yesterday afternoon."

She listened with interest, but anxiety won out over manners. "Forgive me, James, but I cannot continue on. I cannot walk another step or converse in a normal manner, until you tell me what you know of my family." She tightened her grip on his arm. She had not planned such an emotional outburst, but standing so close to someone recently from home, who had surely spoken with her dear ones there, unsettled her. Tears she did not expect or want threatened, and she willed them to halt while she hurried on with her questions.

"Have you seen my father? Do you have news of Julia? I am certain she is on her way. I have been expecting her at any time."

"I did not know Julia anticipated the journey," James said, "but I have seen them, talked with them—"

"Did Father appear in good health? Did he send a message?"

"I spoke with him after church on a Sunday morning last October. In truth, I am here tonight on a special mission from your father. When he learned I intended to come to St. Louis, naught would satisfy him, until I agreed to find you, ascertain the state of your health, and send him a report by the next post. I also promised I would watch over you, if you were in any need. My mission tonight was to deliver his special message to you."

James turned and faced her. "Miss Anne Carty, your father sends you his love."

"Thank you." Anne leaned closer, that persistent tightening of her shoulders easing after hearing his encouraging words. "And my mother?"

She could feel her tension return when he told her Nell Carty had not been at church. Her steps slowed. Illness alone would keep her mother from Sunday mass. There was one thing more, a truth she did not wish to recognize, yet she realized she must. Her mother's absence had allowed her father the opportunity for the extensive conversation with James.

The Duff family was one of the few in Wexford County able to provide additional schooling for their sons. James and his brothers had been sent to Dublin to stay with their cousin. The young priest tutored them and arranged for them to study along with the seminarians at the order's small school.

The boys' advanced education had not impressed Nell Carty. She showed nothing but distain for the Duffs, a family whose name had not been recorded in the parish register since the time of its inception as had those of Anne's Carty and Doran ancestors. Even worse than their recent arrival in the county, an even more grievous blot on the family's respectability, was the fact that James' father, now a blacksmith, once owned the pub located in the center of town.

This pretention, subscribed to by her mother and some women of the village, was beyond Anne's comprehension. Many of these righteous women, including on occasion even her own mother, had the drink brewing in their own cellars, at times. She wished for the courage to mention the kindness of Mrs. Duff and the excellent scholastics of James and his brothers, but she had learned long ago not to disagree with her mother. She had never ventured to say anything in the Duff family's defense. In the midst of her efforts to shake these embarrassing recollections from her mind, James interrupted her thoughts.

"Do you remember the afternoon I kissed you after the choir social?"

Warmth crept from Anne's neck to her face, making her thankful for the darkness all around her. At home, no young girl would speak of a kiss. She had certainly not mentioned it to her mother. Had she even dared to say such forbidden words, she would have found herself on her knees in a convent somewhere in Ireland, rather than on a stroll along a snowy St. Louis street with a handsome young man. This was her new life, though. She was in America. She determined she would push aside her strict and proper upbringing and speak her mind.

"How could I forget? You surprised me." In truth, speaking of that long ago kiss caused a pleasant shiver to rush through her.

"It pleased you," he said. "I'm sure of it."

"You startled me."

"Still, you did not run from me." They both laughed.

They were nearing Dempsey's, and Anne invited James in for supper. "Walter and Mary welcome guests. Their table is often crowded with friends of the boarders, one or two priests from St. Vincent's, or some poor immigrant family. You will see—recent arrival from home that you are—you will receive royal treatment."

Inside the shop, they struggled out of their wraps and cleaned their shoes on the sturdy mat Mary placed beside the door. "I've invited a friend for supper." Anne stepped toward the dining room and called to Walter, who stood beside the table. "It is James Duff from Blackwater."

Walter hurried out to greet them. "Aye, come in, James, come in. We're pleased to have you. Sure, we only awaited Anne's return before we all sat down."

While the two men shook hands, Anne used the moment for a brief, careful observation. Both were tall and broad-shouldered, more so than most young Irishmen, but the physical similarity ended there. Walter appeared robust with ruddy cheeks and abundant wiry, brown hair. James, several years his junior but surely not well fed like the folks at Dempsey's, looked lean and hollow of cheek, his sandy hair beginning to thin.

They proceeded into the dining room, where Anne began the formalities. James had been introduced to Mary, Cara, William, and Eddie, when Grace came through the doorway from the kitchen with a platter of beef. James's greeting took her by such surprise her tray began to slip from her hand. He and Walter rushed to steady it for her. Meanwhile, Anne explained to the others that James was from their home village and had been in school with Grace and her sister Julia. She reminded Walter and Mary of his acquaintance with their aunt and uncle in Blackwater.

"Welcome, James! You must come and sit beside me at the table," Mary said. They were all finding places and settling in when Ellen and Kitty arrived. Introductions and explanations began again, and nothing would do until Ellen knew all she could glean about their guest.

"So, Mr. Duff, you're from County Wexford," she said. "Are you related to the Dempseys, or Donahoos, or the Cartys? Are any of you cousins?"

"We're none of us cousins." Anne could not seem to escape embarrassment this evening. Warmth again crept beneath her collar.

"I have made you blush, Anne." Ellen's bright blue eyes were gleaming now. "Were you two sweethearts back home? Is that it?"

James interrupted Ellen, and began to tell them about her fall.

What a grand relief. With the subject changed, Anne relaxed a moment. Then, realizing they were now discussing her well-being, she tried to make light of the mishap, insisting it was nothing. She urged Ellen and Kitty to sit down to supper.

"What do you remember of this girl from your childhood, James?" Walter's eyes twinkled. "Has she always experienced, difficulty remaining on her feet? Or, is it only our St. Louis streets that cause her trouble?"

Everyone laughed. James looked toward Anne, his grin a little hesitant. When she laughed with them, he appeared to relax.

"It is your turn to wait a bit for a story, James," Anne said. "I may find time to tell of my tumbles on the streets of St. Louis, later perhaps. For now, Mary's delicious potatoes await."

The room quieted then, while Walter said the blessing. With the prayer finished, he reached for the heaping platter of beef before him and began to pass it to Ellen. An expression of chagrin crossed his face.

"Begor—! Our aunt did write us you were on the way, James. It has been several months, has it not? I apologize for not passing the letter on. I should have realized you and Anne and our little Grace would know one another."

"It is no matter," James said. "I am pleased I have found you all, at last. What a comfort it is to be in company with folks from home."

He turned to Mary. "I thank you for the fine supper. Sure, I have not enjoyed such a grand meal in a long while. I do bring news of your Uncle James and Aunt Anne Dempsey. I visited with them after church on a Sunday last fall, and they each sent you their love."

While James talked, Anne could not resist another perusal of him. His eyes, glistening in the candlelight, were the deepest, truest green she had ever seen on a person. His smile, warm and sincere, took in everyone seated around the table.

"On that same day, Grace," he continued, "I spoke with your father and your brother William. They sent a letter I will bring you tomorrow."

Grace nodded. The talk of home did not elicit a true smile, but the girl did appear brighter this evening than at any time since their arrival at Dempsey's. Anne's hopes rose for a recovery of the girl's spirits.

"What are your plans, James?" Walter asked. "Will you remain in St. Louis?"

"I do plan to stay. My first business must be employment and a place to live. I won't need much, but the rooming house where I spent last night proved dire. I am hoping you will have a recommendation on that and advice on where to find a position."

They moved to a discussion of how they could help James settle in. Eddie and Will promised to speak to their landlady on his behalf, and Walter and Mary offered advice about work.

With the rain and gloom of the past weeks replaced with bright snow, and now with the addition of a charming guest, Anne sensed the melancholy had lifted. Though his presence reminded them all of their poor families back home, James's safe arrival brought hope.

Chapter Nine

March, 1861

Anne's evening excursions to St. Vincent's became an adventure after James Duff's arrival in St. Louis, as he often met her somewhere along her way. While they walked the streets of the city together, they used the time to become reacquainted and renew the friendship they enjoyed back home in Blackwater.

They never lacked for subjects to discuss. There were always things to laugh and tease over. James seemed to enjoy Anne's stories of her customers in the bakery and of the immigrants arriving at the mission each week. What a grand surprise it had been to discover he shared her interest in books and wished to discuss those she and Mary and Mrs. Flynn were reading.

"Before I left Ireland," James said, when he bid her farewell at the door of the bakery one evening, "my brothers presented me with a book of verse by the American writer Longfellow. I treasure the book more than any possession I own. I will bring it for you. Such great readers as you all are, you will enjoy the fine poetry."

While they climbed the hill to Dempsey's, on another chilly, windy evening in early spring, he told her of how he missed their home. "I so long for Ireland. Sure, I never knew I loved those muddy lanes and green hills until I had left them."

"I understand what you are saying." Anne patted his arm. "Even after being here for nearly two years, I still pine for home. It feels strange to stand on this ground in America."

"While I dreamed of coming here, I never even considered that once in America I would be hankering for home," James said. "I did not anticipate these feelings.

"When I returned from school and learned you left Blackwater, my one wish was to come after you. My mother had fallen ill, though, and with my brothers away, I could not leave my da to care for her alone. After her death, he urged me to go. My brother Daniel remains at school in Dublin, but Ned is back at home, already saving for his passage. With God's help, they will all be here one day. Then, we will have less cause to be homesick."

"I was sad to hear of your mother's death." Thinking back on the good woman's many kind deeds, Anne shared her remembrances with James. "She was a dear person. She always offered us children a hug and a treat. You must miss her."

Prompted by James' caring words for his family, she told him a little of the burden she had carried with her from Ireland. "My father placed an obligation upon me: to bring the children to America and create a home for them here. The task appears impossible. As each month passes, anxiety over my inability to fulfill my father's wishes and concern for the children's welfare consume my life and my being."

"You must not fret," James said. "Haven't you done a grand job here? Sure, your father deserves praise for his persistence with educating you, and the care the Dempseys provide is commendable, but your own accomplishments are most impressive. Why, you've won a fine situation for yourself. A young woman in charge of the accounts for the bakery? The idea of it would be impossible back home. Even here in America, it is a grand thing."

Anne appreciated the cover of the dark night. Her cheeks had grown warm. Had James' words of praise caused her to lose all control over her emotions?

"Take heart, my girl, you will succeed. You have already sent passage money for Julia." James shifted his arm and drew her close. "When she arrives, won't she be eager to share your task?

"When I observe the lives of drudgery so many young Irish girls here are forced to endure, cleaning rich people's homes or slaving in factories for paltry wages, my heart aches for them. Grace Donahoo is one example. Yet, she is fortunate to hold a position at the mission rather than at one of the filthy establishments so many of our girls have fallen into."

As they neared the bakery, Anne related the story of her Uncle James in Oregon and his lack of response to the letters she sent him the past summer and again at Christmas. She also told him of her experiences with Dermot Fortune.

"I am not certain how long ago Mr. Fortune left Ireland and came here to America," she said, "but his father and brother still live outside of Blackwater. I know nothing of his brother, but I do remember his father, a kind little man. This St. Louis son is a different sort, that's sure. While I try not to think uncharitable thoughts of him, he makes it difficult.

"I have not encountered him since I withdrew the money for Julia's passage, but many stories of his doings have been passed around in the bakery. Some say he disappeared from the city ahead of the law. Another report is he's headed east to gain a profit from the war. Wherever he is, I am desperate for him to return. My uncle placed Mr. Fortune's name on my account, and I cannot remove the funds without his signature."

James seemed reluctant to discuss her uncle or her impending journey to Oregon, but the mention of Mr. Fortune held great interest for him. "When Walter and I finished up some construction work on his new building last evening, we walked to the corner for a pint. Well, he bought me a pint. He does not indulge, you know. At any rate, he spoke of a man who possessed control of your savings. Fortune? Is this the same man? I gained the impression Walter does not trust him."

"The very one," Anne said. "Walter wishes to help me in my dealings with Mr. Fortune, but feels he holds no authority to interfere, since my father and Uncle James entrusted my funds to him. He did attempt to impress on the man how important it is my savings remain safe. He even discussed our concerns with Father Burns. Father extracted a promise from Fortune that my meager account will remain secure."

"Well, I am not bound by the agreement between your uncle and Fortune. I consider my pledge to your father that I look out for you allows me license to intrude." James opened the shop door for Anne. Once they were safely inside, out of the wind and cold, he helped her off with her coat. "Walter claims Fortune has now returned to St Louis. I think it is time I meet the man. Walter says he is married. Do you suppose we could prevail upon Mary to invite him and Mrs. Fortune for a Dempsey supper? Perhaps, with an ample dose of honey and Mary's fine victuals, we could observe this Fortune fellow at close hand."

Mary, of course, approved the scheme and planned a special meal. When the evening finally arrived, what Anne once considered a reasonable idea now made her uneasy. She hurried to deliver her baked goods to the mission, and then, wishing to ease her jittery feelings, ran the entire way home. She went right to work, helping Mary and Cara with the meal preparations. She was adding the finishing touches to the table setting, when Walter entered the dining room. She decided to broach the subject with him.

"I am anxious about this evening," she said. "I have tried to ignore Mr. Fortune's unkempt appearance and look past his expressions of disregard toward me. Still, he makes me uncomfortable. His smile is false, and his eyes never quite meet mine. Each time we part company, I find myself sighing with relief."

"Aye, I agree," Walter said. "But will it not prove interesting to note Fortune's manner in a social situation with his wife? I have never met her, but Mary assures me that, while quiet and retiring, she is a respectable woman."

"She is a good little person." Mary entered the room holding a tray filled with serving utensils, a tall stack of linen napkins and a silver pitcher. She placed her heavy burden on the sideboard, and she and Anne busied themselves, arranging each item to their satisfaction.

At the appointed hour, James and the Dempsey regulars were all in attendance when Anne ushered the Fortunes into the dining room.

Walter made the introductions and urged everyone to take a seat. Eileen Fortune, a pale, thin woman, who appeared a few years older than Mary, nodded in the appropriate places, but spoke little. Her husband, dressed all in black, his hair and beard better groomed than on their last meeting, exuded politeness and graciousness.

"Good evening, good evening!" He moved around the table to greet each one seated there and rushed to hold chairs for the girls who came up to sit near him. He quieted only momentarily, when Father Burns entered the room.

"God bless all here," Father called out as he came through the door.

"God keep us all." Everyone in the dining room recited the refrain to the familiar prayer.

Father Burns barely had time to settle in at the table and offer their thanksgiving for the meal, before Fortune's exclamations began anew. He praised the fine table and each adornment of the dining room. When they began to eat, he elicited a look of great surprise from Mary when he spoke to her directly. He complimented her on each dish, exclaiming over their texture and taste, elaborating on his enjoyment of each bite. In contrast to these courtesies, he never once addressed his wife, though she sat beside him.

Anne wished to be an observer, to listen to the conversation and perhaps learn more about Mr. Fortune. The man apparently thought otherwise, for he soon turned his attention to her.

"My dear Miss Carty, how are you faring? I pray your parents are in good health?"

"They are well, thank you." She held her voice steady and forced a smile.

James and Walter managed to gain control of the conversation, and from then on, she was allowed to sit back and listen to their exchange.

"Well, Dermot, Anne reminds me your father lives not far from my uncle and aunt in Blackwater." Walter matched Mr. Fortune in friendliness, but did not allow pleasantries to interfere with their quest for information. Walter held the meat platter for Mrs. Fortune, seated beside him, and after favoring her with a warm smile, he turned his gaze back to her husband. "She also tells me your brother lives near their place, but I do not believe I have made his acquaintance."

In his eagerness, James almost spoiled the scheme. Anne held her breath when he pushed into the conversation, permitting no opportunity for Fortune to respond.

"Tell me," he said, "what business are you in, here in St. Louis?"

"I practice law and I operate a small real estate venture," Fortune said. "I also work some with immigrants, setting them up with business opportunities." He then shifted the conversation back to James. "I believe your family also resides in Blackwater. I trust they are well?"

And so the evening went. James and Walter interrogated Fortune about his business dealings. He resisted divulging information, giving brief responses and then moving the conversation away from himself. He inquired about the bakery business, questioned Father Burns on parish matters, commented on the approach of war, and asked each person at the table about their home and family. His interest seemed inexhaustible. His controlled, measured expression never wavered. Still, Anne held her doubts of the sincerity of his intentions.

When their guests had gone home, Anne and James sat in the dining room with Walter and Mary. James made no attempt to hide his thoughts from her.

"I do not trust the man. I hold no evidence against him, but I've talked to some around town who claim they have been defrauded by him. They tell me he charms people out of their money, leaving no proof of his misdeeds.

"Walter assures me that, since Julia will be twenty-one in a few months, your account could be placed in her name. You must remove your funds from his grasp, that's sure."

"I have respected your Uncle James' wishes until now, Anne." Walter stopped and sipped his coffee, his next words coming slowly, as if chosen with great care. "I am worried about your savings. Fortune's confident talk does not deceive me one bit. He may be in dire financial trouble. Even with the promise he's made to Father Burns to hold your funds safe, he may not be able to keep his word. He's been seen around town with some disreputable fellows, and it is rumored he is involved in their shady dealings. If he owes them money, he may not be able to extricate himself from this trouble."

Anne nodded. "I agree with you both." She turned to Walter. "I would appreciate it if you would place your name on the account until Julia comes."

One evening, a week after the dinner with the Fortunes, Anne left the mission and stepped out into an eerie, smoky mist. In the few minutes since she entered the church building, delivered her baked goods, and set out again, a heavy fog had settled over the streets leading up the hill from the river. Shivering, more from concern than chill, she shifted the empty baskets to one arm, stretched out her other arm, and trailed her fingers along the wall to keep her bearings.

When she rounded the corner, she was met with a fog covering now so dense she hesitated to move away from the building and proceed on her own. In the midst of her indecision, she noticed a dark shape moving toward her. It appeared to be a man. *Could it be James?* The form approached quickly. For an instant, her mouth went dry and her lips trembled. The next moment brought grand relief. Even with his face still a blur, she recognized the familiar silhouette and grew confident that it was him.

"Ah, my girl, hello. Have I not come just at the right time?"

"James! I am so happy to hear your voice. With this dreadful fog, you were well upon me before I recognized that it was you."

"I surely did not intend to startle you." He relieved her of the baskets and placed his arm around her waist.

They had drawn so close she could now see his smile and the familiar sparkle in his eyes. Then, within the cover of the thick fog, he bent down and kissed her—a gentle kiss, a soft brush of his lips against hers.

Anne's heart pounded. The kiss warmed her insides, and the protection of his strong arm soothed her anxiety and sent her spirits soaring.

"Come, my dear," James said. "Won't we make our way together?"

Her thoughts rushed between confusion and joy, as engulfed in the haze, they clung together and moved with slow, cautious strides. Following the faint glow from the gaslights, they climbed the hill toward the bakery.

The training of her childhood swirled in her mind—*Push him away! Run!*—but her mother's warnings of danger seemed a lifetime ago and so far away.

Was she overwhelmed with loneliness and overcome with the new anxiety brought on by the fog? Or, did James Duff's strong arms not provide comfort and protection such as she had not known in her life before? And, was he not the most wonderful man on earth?

If only Julia would hurry. She needed her big sister's advice desperately.

Chapter Ten

April, 1861

On a grand spring day, with the breezes growing gentle and the sun inching nearer to the earth and warming all in its path, a young woman entered the shop and introduced herself. "I am Kathleen Casey." In the next moment, she delivered the message Anne had waited so long to receive. "I sailed with your sister, Julia. She will arrive here Tuesday next."

Anne came around the counter. She couldn't resist, she hugged the girl. "Oh, how wonderful!" The joy of the message filled her being, making her wish to dance and whirl about. She pushed back the urge, and instead, contented herself with seeking further information. "Is Julia well?"

"We were all exhausted from the voyage, Julia included." Miss Casey paused for a moment, shaking her head. "I know you have not forgotten the desperate conditions on those ships. The ordeal is so recent for me it is difficult to even speak of it. Traveling with the other girls proved a blessing. We were a party of three, you see. We helped one another survive. And, your dear Julia is faring well.

"I worked in a shop in Cork with your Aunt Elizabeth, and she arranged for Julia and me to meet. We encountered another young woman there, Sarah Kelly, the sister of our employer. And so, the three of us sailed to America together.

"My uncle who lives in New Jersey purchased a train tick-et for me in advance, and I left New York City the day after we landed. I will be going on to New Orleans tomorrow. The other girls could not obtain tickets until next week, but they will wait together and Sarah will travel as far as Chicago with Julia." Miss Casey smiled at Anne. "When they waved me off at the train station, I promised I would stop here and inform you of her arrival date. I trust my coming eases your worry."

Memories flooded in, of the dreadful hotel in New York where she and the Donahoos stayed—the noise, the filth, the stench of the place. Anne sobered for a moment.

She could not remain subdued for long. A shimmer of excitement coursed through her. At last, her dear Julia would be here, sitting with her at the Dempsey's table, climbing the stairs to their attic room, Julia laughing, running ahead, and then finally, settling in on her bed, relating stories of the children, telling of the state of Jimmy's health.

With a jolt, Anne remembered her visitor. "You are most kind to come," she said. "I thank you with all my heart for bringing this grand message. My mind is eased, indeed. Sure, your family in New Orleans will rejoice to have you safely with them, as I will when Julia is finally here at my side. Will you join us here at Dempsey's for supper this evening?"

"I would love to, but I must decline." After a few moments of discussion about her early morning departure on a riverboat and the time of her expected arrival in New Orleans, Miss Casey fastened the buttons of her coat and pulled her shawl close around her. "I am sorry I cannot spare the time to come back for supper. I must spend each possible moment in preparation for this last portion of my journey."

When Anne inquired if there was any help she or the Dempseys could provide, Miss Casey again politely declined. "I do not believe I will need any assistance." In another few moments, she was out the door and on her way.

At noon on Tuesday, Anne paced on the platform at the riverfront. She moved to the end of the dock, stamped her feet, and then returned to her original spot. A wide range of potential problems and questions filled her mind. Would the tiny attic room upset Julia? Would they find a suitable position for her? Had Julia changed in the nearly two years since she had been in her company? Had she, herself, changed? Would she even recognize her sister?

A smattering of people came to join Anne. They all appeared absorbed in their own concerns. An hour went by, then two hours. No one spoke. No one asked a question about the length of time required for crossing the river or the expected arrival time. In any case, none of her fellow bystanders appeared qualified to answer such questions. The atmosphere on the riverfront remained quiet and calm.

Another quarter of an hour passed, and then a young man with a bullhorn appeared to announce the imminent arrival of the ferry. With the passage of a few, brief moments, workmen materialized from all sides. Doors were pushed open and planks thrown down on the riverbank in the direction of the water. Anne secured her place on the platform. She shaded her eyes and scanned the distant shoreline, straining to make out any sight of a vessel across the river.

Soon, she could see what she believed was the ferry, no more than a dot, now separating itself from the scenery along the riverbank. The tiny splotch grew in size as it approached. Things changed quickly now. People came toward her from all directions, crowding near and jostling her.

The ferry pulled close to shore. How different the operation was from what she remembered of her experience on the ferry almost two years ago. The workmen quickly secured the vessel with ropes and then rolled back the heavy gate. Passengers streamed forward. The crowd surged around her, but Anne had been waiting a long time for this moment. She settled herself in her place and did not allow anyone to push her aside. She scrutinized the face of each woman who moved down the gangplank.

At last, Julia walked toward her. Their eyes met, and with each step that moved her closer, Anne felt and shared her sighs of relief.

"Julie! Julie!" Struggling forward, and in her excitement reverting to her sister's childhood name, Anne helped her maneuver along the uneven wooden ramp.

"Anne, I am thrilled to see you. How I have missed you. Everyone at home misses you so." Julia's golden brown curls bounced beneath her cap, her pale blue eyes sparkled, and a smile illuminated her fine, delicate face. Anne did not miss the weariness beneath the smile, the slight slump of Julia's shoulders, and the hesitation in her usual jaunty step. She observed the grime that clung to her dress and bonnet, now dampened by the spray from the river crossing. She shook her head in puzzlement at the unusual, voluminous frock she wore. Yet, with all the disarray of her clothing and the heartbreaking signs of fatigue, was Julia not the prettiest girl ever to arrive in St. Louis? When they embraced, Anne did not wish to let her go.

Julia held only a small valise. "Your trunk was delivered to Dempsey's the day before yesterday," Anne said. "It has been installed in our third floor bedroom already."

"By the grace of God," she said, relieving Julia of her bag, "you appear in good health. Though you must be exhausted, you look fit. I cannot believe you are here at last." She continued to clasp Julia's arm, and clinging to each other, the valise dangling between their locked arms, they began their walk. "Please, tell me about your crossing and the news from home."

"Your descriptions of the hardships of your own journey proved accurate." Julia's expression sobered, as she began telling of the trip. "In spite of your warnings, I continued to dream of coming to you, experiencing the adventures you've had, and observing the sights you have seen. While I longed to be on my way, I could never have imagined such dire conditions unless I lived through them on my own. The voyage proved dreadful—the hard berths, the noise, the constant rolling and jolting, and the misery of the poor sick people. The frightful hotel in New York is another experience I wish to erase from my mind. I must think of other things until I have forgotten it all."

"Was the train safe? You know, the war has begun in earnest here and we received reports of renegades raiding the trains."

"I observed nothing of concern. Uniformed men filled the train, but all appeared peaceful."

"Please, please, tell me about everyone at home," Anne said.

"Our poor parents work hard, like always," Julia said, "but while Father manages to remain cheerful, Mother's sadness never wanes. I cannot fault her for it. There is much to be sorrowful about: the few provisions remaining in the cellar, Jimmy's medicine becoming near impossible to obtain, and the taxes owed, new taxes levied—the taxes, always the taxes. Living with gloom all about is hard on the young ones, though." They turned the corner now and began to climb the hill toward the church, but Julia talked on, not seeming to notice any change in their pace or their surroundings.

"Kate spends much of her time at Uncle Martin's, helping Aunt Catherine with the children, but she finds time to sew. She is an excellent seamstress, more gifted even than Mother, I believe. She possesses a flair for the design of garments. It is difficult, though, to obtain fabric for any clothing, even for those with the means to purchase goods.

"Jimmy has grown weaker than he was when you left home. It proved hardest to say good-bye to him, the poor dear fellow, sitting in his chair, wishing me well, and writing out messages for you." Julia seemed unable to go on now, and they walked on in silence for a time. In a few moments, she appeared to recover, and with a small smile, she went on with her descriptions of their family.

"Our Lizzie, and Maura, and our wee Mag—she is four now, not such a baby—are all bright, healthy girls," Julia said. "Michael has grown into the fine boy we all knew he would one day become."

Anne dropped her sister's arm for a moment, and as they continued to walk, she transferred her valise to her right hand.

"Will we have them all here with us, in time?" Julia asked. "Sure, it would be grand."

"I pray it will happen," Anne said.

"This is the loveliest place I have encountered since I left Ireland." Julia began to notice her surroundings and observe the foliage and colorful blossoms. "Though there are many buildings and crowds of people, every available space is filled with marvelous trees and bushes, and look over there, those brilliant yellow blooms. And, what of the fine trees across the way, loaded with full white flowers with green pushed forth at the tip of each limb? Have you learned their names? I know we mean to go on to Oregon, but I do think we would all love St. Louis."

"It is a beautiful time here," Anne said. "Last Sunday afternoon, we all rode out into the countryside with Walter and Mary Dempsey. Mary is our garden expert, and with her guidance, we gathered wildflowers for our table and purchased plants from a farmer to put in around the building. It was splendid.

"I must warn you, though, when it rains, you will see the flow of mud. Ah faith, I should not talk of mud now. Let us enjoy this glorious day God provided to welcome you here." Anne gave her sister's arm a squeeze. "I am happy you have come on any day. Have I told you that?"

The strange looking garment her sister wore had been distracting Anne from the moment she stepped off the ferry. She could ignore it no longer, nor could she suppress her next question. "I did wonder about your dress, Julia. Sure, it cannot be of our mother's making?" The gown, though fashioned of a sturdy brown fabric, was decorated everywhere—arms, back, bodice, skirt; neckline to hemline, shoulder to wrist— with deep, swooping ruffles, which caused the slender Julia to appear twice her size.

"Aunt Mary gave it to me," Julia said, "pronouncing it stouter than my old gray. With my Sunday dress packed in the trunk and Mother insisting we would not want to injure Aunt Mary's feelings, there was naught for me to do but bring it along. Well, I wore my faithful gray all along the entire crossing. When we arrived in New York it was filthy, beyond cleaning with the specks of soap and water the hotel allotted to us. So, I was forced to adorn myself in this field of giant ruffles.

"Kate suggested that, once on the ship, I toss this thing into the ocean." Julia paused a moment and bent down.

"See how useful these ruffles are. At the last stop on the train, I purchased a treat and stored it here in my skirt." She untied a knot in a deep ruffle at her knee and produced two rolls.

"Oh my, Julia." Anne couldn't help but laugh. "You have purchased biscuits, and here we are on our way to your new home at a bakery." In the next moment, the two girls were laughing together. During the last two blocks of their walk, they hugged, and giggled, and then hugged again. They reached Dempsey's in great high spirits.

The women of the neighborhood had once again assembled in the shop to welcome the newest arrival from Ireland. They all enjoyed cups of tea and Mary's special cakes and satisfied their need to learn any news from home Julia could pass on to them Then, Mary shooed the girls off to settle Julia in.

Once they were in the attic room, Anne realized she need not have worried over her sister's reaction to the small space.

"A bed of my own, and—praise be—a real mattress, and this splendid wardrobe. 'Tis wonderful." She moved across the room to stand before the massive armoire and brush her fingertips along its surface. "What beautiful wood, and so roomy, large enough for our entire family's clothing. How grand!" Excitement brimmed in her eyes, as she exclaimed with pleasure over everything.

"Ah, we have our own windows." She stopped a moment to gaze out. "I believe I see the river in the distance. Is that our church? I can imagine the brilliant view in the morning. Oh, I never dreamed it would be so fine." Once begun, she could not seem to slow her words or stem her commendation for each thing that caught her eye.

"I love everything at Dempsey's, this cozy room, the bakery, the wonderful people, but what I cherish most, is being with you." Julia reached out to her, and Anne felt chills at her touch. After almost two years of waiting and longing, difficult as it was to believe, Julia had arrived, and the proof of it held her hand and continued to talk.

"You are still my dear little sister," Julia said, "with your rosy complexion and your wondrous soft hair and fine eyes. I prayed the bond we shared back home would remain strong and our affection for one another would hold firm. Well, here we are together again, after almost two years, and it's as if we had never been apart."

"Oh, Julia, I have missed you so." Anne wrapped her arms around her sister and held her tight. Then she stepped back. She did not wish to end this joyous time, to leave and break the spell, but she had obligations. It was time to return to her post in the bakery.

"Now dear, I must hurry down to the shop to help Mary. At dusk, I will leave for the mission, as is my custom, but you rest here until supper. I am sure you are exhausted, and your welcomes to St. Louis have only begun. We will be enjoying a special meal Mary is preparing for tonight. Grace Donahoo is waiting to renew acquaintances with you, and there are the other Dempsey girls and Walter and his helpers to meet. It will be a grand evening."

While Anne worked in the bakery, each lady who came in questioned her about her sister, reminding her again and again of the blessing she was finding difficult to believe.

Must she pull at her hair or pinch her flesh to jar herself into full acceptance of Julia's presence in St. Louis? When she herself had come, the realization that she was in America had taken a long time to sink in to her consciousness. With the passage of each month, she had begun to accept that the roads she moved along were in St. Louis and not Blackwater, the building she worked in was Dempsey's Bakery, and this was her home. Julia would soon be experiencing the same such confusing and at times painful emotions.

What a wonderful, unbelievable day. Her dear Julia had come at last and was right this moment upstairs resting in their attic room. Anne was no longer alone, and she could not find a thought or image grave enough to push away her smile. Her happiness was difficult to contain and she worried she may burst into song and frighten her customers away.

When the time came to fill her baskets for her walk to St. Vincent's, Julia joined her. "I know you advised me to rest," she said, "but I am too excited to be still." She had scrubbed away some of the residue from her long journey and changed to her Sunday dress. Though the frock appeared a bit wrinkled and worn, Julia now looked her familiar self. "I have many a thank you to offer our great, good God, and I would appreciate the opportunity to visit the church."

Arriving at the mission, the girls discovered Grace had finished for the day and left ahead of them. Anne sighed. Could she not even wait a few minutes to greet her old friend? Bridget Rice was on duty, though, and Anne prayed her warm welcome would make up for any disappointment Julia may feel over missing Grace.

"It is grand you've come." Bridget helped the girls lift their heavy baskets to the table, all the while talking to Julia. "You look well. Sure, you'll be rested and ready to help out here at the mission in no time. We will likely work together one day soon."

She turned to Anne. "Is it not splendid? Julia is here in time for the church social?"

Bridget moved her attention back to Julia. "You will want to be refreshed by Saturday. Our gatherings here at St. Vincent's are wonderful affairs with music and dancing. So many of our friends will be there, and they are all waiting to meet you. Are you nimble of foot like your sister?"

"Ah, so she's demonstrated her dancing skills, has she?"

"She has amazed us all."

"'Tis not fair." Anne placed her hands on her hips. "You two have already joined forces against me." She could not hold back her smile, though, and everyone in the room appeared enveloped in her joyous mood. Workers and immigrants alike smiled and laughed along with her.

In the midst of their merriment, Father Daly came out to meet Julia. "It may be a good time to introduce Julia to the pastor," he said. "Father Burns has been at work in his office all afternoon and I suspect he has had his fill of the paperwork by now."

The girls climbed the stairs to the rectory office and found Father Burns seated behind a large, overflowing desk. He arose from his chair, at once, and greeted Julia warmly.

"Anne told me of your work in your parish in Blackwater. Sure, I would welcome your assistance, but I have funds for but a few hours each week. Now, there will be no more talk of employment tonight, Miss Carty. Rest and regain your strength, my dear, and we will speak again next week."

They left Father Burns and made their way along the hallway that led them back to the mission. At last, they started for home. It had been a long day for both girls. Anne felt weary, but her sister, appearing rejuvenated by her brief rest, ambled along, a decided bounce in her step. At every few paces, she rolled her head from side to side and exclaimed over her prospects. As they neared the corner at Park, she stopped and leaned toward Anne.

"I am thrilled. I never dreamed I would obtain a position so soon."

"Father Burns cannot pay a full week's wage, though. We must find additional employment for you."

"But, do you not consider half a position a great success for my first day? Perhaps tomorrow I will secure additional work."

"You are so right. Any work at all, is an amazing feat for your first day in the city," For the second time in the passage of a few hours, the sisters walked along, arms entwined, laughing together. Anne sighed. She had been missing the grand pleasure of Julia's company for a long, long while.

When they reached Dempsey's and passed through the shop to the dining room, the aroma of the fine meal Mary prepared for Julia's first evening filled the air. Anne's energy revived. She introduced her sister to everyone, and once again, she chided herself for her foolish worries. Julia's exuberant response to each of her friends and their delight in her pushed aside all her concerns.

"Grace, it's grand to see you!" Julia said when she discovered her old friend. "It has been a long time since we sat beside one another in school."

"Ah, Julia, you have come at last." Anne noticed the tears that filled Grace's eyes, while Julia related all she could remember of her last meeting with the Donahoos in Blackwater. As they continued to talk, Grace's countenance began to brighten a bit. For a moment, a genuine smile crossed her face, the first Anne had seen from the girl in many months. She noticed the folks around the table agreed with her. They were all nodding toward Grace and smiling along with her. Perhaps Julia would, indeed, help the poor, sad girl recover from her disappointment.

In the midst of the introductions, the reunion, and a shower of questions for Julia, James Duff arrived. His cordial greeting to Julia brought a feeling of extraordinary pleasure to Anne.

"I expected to find you in St. Louis, James," Julia said, "but to meet you here on my first night in St. Louis is a grand surprise. I've brought along a letter from your family." She turned back to the others. "I have one for you, Grace, and another for Walter and Mary."

Walter made special note of the happy occasion, including in his blessing a prayer of thanksgiving for Julia's safe arrival. Anne's own joyful mood sobered when he added a prayer for their families and mentioned the desperate conditions back home.

When the prayer ended, Julia acknowledged the sad situation. "Crops failed all over Ireland last year, and large families in particular cannot obtain enough food to satisfy their children. We must not rest until we bring our dear ones out of that desperate place.

"Why, when I look around this bountiful table, my heart grieves for my poor parents and many others like them who struggle to feed each *wee wane*—oh, forgive me." Julia shook her head. "I intended to say each small child. I know we are meant to use the American terms. I will try to remember." For a moment, she covered her face with her hand.

Anne leaned close to Julia to offer her comfort. Everyone around the table joined in, assuring Julia it would take some time.

"Even after so many years, I still revert to a *begorrah* now and then," Walter said. Everyone at the table became more animated than usual, telling of their own experiences, murmuring assurances to Julia.

"I dunno." Ellen dipped her head for a moment. "I would love to capture that touch of home for myself. It thrills me to listen to Julia's talk. I worry I will forget my dear Mother's voice and her favorite expressions." She turned to Julia. "Don't you worry, your speech is fine. You'll lose the sound of home soon enough."

Julia needed only that slight encouragement, before her bright smile returned and she moved to telling the adventures of her journey. Anne watched in amazement. Her sister had revived her own spirits and was managing to uplift them all.

By the time Mary and Cara began serving dessert, Anne realized Julia's strength had begun to fade. She was attempting to remain alert by pressing her arms into her ribs, but she was having difficulty holding up her head.

"I believe it is time Julia and I retired to the attic room," she said.

"I agree," Mary said. "Julia must rest. It will be some time before she recovers from her difficult journey."

Even as Anne guided her to the stairway, Julia, leaning heavily on her arm, continued to talk. She thanked Mary for the fine supper, apologized for not helping to tidy up, and assured the girls she would be fully recovered the next day.

Once in their room, Anne helped her sister find her nightgown in the trunk and prepare for bed.

Still exclaiming over everything, Julia nestled into "the most comfortable mattress I have ever rested on," with her head propped on a pillow "soft as I have touched in all my life.

"I cannot rest, until I share one more thing with you." Julia attempted to sit up, but exhaustion triumphed at last and it took an enormous effort for her to speak. "Please search to the bottom of my trunk, and you will uncover a gift from Father."

Buried beneath Julia's undergarments and two pretty quilts she said Aunt Mary made for them, Anne uncovered something special. Her father had sent her *Volume One: The Tragedies of William Shakespeare.*

"Oh Julia, Father is so kind." Anne had not forgotten how he treasured the few precious books he owned. He had remembered her love for the Shakespeare books, though, and sent one to her. As she held the precious volume close, she could almost feel her father's presence beside her. She must somehow impart to him what delight this dear bit of home brought her. She would try to express her appreciation in her next letter.

Julia took her hand, and the tears they shared were an equal measure of sadness and joy.

Chapter Eleven

Blackwater

Dear Anne,

I was in great trouble about you since Julia went away. There were such bad accounts from America. I am glad to hear Julia is with you. Dear Anne the times are bad. We had a bad crop. I was not able to pay our rent. My Dear Child, I'm sorry to have to say we are heavy in debt. I need not say any more about that. Julia knows the way she left us.

Dear Anne, I hope the times will be better and your good letter has given me great pleasure. We were all rejoiced to hear that you are doing well. Tell Julia that Rev. Father Furlong inquired for her. Kate is a good girl. She is going to school. Lizzie is coming on well now and Maura and Lizzie are always speaking of you. Jimmy is getting very bad.

Mary Murphy is going to Dublin in January to school. Kitty Read is home. Ellen is the same thing. William Doran never was so bad as he is now. He is a great annoyance to his family.

I believe I have no more to say. I remain your mother,
    Nell Carty

    My Dear Anne, I know your cousin, Edward Carty, has reached your uncle by this time. When you go there be careful of him, as I understand before he left he told a person when he would see his uncle he would settle us. You know we never deserved any ill will from him, but God who sees all things will, I trust, render harmless his Irish tongue. N.C.

July, 1861

    Anne sat at her work table in the bakery. She and Mary had been engrossed in accounts, but they became distracted by Julia, who had begun telling Cara a story about their Uncle Martin. At Cara's puzzled look, Anne lowered her head to hide a grin.

    "I've no family ata'l, here or back home, you see." Cara shook her head. "'Tis hard for me to make out... so many people...all of one family."

    "In truth, it is quite simple." Julia patted Cara's shoulder for a few moments. After obtaining a slight nod and a relaxing of the bewildered look from the poor, confused girl, she went on. "Uncle Martin and Uncle Pat Doran are our mother's brothers. Uncle Joseph Read is the husband of Mother's sister, Margaret. There is but one Uncle James, and I am sure you have heard of Father's elusive, older brother in Oregon.

    "There are two Uncle Williams. One is William Carty, Father's fine upstanding brother, who prepares to leave for America any day with his wife, Elizabeth. The other William, another of mother's brothers, is the eejit uncle who drinks. He lives on a farm a few miles south of our village with his wife,

Eileen. We seldom see her. Father says she often suffers with a blackened eye. Mother says, 'Now John, you hush.'

"Then, there are the aunts. There is a Mary on each side of the family: Aunt Mary Kelly, a widow, and Aunt Mary Doran, a spinster. There are two Catherines, one is Father's sister and the other is married to Uncle Martin. Another Elizabeth, father's youngest sister and everyone's favorite, lives in Cork and enjoys a life of adventures."

Julia appeared surprised to see them all laughing, but she could not be diverted from her journey along the family tree. She held up a plump currant roll and attempted to draw them all into her next scheme. "Now ladies, I hold here a special treat, a reward you will receive if you name at least ten Carty and Doran cousins living in Blackwater."

"Aye, if you are not a scamp for sure." Mary wiped away tears. "I could spend the morning in a grand attempt to name Margarets, Marys, Elizabeths, and Annes, and perhaps a James, a Michael, a Patrick, or two. And then, what would be my fine reward? A treasured biscuit from my own oven? I thank you, though, my dear, you have cheered us all. I've not enjoyed such a good laugh in weeks."

It pleased Anne to see them all—Cara included—wearing broad smiles as they returned to their tasks. What pride she felt in the way her sister comported herself. When not assisting Father Burns, Julia helped Anne in the shop. With her sunny nature, she spread cheer throughout the place, yet she worked harder than anyone.

Mary had offered to pay Julia a salary, but Anne would not hear of it. "You and Walter have already extended such kindness to us. We will not take advantage of you," she said.

After some discussion, they agreed Julia would receive room and meals for her work, an arrangement that satisfied Anne, thrilled Julia, and pleased Mary. She remarked many times how fortunate she was to be blessed with another excellent Carty sister for a helper.

When the girls retired to the attic room that evening, Julia made a confession to Anne. "I miss our family with a longing surpassing what I ever imagined I would experience." As she spoke, her eyes rested on a tiny container on the writing table.

"Oh Anne, here is the cracker tin you kept your savings in when you were at home." She held the little box in one hand and stroked it with the other, as if wishing to draw forth some spark of home. She broke into sobs, and minutes passed before she spoke again. "How strange this is. While I was at home, impatient to come, it never occurred to me that I would suffer this homesickness."

"I, too, pine for our dear ones." Anne moved from the writing table to sit beside Julia on her bed. "In those first weeks after my arrival here, I was frantic, missing you all, longing for you. I would rest in bed at night, thinking of everyone, trying to picture each one: Jimmy in his chair before the fire; Mother at the table, her head bent to her sewing."

Anne gathered her courage and moved to the one question that had weighed on her mind and heart since the day she left Ireland. "While I longed to have you here to share each new thing I experienced, I worried you were angry with me. I prayed you would forgive me for leaving Ireland ahead of you." Anne searched Julia's eyes, seeking her sister's understanding.

"There was never anything to forgive," Julia said. "I suffered a dreadful disappointment when Father sent you out first, but he made the decision, not you. I knew you did not want to go. The many months I waited for my turn to come seemed an eternity. I dedicated myself to gathering fare money. I tried to emulate you, practicing thrift and spending as little as I could. Still, when it came time to go, my efforts proved fruitless. After I purchased the necessities for the journey, I had little money to bring along with me, save what you were good enough to send. Though it pained me to do so, I was forced to concede that you were the perfect person to lead our family to America and Father's judgment had been sound.

"Ah, Anne, we are both here now. Could we not ignore the two years we were apart and pretend we came together after all."

Relief and joy flooded through Anne at the understanding words she was hearing. "If I had broached this subject with you before I left home, your reassuring words would have eased my worry. They warm my heart even now." She leaned in close to Julia. "I suppose I was so troubled about leaving, I could not think clearly."

"Well, we've been given a new beginning. Let us learn from our foolish lack of sharing with one another. We must resolve to confide our happiness and our cares, holding nothing back. We are both missing home, and now we will pine for our dear ones together." Julia hugged Anne vigorously.

"I picture our tiny cottage," Julia closed her eyes, moving back to the remembering. "I imagine I see our girls' loft spread across the top of our parents' bedroom partition. I see Michael's head peeking out from the boys' loft above the dining room table at the other end of the room."

Anne looked up at her sister, nodding her agreement. "Many long nights, as I waited for sleep to rescue me from my loneliness, I felt sure I could hear the children's laughter. I still believe Father's voice calls to me. With time, the pain eased. Now that you are with me, I expect the wild fancies will leave me entirely."

"Sure, we are blessed to be together." Julia's face brightened. Nothing—homesickness, worry over their parents, concern about employment, the constant talk of war—seemed to dampen her spirits for long. In a moment, she pushed aside the memories and moved to a new topic.

"And, what of our fine looking Mr. Duff? He is handsome, with his tall, strong frame and his ever present smile. You cannot deny it, Missy Anne. Has he been walking you home from the mission each night since he came here? And, have you noticed his eyes searching you out, no matter who is present in a room?"

"Oh Julia, I am desperate to discuss this very thing with you." Anne rushed to unburden her heart, telling her sister of the first kiss, a few subsequent kisses, and of James' assertion that they would build a life together.

"Though I teased you about James," Julia said, "I also wondered about Walter. Your letters were filled with talk of the Dempseys." A fresh, new light appeared in Julia's eyes. "I imagined I might arrive here and find you betrothed to him. When I noticed your attachment to James, I must say, it came as a surprise."

Anne shook her head. "Walter is a fine man, that's sure, but, he's shown nothing but friendship toward me. Then, when James arrived, I confess, he immediately captured far too many of my thoughts.

"I believe Mary had the same idea about Walter as you, and I worried she would be disappointed. I would not distress her for the world. But, Mary favors James over most all of the guests who come here for supper. He teases her and makes her laugh. And of course, she appreciates the help he is giving Walter with the renovations to the new building. I do believe she is nearly as fond of James as I am."

"Exactly how fond of James are you?" Julia looked into Anne's eyes, and though she did not squirm, her sister's gaze touched deep within her. The feelings she had been holding locked in her heart since James' arrival in St. Louis were slowly beginning to slip out.

"At first, James was someone from home. He told me of the talks he had with all of you before he left Ireland. We reminisced about school friends and teachers. We talked about long ago outings and places we had explored as children. His voice brought the sound of home to me. Do you see?"

Julia nodded, but she motioned for Anne to continue.

"Well then, he began to arrive at the mission on many evenings to walk me home. I looked forward to seeing him. Our talks became ever more important. James listened attentively to what I had to say. He was truly interested in hearing about my work here at Dempsey's. It felt grand to stroll beside him and hold his arm. As the weeks passed, my feelings of friendship toward him began to change. When he smiled down at me, my insides would begin to bubble."

"Bubble?" Julia giggled.

"The emotions are difficult to explain." Anne grinned.

Julia threw herself on the bed, dissolved in laughter. In a moment she sat up again and prodded Anne for more of the story. "Then, talking to James turns you into a pot of soup simmering on the hearth?"

Anne edged closer to her sister again. She attempted to suppress her own chuckles, but failed. "Not necessarily simmering. Some bubbles are light and cool."

"Well, thank you for sharing these mystifying feelings with me. Now, I will know the moment I fall in love. When I begin to bubble, I will recognize my condition for sure."

Anne sat up straight, attempting to calm her mood. The topic she now wished to discuss with her sister was a more serious matter, one she had been wishing to talk over with Julia since she arrived in St. Louis. "James maintains he came to St. Louis with the express purpose of finding me. I believe he will propose marriage when he obtains a permanent position. What will I do then? You know, I cannot think of marriage until we bring the family to America.

"I did try to talk to him, to explain the whole of our obligation to the family. Still, I hesitate to speak in such plain terms. I do not wish him to think I am forward. You know, Mother says—"

"We cannot mind what Mother says now. Ah here, only minutes ago I sat right here, dissolved in tears because of missing her." Julia rose and walked to the window. Sighing, she turned back to Anne. "'Tis another matter altogether. Our situation is so different from what our lives were at home, and Father and Mother are not here to advise us.

"Faith, I'm happy I have come." Julia squared her shoulders. With one arm at her waist and a fist resting under her chin, she paced the room. Coming to a sudden stop, she faced Anne. "You are not alone anymore. I promise my help and support, and I mean that with all my heart. Though I did not make the pledge to Father that he demanded of you, I, too, yearn to have the children with us."

Anne attempted to explain her strange agreement with her father, wishing that in the process she would be able to sort it out for herself. "When Father said I must set aside my own life and I made the promise to him, our discussion ended. He assumed I would carry out his wishes without further question, and I, so accustomed to doing his bidding, never even asked him to elaborate. He said I must make a home here for the children. But, once I arrived in St. Louis, there seemed to be a change in his demand. Now, I also seem to be responsible for sending money home each month, as well as providing passage money for each of the children.

"Am I never to marry? Never have a child of my own? How foolish I was to take on this task without asking these questions. At only sixteen, marriage and children were but dreams of events and happenings belonging in the distant future. Now that James is here—and him speaking at every opportunity of building a life with me—the questions appear more pressing."

"Well, here I am, all of twenty years old," Julia said, "and I never dared to have these same conversations with Father." She shook her head in agreement with Anne. "Before I left home, he told me he loved me and would miss me, and that was the end of our talk."

"Throughout our childhood, he showered us with kindness and affection," Anne said. "Surely, that will never change." She felt a need to defend their father. She paused a moment, remembering the gentle, affectionate parent he had been.

"He was loving and kind," Julia said, "but he should have discussed these matters with us. He should have expanded upon his plan for us. How long did he foresee it would take to bring all of the children out? Did he and Mother plan to come?

Were we to remain unmarried until that day? I am sure he did not intend that we never marry. Would not a husband for you, and perhaps one for me in the bargain, add assistance toward bringing them all out?

"We should have persisted with these questions ourselves, but we did not. Here we are now, on our own and without direction. I believe we must act as we see fit.

"So, my dear sister, here's what you must do." Julia patted Anne's hair and then rubbed her hands along her arms. "Speak to James from your heart. I have studied his character some, both here and at home. I observed him at church a few times last summer and I admired his kind and solicitous demeanor with his father and young brothers. And, you cannot question he cares for you. Anyone who knows him at all can see it. He will wish to share this burden with you. I am certain of it.

"And, are you praying about all of this? Have you asked our heavenly Father for his guidance?" Julia looked into Anne's eyes until she squirmed and turned away.

"Of course, I pray every day." That was not Julia's question, she knew.

"But, have you placed the whole of this dilemma in His hands? Or, are you attempting to climb this entire impossible mountain on your own?"

"You are right." She could not fool her sister. Julia knew immediately that she had fallen into her old habit of taking the full burden on herself. "You are a gentle and tender reminder to me that I must place my trust in God. Will you help me?"

"Of course, I will." Julia knelt beside the bed and joined Anne's hands with her own. Together, they offered up their petitions and asked for guidance. Anne ended their prayer by pouring out thanks for the safe arrival of her dear sister.

Chapter Twelve

Blackwater
12th July 1861

My Dear Children,

I received your most welcome letter of the 9th. It gave us great pleasure to hear you were well and in good health as we are all at present, thank God.

This has been a hard year in Ireland. The crops are bad and greatly short of the usual compliment in every kind of grain which leaves a great many distressed and will for this winter and in consequence of same my crop being so bad I was not able to pay my rent.

We are happy to hear of you being in good health and good situations and that all dangers of the war appear to be removed from you, at least you say nothing about it in your letter. We got the slip of paper sent in James Dempsey's letter and also the two newspapers. You may tell Grace Donahoo that her father is just alive and I believe not much more.

Let me know if you delivered the slip I sent in my last letter to Mr. Fortune and if you received any kindness from him or how he treated you. Your brother Jimmy's health is just the same as ever. We would wish to be remembered to Walter Dempsey and his sister and also wish you to thank them in our behalf for all their kindness to you.

William Doran is now stark staring mad, and roving about night and day. He and his wife are living still on the same stretch and he has given her a broken bone. Kitty remains home still and Mr. Stapleton has lost his senses and turned fanatic.

I conclude by praying for God to protect you, and remain your affectionate father,
John Carty

August, 1861

On one of the warmest afternoons of the summer, Anne stood on a ladder with a pail of water in one hand and several soft white cloths draped across her shoulder. She had been cleaning the bakery's broad front window when Julia burst through the shop door, returning from her work at the church.

"Good afternoon!" With a brilliant smile spread across her face, Julia walked right up to the ladder and extended her arm to help her climb down. Descending each step, slowly, cautiously, Anne looked into her sister's bright eyes. Clearly, the tale that caused her face to glow and her smile to near explode would not wait another moment to be told.

Before Anne's feet touched the floor, Julia began with her story. "As I worked in the office this afternoon, Colonel Joseph Scones, a Union Army officer, arrived to talk with Father Burns. Father introduced me to the Colonel and then began to extol my virtues."

Julia leaned an elbow on the bakery counter. "He called me the hardest working girl in all of St. Louis. 'I hand her notes in my terrible scribble, and she turns out letters to the archbishop and lists of parishioners, contributions, and merchants' bills in her fine script.'" Julia imitated the priest's voice and inflections to perfection.

"'She writes out my Sunday sermons, improving them a little, I suspect. She helps at our mission, keeping track of supplies and paying bills for Father Daly. Though she arrived here but a short time ago, she's become indispensable to us both.'" Julia laughed. "Lord bless me, with all this fine praise, I believe I have come near to sainthood."

Anne placed her heavy pail on the floor. She shook her head, wondering where Julia's enthusiastic tale could be leading.

"Here's the best part," Julia went on. "Colonel Scones exclaimed how helpful it would be if he had my assistance himself. I know Father Burns held some reservations, wishing to guard my respectability, and at the same time, worrying about retaining my help with his own work. He could have refused, but he responded with his usual kindness.

"While I listened to the two men talk, it occurred to me that I could not work for the Union Army at the church office. With the strife in our parish over the war, my working for Colonel Scones would anger southern sympathizers, and the fact that he is English would rile the entire congregation.

"Already one thought ahead of me, Father Burns suggested Mr. Lane next door might allow me to use the small area adjacent to his wife's laundry for the work. They walked over to speak with him, and things were settled in a matter of minutes.

"I will now work for both men. Mrs. Lane will watch over my virtue, and I'll suffer only the slight inconvenience of a short walk between the two buildings." Julia took Anne's hands, and in her excitement, gave them a hard squeeze.

"Well, if Walter agrees I should do it, that is. I suppose he will approve of my supporting the Union Army with my work?" Julia's look shifted from joyous to uncertain. "I must admit I have avoided all the talk of war since I've been in America. I do not understand the conflict at all."

"I must confess, I am no more knowledgeable on the issues than you" Anne said. "I, too, read only the occasional newspaper, but I do feel confident Walter will approve of your working for the Colonel."

"Walter is for the Union, I know." Julia said. "I will follow his lead in this."

"As will I, for now." A resolute feeling settled over Anne. "I must increase my efforts from this time forward, read all I can, and make a determination for myself."

"At any rate," Julia turned back to her new employment situation, "with two positions, I will earn a full salary. Bringing the children out and supporting our family on both sides of the Atlantic will be a shared mission."

While the girls cleaned up after dinner that evening, Anne told them of their struggle to alter Julia's ruffled dress and make it into a suitable frock for her work at the rectory and for the colonel.

"I will be happy to help you," Ellen said. "You will help, too, will you not, Kitty?"

Kitty nodded with enthusiasm.

"Oh, thank you both," Anne said. "Julia and I are attempting to save for passage for our sister, Kate, and purchasing a new dress right now is out of the question."

"I wish I could join you," Mary said, "but I must rest a bit. Walter now begins to bake before my eyelids even close for the night. I have something to contribute to your get-together, though. Several comfortable chairs were left back by the previous owner of our new building. I'll ask Will and Eddie to move chairs to both of your rooms."

"The attic room looks as if it has been transformed," Ellen said, after the girls climbed the stairs to the third floor.

"You have all been up here many times," Anne said, ushering them inside.

"But, your new quilts are lovely." Grace brushed her hand across the soft covering now spread across Anne's bed.

"And just look at these chairs the boys have placed up here." Kitty rushed across the room to sit down. "Imagine, someone moved and left these fine chairs behind."

They made Julia's frock over in no time. "You girls are marvelous," Anne said to Ellen and Kitty. "With your expert guidance, the problem of a work dress for Julia has been solved."

"Whatever will we do with the yards of ruffles we removed from my dress?" Julia giggled as she rolled the leftover material into a huge mound.

"A large pillow," Ellen suggested.

"Or, a few lumpy soccer balls," Kitty said.

"Please stay and visit with us for a while," Anne said, amid the laughter. They sat together, for a time, their pleasant conversation seeming to banish their loneliness and their cares. They did not even appear to notice the heat of the small room,

Each evening after dinner then, one, two or sometimes all of the Dempsey girls visited the attic. The little room, once a retreat for Anne, became spirited and merry. There were few quiet moments now, and the additional chairs left little space to move about, but she did not mind the change. Sure, the return of her beloved sister to her life and the friendship of the Dempsey girls helped to push away her terrible homesickness. Their friendship and caring more than made up for her small loss of solitude.

Chapter Thirteen

Blackwater
12 Sept. 1861

To Miss Anne and Miss Julia Carty,
My dearly beloved children, I received your kind letter. I wish I had you both at home rather than near to dangers or difficulty in a strange country.

We are well, thank God, but it caused us a great deal of anxiety to think you are situated in a country at the brink of war. My beloved children your Mother and I would sacrifice everything to get you right but what can we do the wide Atlantic roles between us. If you could come home, oh how contented would we be to have you both home under our auspices and within the grasp of our embraces. Alas, it is not the will of Divine Providence.

My beloved children, I wrote a letter to your Uncle James and posted it the 1st day of June. Your cousin Edward wrote to his father from Vancouver Island after leaving his uncle. He stated his uncle got married.

I was speaking to James Dempsey and he wishes to be remembered to his nephew and niece. The corn crop looks very bad here and the old disease is on the potatoes. Tell Grace Donahoo that her father is gave up by the priest and doctor.

Dear children, your state is very bad and in another sense ours is not much better. I fear from the look of my little crops that I will have to sell the cow about Michelmas.

Let us know about the war and state of the country as we will be uneasy in our minds until we hear from you. I hope you will have better news for us the next time.

We conclude by all sending you our love. God go with you and protect you,

John and Nell Carty

Dear Anne,

Lizzie was confirmed the 23rd of July last. You want to know how I am getting on, my health is the same as usual. You also want me to not fret for you but I cannot help fretting for a troubled mind finds no rest. Kitty Read is living in Wexford and Mr. Stapleton has a situation in the newsroom.

Nell Carty

October, 1861

Since she arrived in St. Louis, two years ago, Anne's life had encompassed little outside of the bakery and St. Vincent's. Now, the talk of war intruded into even her protected existence. She and Julia mentioned little of it when they wrote to their family, but their attempt to keep their parents from worrying about their safety proved futile. It had become a common practice among Irish immigrants to send newspapers to the folks back home. The papers were passed around from cottage to cottage, each page filled with the worst possible accounts of the battles. Any information omitted from the girls' letters would be filled in from the papers.

"Our parents will surely read of the exchange of gunfire between Union troops and Confederate-leaning State Militia at Camp Jackson last week," Anne said to Julia. "But, I fervently pray this incident unfolding before us right now will never be written about in a newspaper that makes its way back home."

They stood together, watching as James carried Ellen in and placed her on a cot in the alcove off the dining room. She appeared to be experiencing terrible pain. She held her hand across her mouth, likely trying not to cry out. Splotches of blood covered her dress and what appeared to be James' work shirt that had been drawn across her knees.

In the next moment, the doctor arrived and went right to work tending to her, assisted by Mary.

"What do you suppose could have happened?" Julia asked.

Before Anne could answer, Walter rushed through the dining room to fetch water for them, and Cara hurried out right behind him.

A tearful, shaken Kitty had been settled in a chair beside the fireplace. Anne held her hand, and Julia and Grace gathered around them. After some coaxing, she told them she and Ellen had been returning from work at the time of the incident. She could not tell them the extent of her injury. She knew only that the wound Ellen sustained was to her leg. She then dissolved into tears, and long minutes of soothing words and encouragement were needed, before Kitty began to speak again.

"We left the garment factory and walked to the corner to await the omnibus." Once begun, the sad shocking words poured from Kitty. "The wind blew our wraps about and stung what skin we could not keep covered. And so, we decided to head north on Second Street to meet the bus rather than remain still and allow the fierce cold to torment us.

"At the first intersection, a terrible rumble erupted. A troop of soldiers charged up the side street, and rounded the corner. They headed north at great speed, pushing all manner of heavy equipment along before them. A crowd spilled out into the street. People ran to keep up, shouting at the soldiers and at each other. 'Twas a frightening moment, that's sure."

"Oh my goodness!" Grace commenced to rock back and forth.

Julia had left the room to prepare tea, and she now returned with steaming cups for them all. The sisters were kept busy, Anne assisting Kitty to sip from the cup held in her shaking hands and Julia attempting to soothe Grace.

Minutes passed. As they sat quietly, drinking their tea, Anne pressed down hard on her right knee to keep her foot from jiggling and her toe from tapping. After Kitty consumed most of her tea, she could wait no longer. She leaned over and whispered to her: "Go on, Kitty dear."

"I jumped back and tried to pull Ellen with me. I called out to her, but you know how her hearing has been damaged by the dreadful factory noise. With her head lowered against the wind, she neither saw nor heard the commotion.

"She broke free of my grasp and pushed on. When, at last, the groan and creak of the carts drew her attention, she tried to back away...but you see...it was too late. A wagon swung out of control, caught her leg, and pitched her to the ground.

"Ellen was stretched out in the road, covered in blood. I dragged her as far away from the crowd as I could manage. I knelt down beside her, screaming for help. At that moment—led by an angel, I will forever believe—James Duff himself appeared."

Anne took in a sharp breath. James—her James—rescued Ellen and Kitty? She lowered her head, distracted by her bold thought. Was he her James?

Paying no notice to Anne's reaction, Kitty went on with her account. "He took hold of my shoulders and forced me to look away from Ellen and face him. 'Kitty, stop those wails!' he shouted to me. 'Run home for Walter. We need the wagon.'

"As luck would have it—perhaps it was that same angel bringing a second miracle—a man James knew rode up to us on horseback. 'Jonsey, take this girl home to fetch help,' he said.

"He shouted to me, once again. 'Take up your skirts and go. Hurry!'

"We arrived here just as Eddie commenced to turn the horse and wagon into the stable. 'Eddie, stop!' I waved my arms and called out to him. 'We need the wagon. Ellen is hurt.' Eddie turned our way with a perplexed look.

"Desperate to be understood, I pummeled Jonsey's shoulder with my fist. I do not know where my strength came from. 'Hold him here,' I said, 'I'll locate the master.' I jumped from the horse, left the two men in the street, and ran.

"I raced through the shop, by then near done for. I found Walter here in the dining room, and no longer able to speak, I seized his arm and pulled him out to the street. Then, I was forced to sit on the stoop, while my breathing returned to normal and Jonsey told Walter and Eddie what happened."

Kitty's entire body had begun to shake, and Anne pulled a quilt from the closet and wrapped it around her. While the girls exclaimed over the sad incident and tried to console the poor girl, Walter returned to the dining room and took up the story.

"With Jonsey in the lead," he said, "we set out in the wagon. In only a few minutes, we found James, sitting in the street with Ellen's head cradled against his knee.

"He had tied a cloth around her leg to stanch the flow of blood. Along the way home, he sat with her and adjusted the pressure on the tourniquet."

Mary and Cara entered the dining room after helping to care for Ellen, and Anne began to question them immediately. "How is she?"

"Awake, but drowsy and fretful," Mary said. "She will likely endure weeks of pain and discomfort before her wound heals.

"She is also suffering great distress, worrying she will be dismissed if she cannot appear for work." Mary shook her head. "I wish I could reassure her, but I know the reputations of those dreadful factory managers. They care for no one but themselves. They hold no concern for anyone's pain or misfortune. With an injury such as Ellen's, I am sure the convalescence will be lengthy. She will likely lose her position.

"I'll obtain cloth to keep her occupied, at least for a time." This new idea brought a spark to Mary's eyes. "Won't we all be pleased to wear new aprons and work clothes sewn by Ellen's own hand? And, with few immigrant girls coming out now because of the war, perhaps a need for seamstresses will arise. We'll hope for the best." Mary left again to tend to Ellen, and Cara followed along to help.

Kitty's tears began anew. "I am to blame. It was me who suggested we walk instead of waiting on the corner for the omnibus. I should have been able to pull Ellen back when she did not hear the racket. Then, when she fell to the ground, I was in a panic. If James had not come along, I might be sitting in that street still, wailing like a child. He must think me a fool."

James entered the room in time to console her. "Now, Kitty, no more tears. You pulled Ellen out of the melee, and you sent help to us in record time. You are a true heroine. I know everyone here is amazed at your bravery. When Ellen realizes all that happened, she will be grateful to you, indeed."

Anne and the others joined in with praises of their own, and at last, Kitty raised her eyes and favored them with a brave smile. When Julia and Grace took the poor girl upstairs to bed, Anne stayed behind to speak with James.

"You did a wonderful thing tonight. Thank you."

"No thanks are needed, except to God, who directed me to take that path," James said. "I do not often walk that way.

"Ellen and Kitty encountered a troop moving toward the site of a skirmish at Fifth and Walnut Streets. While I waited for Walter to fetch us with the wagon, some bystanders told me a group of reserve troops had been attacked by a crowd of angry secessionists."

"Women are not safe on the streets, now," Walter said. "I know what happened tonight was an accident. Still, with Dempsey's supplying bread for the Union Army and Julia working for Colonel Scones, we're all in danger of reprisal from Confederate sympathizers. You girls must not go about alone, Anne. We cannot take foolish chances."

Anne nodded to Walter. A distant memory slipped into her mind. She thought of the evening over two years ago, when she had bowed to her father's wishes. Father had acted then as he thought was right, just as Walter was doing now. And, then as now, the changes their directives caused in her life were hard to bear.

A week later, Ellen held court in the dining room, her poor injured leg propped on a footstool and cushioned with pillows. She spent a good deal of her time entertaining them all with her fine humor and her grand singing.

"I cannot just sit here and provide entertainment for all of you," she said. "Please bring me your mending, or if it is a new garment you need, bring me the cloth and I will set right to it. I must keep my hands occupied."

With Ellen on her way to recovery, things returned to nearly normal at Dempsey's. One serious exception had been made to their routine: the girls were no longer able to walk about on their own.

For the past two years, the nightly walk to the mission to deliver the day-old goods had offered a few glorious minutes of freedom for Anne. Each evening, she thrilled anew to the opportunity to walk the city streets, examine new buildings being erected everywhere, and observe the constant stream of people passing along the roads at any hour. These brief interludes, moments alone with her thoughts, were the best part of her day, and truly, her favorite thing in her life in America. She would miss this small bit of liberty.

Chapter Fourteen

November, 1861

On the second Tuesday of the month, Julia celebrated her twenty-first birthday. Supper at Dempsey's that evening was a festive occasion. Mary and Cara prepared a special meal, and Walter and his helpers worked with Anne to bake a beautiful cake in Julia's honor.

Anne's heart skipped to see James come through the door just after Walter offered their prayer of thanksgiving for the grand fare.

"Let us take time out this evening and celebrate," Julia said, as James settled in at the table. "While we enjoy this grand meal, we must concentrate our thoughts on the good times and share stories of work and family and dreams."

"Just imagine, Anne, a birthday cake," Julia said, when the dessert had been served. "Wouldn't the children at home love to celebrate their birthdays with such a marvelous treat?"

Anne had no opportunity to answer her sister. Walter had turned from the celebration and he was concentrating his attention toward her. She noted his change of tone, a strong voice she had not often heard from him.

"It is long past time that you remove Mr. Fortune's name from your savings account and replace it with Julia's," he said.

"I agree with Walter," James said. "Dermot Fortune cannot be trusted. "Please make this change now. If Fortune is in financial trouble, as we have heard from all quarters around the city, he may disappear."

Anne nodded her agreement. "Now that Julia and I are earning a fair wage, we have already replaced the money I used for her passage. We have also put enough aside for Kate's fare. The funds Uncle James sent me, now over two years ago, remain in the account, and our combined savings comprise a considerable sum. I intend to secure the money in one safe place, remove Mr. Fortune's name from the account, and end his influence in our lives forever more.

"I have been remiss. It has taken me far too long to make this change, but I will see to it as soon as you have the time, Walter."

"I will find the time, Anne," Walter said. "Tomorrow."

Anne, Julia, and Walter climbed the steps to Mr. Fortune's second floor office the next morning. They discovered a locked door and no sign of the man anywhere. Walter took charge then, leading them on a search for the bank manager.

"Fortune is not here," the manager said, when they located him in an office at the rear of the bank. "We have not seen him for weeks."

Anne assumed the worst possible reasons for his absence. She recognized the same apprehension spread across the faces of Walter and Julia.

After some persuasion, the manager offered more information. "His rent's not been paid for two months. Last week, Mrs. Fortune also came here to inquire after him. She has not received word from him for some time."

When they explained their mission, he offered a suggestion. "In Fortune's absence, you could establish a new account in Julia Carty's name and secure the young women's current funds there. I will then petition the bank to remove Mr. Fortune's name from the first account and transfer Anne's previous savings to the new one." He led them over to the bank teller and then left to find the proper papers for the process. In a few moments, he returned, looking grave.

"My sincere apologies, Miss Carty. I must inform you that your account is closed. The funds have been withdrawn."

"That cannot be." Anne pulled her shoulders, to her full height. She looked directly into the manager's eyes. "I have deposited our savings each month. Surely, you have witnessed me coming into the bank. The money must be here."

With these firm words delivered, her confidence dissolved quickly. Anne lowered her head, turning her thoughts inward, chiding herself for her foolish inaction. She had received sound advice about removing the money from Fortune's control from both James and Walter. She should have heeded their warnings. Now, the money was gone. *Oh my word, what have I done?*

"Anne? Your cheeks have turned pink." Julia moved closer and took a firm grip of her arm.

"I am not about to faint. I am just angry." She turned to Walter and they exchanged a knowing look.

"Fortune," they said in unison.

"That dreadful man cannot have gone far." Julia turned her attention to the manager. "We must locate him."

Walter slapped the countertop, bringing startled glances from several people standing near them. "Notify the law!" At his shout, a murmur of voices spread through the room.

"I have already sent for the sheriff," the manager said. "A search will begin at once. Do not worry, he will be apprehended!"

Chapter Fifteen

Blackwater
January 27, 1862

Dear Children,

I received your letter the 13th January last and a remittance of four pounds, for which I am sincerely thankful to you and for which I wanted very bad and from the state I was in I was obliged to sell the cow. This country is distressed and a great many farmers are put out of their lands by the bad crops and loss of the potatoes. It is the worst year we had since the public works and it appears this summer will be a very hard time to get support. We are sorry for the state of the country you are in on account of the war and we think very hard to expect any assistance from you only we are so distressed. However your remittance gave us great relief. I had no crop this year and was not able to pay one-half years rent. We are glad you are in good situations and good health and the country agrees with you. We are all in good health, thank God, except for our Jimmy. He is no better in his health. The children are going to school continually.

Let Walter Dempsey know that James Dempsey and family are well. Tell Grace Donahoo that her father posted a letter two months ago. Do you know any Murphys of Gary, Indiana? Daughters, we had no letter from your Uncle James nor don't expect one.

Remember us to Walter and Mary Dempsey. Joseph Read is gone mad through the country. Kitty is at home still and her husband W. Stapleton is gone and we do not know where.

We give you our love and expect you will do well. No more from your loving parents,
John and Nell Carty

February, 1862

On a cold and blustery winter evening, Anne and Grace were leaving the mission, when James Duff approached driving Walter's carriage.

"Eddie went off to make an unexpected delivery to Camp Bennett, and since I was at Dempsey's helping Walter, I volunteered to collect you." He handed them in and spread his cloak across the side opening of the carriage to create a barrier against the strong wind that nipped at their faces.

"We must wait for Julia," Anne said. "It will not be long."

"Of course," he said. "I only want to move you girls out of this bitter cold."

James appeared agitated, but she did not think it was the wait that caused him distress. What could be upsetting him so?

He attempted to make them comfortable. Finding a blanket on the floor of the carriage, he handed it to Anne. Recovering a heavy sheet of cardboard from the back seat, he placed it across the rear window to further shield them from the wind. Then, he turned his talk to the subject she had been trying hard to forget.

"It is that devil Fortune I'm thinking about. I cannot erase his treachery from my mind. I should have protected you from him. If he comes near the city again, I will be in wait. A quarter of an hour with him is all I'll need." James bunched his fists as he turned to face Anne. "You must allow me to reimburse you for the money he took. It is my responsibility."

"You cannot take this burden on yourself." Anne straightened her shoulders. "As I have stated many times," she said, "the fault belongs to me alone."

She also hesitated to discuss the matter in front of Grace. She did not wish to burden her already troubled mind with the Carty family's worries.

Since Walter declared his edict of the girls not walking home alone, the poor girl had been forced to accompany them in the carriage. Though Grace's sad countenance showed no signs of lightening, Anne prayed this new practice of moving about the city streets together could be a step forward for her. A return to a bit of normal connection and interaction with people who cared for her would surely help advance a recovery of her spirits.

"I am accountable." James persisted in bearing the blame for their loss. Anne attempted to send a message to him with her eyes that she wished to end the discussion, but he did not understand her meaning, and he went on. "I promised your father I would watch out for you. I should have driven Fortune out of town before he defrauded you and escaped from the city."

"Julia and I did not accept Walter's offer of help." Still trying to put the subject to rest, Anne spoke firmly to James. "We will not take your hard-earned money. The sheriff comes to the bakery on occasion to assure me he will continue the search for Mr. Fortune. The bank manager also pledges his help. Both are determined to find him and recover the money. Yet, even if he was detained, Mr. Fortune could not be prosecuted. Despicable though he is, Uncle James placed his name on our account and he has broken no law.

"There is no hope for it. Mr. Fortune and our savings vanished, and our tears and self-recriminations have changed nothing. Julia and I are determined to forget his deception and concentrate instead on building a new fund. We will rise above this disappointment."

"You and Julia are brave girls," James said. "When I find him—"

Anne interrupted again. "Mary tells me Fortune left his wife in an even more desperate state, without funds or means of supporting herself. The poor woman is also being badgered by his many creditors. Walter and Mary offered her a place to stay, but she decided to return to her family home in Illinois."

"If I had him—"

Anne's attempt to shield Grace from the conversation over Mr. Fortune's treachery had gone awry. Her choice of a diversion proved a poor one, and Grace had edged herself into the corner of the seat and bowed her head. She searched her mind for another topic.

At that moment, she noticed her sister approaching and a new subject presented itself. "Look now, Julia is coming, accompanied by a young man in uniform." Never one to keep anything to herself that excited or interested her, Julia had spoken frequently of a particular soldier who worked for Colonel Scones. Having heard his excellent appearance described many times, Anne recognized him as the soldier who delivered work to Julia from the Colonel.

"Anne Carty, Grace Donahoo, James Duff, may I introduce Martin Tobin." Julia beamed.

"I am happy to meet you, Corporal Tobin." Anne leaned out the carriage door to offer the slim, erect young man her hand. "I have heard many fine things about you." The corporal took her hand and bowed to her.

"Good evening, sir." Grace nodded to Martin, but she lowered her head quickly and kept her hands out of view.

"I invited Martin to join us for supper." Julia turned her gaze to Anne for support. "I assured him Mary is always pleased to entertain guests." Martin smiled at Julia, and even in the darkness, Anne could see the softening of his steel blue eyes.

"Please do come," she said. "The Dempseys will be happy to have you."

James shook Martin's hand, and then he turned to helping them all settle in, the men in front, and Anne, Julia, and Grace huddled together in back. "Lord bless me, if you don't remind me of my brother back home," James said to the newcomer. "You even resemble Ned, Martin, correct and proper as you are, in bearing and address."

"It is the result of my schooling." Martin faced the girls, including them in his response. "I arrived in America at thirteen and studied at a military academy in the East, where my uncle served as headmaster. I soon learned my survival there depended on my ability to speak like the other fellows. So here I am, sounding like a Yankee, as I have been told, and I am sure it is too late to change."

"I must add," James said, "your speech also resembles that of our Miss Anne, Miss Julia, and Miss Grace, who do such a fine job of speaking like true Americans."

James seemed to be recovering his good spirits, Anne observed. His eyes gleamed with mischief when he spoke.

"I quite agree." Martin grasped the tone of James' bantering. "On our first meeting, I supposed Julia to have been born right here in St. Louis."

Anne knew both men were teasing. Sure, her customers in the bakery, who had been in the country for a time, would hold a more critical view of her attempts at Americanizing her speech. Tonight it mattered little. What a pleasure it was to be riding along toward Dempsey's with these dear people. James grew more important in her life each day. Her dear sister appeared happy with her two positions and her new young man. Even Grace had begun to show a small measure of appreciation for their friendship.

As they continued on, all appearing in great high spirits, Anne's mood soared, and she felt the others reacting to the fine company in the same way.

When the laughter and conversation quieted, Martin turned to James. "I understand your feelings about your brother. My own brother Bill and I intended to come together, but he died a month before we were to leave Ireland. Many years have passed, but I suffer the loss still. My brother Patrick plans to come soon, and I am most anxious for him to arrive."

As Anne assured him he would, Martin received a warm welcome from the Dempseys. They all settled in around the table, with their guest seated on Walter's right. Then, she noticed the new gas fixtures installed in the dining room that afternoon.

"They cast a lovely glow." She looked around the table to gain everyone's agreement, and they all joined in with her, adding their praises for Walter's latest innovation.

"'Tis a grand addition to the room," James said. "We can watch the steam rise from these wonderful dishes you've set before us, Mary, and our faces radiate with the reflection from the flames."

Walter obviously enjoyed their compliments, but after favoring them with a nod, he moved right to his questions for Martin. "Since there are few immigrants to torment these days, we must rely on the military for information. Indeed, won't we all settle for news of the war?"

Anne shared a smile with Julia, while they listened to the men discuss the latest word of battles and strategies. When they seemed to gain their fill of military talk, Martin turned to a new topic, surprising them by supplying reasons for reminiscences.

"My family home is in Cork, but my cousins live in Enniscorthy and my brothers and I visited there often as youths." He turned to Walter and Mary. "I do not remember your family's shop, but I recall the general area where you lived." They chatted about the Dempseys' former home in Enniscorthy for a few minutes. Mention of the familiar sounding names of Martin's relatives and of roads and sights so beloved to them brought expressions of delight to the faces of the Dempseys.

"Another relation, my uncle Michael Tobin, his wife, and their three sons lived north of Blackwater. I believe the boys have come to America, but I've lost touch with them. Uncle Mike still lives on the farm, though." Martin directed his talk to Anne and Julia. "We sometimes visited a village church a good distance from their place. It may have been your parish church?"

"Faith, I do remember the Tobins," Julia said. "Anne, you know the family. They often attended mass at our St. Bridgid's."

Anne's thoughts flew back to the days of their youth, times now seeming so distant. She could envision them all making the short walk from their cottage to the church on Sunday, crossing the road to the schoolhouse each weekday morning, and running and playing in the church yard. Of course she remembered. "The Tobins came to our church when the roads to Enniscorthy proved impassable."

"Is it not a blessing?" Tears filled Mary's eyes as she spoke. "Here we are a world away from home, and we discover our families live near one another and attend church together on occasion."

Anne turned toward her sister, who seemed bursting with good cheer. She could not suppress a grin when she observed Julia's reaction. No one bestowed more joyful approval to the fine meal, the talk of home, and in particular, the excellent company of their special guest than Julia.

"'Tis wonderful," she said softly.

Chapter Sixteen

June, 1862

If Anne held any doubt of the growing friendship between Julia and Martin, all uncertainty vanished in the next few weeks. The young corporal managed to secure time off to dine with the Dempsey group several times. One evening in March, he arrived with gifts: writing materials for the girls and cigars for the men.

When Anne turned to Martin to attempt to thank him for the gifts, everyone at the table joined in with her. Martin waved aside their expressions of thanks. "I am sometimes able to secure things not available to civilians."

"It is grand that we have been able to secure such a fine array of food," Anne said. "With vegetables and meat growing scarce in the city, it is not an easy thing to obtain enough to feed our large group. I know Mary and Cara have extended great effort to provide it for us."

James was also present for the supper, and Anne's appreciation for the kindness of Mary Dempsey soared, when she thoughtfully included him in the praise.

"Didn't James work with Walter to develop the old, damaged warehouse out back into a marvelous baking area?" she said. "Now, here we have these fine gifts. You lads will spoil us for sure."

Mary turned to Martin and favored him with a grand smile, before she went on to elaborate on James's good deeds.

"This past November, the contractor finished the outside work required to connect the two buildings here. There were many delays. Materials became difficult to obtain and a succession of his workers left to join the army.

"Walter suggested he and James could help with the inside renovations, and after a few weeks of haggling, the contractor conceded. He agreed to use their assistance and reduce the cost. These two men worked at night throughout these past months. The result of their labor would astonish you."

Martin had time to do no more than nod his head in response, before the grand meal came to an end and Walter and his helpers rose from their places. Mary offered a suggestion. "Why don't we walk back to the oven room to inspect what's been done there, and then we have been saving a wonderful dessert we can enjoy later?"

"You go ahead, Mary." Anne began stacking the dinner plates, and Grace jumped up to help. "We will clear away the dishes. We've seen most of the work already."

"Goodness no, you girls must see the most recent improvements. Come along. The chores will wait." They all followed Mary through the old oven room space, where she pointed out Walter's office area and made particular mention of Anne's small desk.

"I do the majority of my book work at the table in the bakery," Anne said. "I use this space merely to spread out papers and ledgers."

They walked on through the area partitioned off to serve as the family kitchen, all admiring the long, narrow windows installed the previous week, and some additional gas lamps. Moving along a hallway connecting the two buildings, they entered the newly renovated section.

When they reached the baking room, Mary held back and allowed Walter to deliver the commentary.

His eyes gleamed as he explained the workings of his new domain. "The army provided these large ovens and the preparation and cooling tables. The two sinks at the back are equipped with the latest method for pumping water into the building. You will all want to see what a fine innovation this is."

Since his arms were filled with a long, metal tray he had just removed from the sink, Walter turned to Grace, who stood beside him. "Come closer, Grace, and demonstrate for us. Press the handle here, and watch the surge of water."

Grace backed away and shook her head, but Cara came forward. "Ah sure, I'll show you how 'tis done. Indeed, I am so thrilled I must no longer trudge out back for water, I've mastered the fine contraption in no time." She provided a brief demonstration, and when she had managed to pump a steady stream of water into the sink, she stepped aside. She dipped her head for a moment, but not before Anne discovered her grand smile peeking through the fingers she held up to her face.

"Och, here I have taken over the blessed thing messell. Sorry, Walter, I did not mean ta steal the limelight."

"Ah now, Cara, you've done a fine job of it." Anne grasped the handle. "I'm sure Walter does not mind. I'd like to try it myself."

"And I would too," Julia said. "After hearing talk of this grand pump all week long, I am ready for a go at it."

When they had each taken a turn at the pump handle and admired all corners of the oven room, Mary led them along a short hallway to an elegant sitting area. "Here you will see one of my favorite places in the entire world." She ushered them inside. "This fine room, once a part of the old oven space, is a bit of home to Walter and me. It's as near to our parlor back in Enniscorthy as we could make it and what I have seen in my dreams all these many years." With a sweep of her arm, she directed their attention to the great stone fireplace, the sturdy carpet, and comfortable furniture and described the effort involved in the installation of each thing.

Mary asked Anne to pull open the heavy wooden door that led to the outside. "Ah 'tis a shame, it is already too dark to see," she said. "Beyond this door, the contractor formed a lovely courtyard and erected a porch, spanning the space where the two buildings are joined. There's ground enough for a fair-sized garden."

"Imagine how grand your fine courtyard will be, my dear lady." Anne placed an arm across Mary's shoulder. "In the first weeks of spring, you will step from your fine parlor out onto the porch, and from that excellent vantage, plan for an ever-changing array of flowers. Meanwhile, can we not all picture Walter sitting out there, enjoying your blossoms, and contemplating additional improvements he and James will make to the place?"

"I find it difficult to comprehend that these two buildings were once old warehouses," Martin said, when they returned to the dining room for dessert. "I am amazed at what you have accomplished. I would be pleased to help with any further work. While I have little construction experience, I did receive some training at cabinetry. Since I was in this country on my own, with my uncle my only family, I spent my summers and school recesses with him in his small place over the carriage house. He saw to it that my free time was filled. I learned some basic carpentry, and in particular, cabinet making."

"We would never turn away a kind offer of help." Walter nodded to Martin. "And, our Mary here will love each cabinet and shelf you create for our workspace."

James later confided to Anne that Martin worked with enthusiasm and expressed appreciation for each thing he learned from them. He also told her how much he and Walter had already gleaned from Martin about cabinets and shelves. It was clear that, as they worked together, night after night, the three men were becoming fast friends.

The weeks passed, and with the evenings growing warm, Anne and Julia and the other girls moved their nighttime visits from the stifling attic room to Mary's new porch. Walter, James, and Martin often joined them after an evening's work.

These gatherings were brief intervals in their long, demanding days. The irrepressible Julia would not allow anyone to mention worries over family, home, and war. Anne and Mary supported her suggestion and urged them all to enjoy the respite.

On one particular night, while Anne stood at the edge of the porch taking in the view of Mary's first blossoms, Julia persuaded Grace to lead them all in song. They sang several familiar tunes, "The Minstrel Boy," and an old favorite of her mother's, "The Rose of Tralee." When Grace's face showed a trace of a smile, Anne decided it was a sign her sister's enthusiasm and good humor were working wonders with the poor, sad girl.

"I must go," Martin said, after an hour sped by. "The desserts Mary sends along with me earn some leeway with the officers. Still, I am required to report on a reasonable schedule."

"I, too, must be off." James stood, and retrieving his cap from a post on the new stairway, he prepared to take his leave. "I have work guaranteed for the next two weeks, and I will begin before sunrise tomorrow."

Anne's favorite time of day came now. As Martin crossed the porch to say goodnight to her sister, she used the diversion to slip away, her heart skipping a beat, and walk to the corner with James. Here was their time for a few moments of private talk.

"Tell me about your day and the work you've lined up for the coming weeks," she said, as they started off.

"It's common labor, nothing more," he said. "I become frustrated over the lack of suitable work available."

On most nights, it seemed to sooth him to speak to her of his discontent over his employment prospects. This evening, though, his spirits seemed particularly low.

"Again and again, I watch men with less education gain better positions and higher wages. Many employers believe the Irish—they call us Micks or Harps—are good for none but the most menial tasks. This barrier appears impossible to overcome.

"On occasion, a foreman will recognize me from a previous job and hire me ahead of the others in line. Then, my hopes rise that one day I will be offered permanent work. Until that time comes, I take whatever I can find, lifting, hauling and shoveling."

They had progressed two blocks, leaning close together, but not touching. She took great joy in these rare moments alone, but, it was time to turn back now.

"America is a grand place and opportunities abound here," James said, as they turned back, toward the bakery, "but where are the good positions for our countrymen? In my brief time in New York, I encountered such hatred toward the Irish. In Chicago, the mood seemed less rancorous, but I have discovered St. Louis to be the most welcoming city. Of course, they want us here to do their hard labor. We are a canny lot, though. We will find a way to chisel out a place for ourselves." They now stood across the street from Dempsey's, and they could delay their parting no longer. They must say good night.

"Pay me not a care, Anne. I've no cause to be complaining. Walter offers me work when there's none available elsewhere. And, here I am holding the soft hand of the prettiest girl ever was. Sure, I am a lucky man."

"Thank you, James. But, I do not wish to hear only the good things. I will share the difficult times with you as well."

"You're a lovely lass, for sure. I wish we could walk together like this every night. There are so many things to talk over." James bent his face close to hers. "I wish to hear more from you. I wish to know your every thought. I want to share your troubles and cares."

"I agree. I would like to stay and talk forever."

If only they could have more time together. His words—no matter what they were discussing—were always a comfort to her. His touch—if only his hand at her arm—brought a delightful thrill soaring through her being. She did not wish to move away from him.

James edged closer. He brushed his lips against hers. For a brief moment, he rested his cheek against her warm skin. "Go now. I'll keep watch until you reach the porch. Good night, my dear."

After looking back, waiting until James gave one last wave and turned the corner out of her sight, Anne climbed the steps to the porch. Everyone had pushed back their chairs by now, preparing to return to work. She slipped into the midst of the group in time to offer her assistance, and she and the others followed Walter and Mary back to the new oven room.

The quantity of bread Dempsey's supplied for the Army increased each week, and the bakery workers toiled almost without rest. While they worked together now, Grace confided to Anne that, in one happy outcome of these long hours, Mary had asked her to leave her position at the mission and help in the bakery. "How pleased I am with this new situation," Grace said, again and again.

"It is a wonderful change. 'Tis surely a sign. God is protecting me. I can feel it."

"I am happy this new position suits you." Anne began scrubbing the trays and stacking them on the table beside one of the new sinks.

Grace faced her, and instead of looking down at the floor as was her usual way, she gazed directly into her eyes and favored her with a small smile. "It is the same cooking and scrubbing I've done at the mission, but in my mind there is a distinction. I am part of this Dempsey family now, one of the women of the house. Keeping our home spotless and preparing excellent meals is a source of pride for me. A bit of my dignity has been restored, you see."

Grace's renewed spirits, Julia's optimism that together they would bring the others out, and her evening talks with James provided a time of contentment unknown to Anne for a long while. The pleasant interlude proved all too brief.

Chapter Seventeen

Blackwater
August 13th, 1862

My two Dear Children,

I received your welcome letter on Sunday, the 11th of August which gives us all pleasure to hear you are well as this leaves us here, thank God for his goodness to us all.

Dear Anne, we received Julia's likeness which gave us great pleasure to see her once more. I hope you will send yours. Dear Anne, you spoke of sending Kate to school but there is no occasion as she is good enough both in writing and sewing. I will get some situation for her until you send for her. Dear Anne, the times are so hard we cannot keep them all at home. Clothes here are dear. Jimmy's health is no better. He is grown very large but is not able to do much. If it was God's will Jimmy have his health, he would be able to assist himself and us but it is all the will of God.

John Carty

*My two dear Children, I hope I have no oc-
casion to remind you of your religious duties
which are the most necessary of all. You are far
away from me and I don't expect to see you till
I see you in heaven. I now conclude with sending you all our love. No more from your mother,
Nell Carty.*

*Dear Anne, I am going to school every day
and all I have to stand for me is to learn all I
can. Dear Anne, I expect you will do all you can
to bring me out with Kate. M. Carty, B.W.*

September, 1862

The bakery had received several shipments of supplies in
the last two days, and word must have circulated through the
neighborhood. With food of any kind scarce in the city now,
people traveled long distances to buy bread and biscuits. Each
roll and loaf sold as quickly as Anne and Mary could wrap
them, and there had been no lull in the shop until every crumb
disappeared. Now that the place had been emptied of baked
goods and customers, they took a moment for a cup of tea.

"What has become of James? Have you had word from
him?" Mary asked.

"I wish I knew where he has gone," Anne said. "If on occasion he works long hours or is employed outside of the city,
he sometimes vanishes for several evenings. Without fail, he
appears at St. Vincent's for church on Sunday. When he did not
come last week and then again yesterday, I began to worry. It
seems he has disappeared.

"His spirits were low on that last evening I talked with
him. He spoke, as he often does, of how discouraged he has
grown over the lack of decent jobs and suitable wages." Anne
could admit this much to Mary. Everyone at Dempsey's knew
of James's concern about finding a good position.

The worry that now filled her heart, so fresh, and raw, and private, could not be shared with anyone, not even Julia or her dear, kind Mary. On the last evening they walked together, James had spoken of how much he loved her. Surely, he would not have changed his mind in these two weeks? After declaring his love, he would not turn away from her. She could not believe that of James. He was no Will Stapleton.

"Oh my. He would not leave the city to find work, would he?" Mary's question jolted Anne's thoughts back to the present.

"I do not think he would. He has been determined to make a place for himself in St. Louis." While Anne attempted to address Mary's concerns, she also tried mightily to push aside her own disquiet and thrust away any foolish doubts of his devotion. "I suppose we just must wait."

Anne did not have long to contemplate James' words or wonder over his whereabouts. The evening after she and Mary spoke of his absence, Martin arrived at the door of Dempsey's with the answer. They had already finished their meal, when they heard his knock. Mary rushed out through the bakery to unlock the door and welcome him. The girls were cleaning up out in the kitchen, and Anne could hear Mary insisting it would take her no time to make up a plate of supper. As they made their way through the house, Martin assured her he had already partaken of his evening meal.

He greeted them all, sending a special little smile toward Julia.

Then he turned his attention to Anne. "I have been away from the city for two weeks. On my return to the barracks, I discovered a letter from James, another note for Walter, and this package for you."

"I am obliged to you." Anne nodded to Martin. She tried to offer her thanks, but she knew her expression fell short of a full smile. "If you will excuse me, I must go to my room. I have some work I must finish this evening." Moving slowly but deliberately, Anne backed out of the room.

Martin looked a bit surprised, but polite and courteous, as always, he favored her with an understanding nod. The girls all turned her way, not hiding their quizzical expressions. Was she not the one who always insisted she must stay until the last dish had been dried and the place returned to perfect order?

She nodded to the Dempseys, who stood in the kitchen doorway behind Martin. "Mary, Walter, I bid you good night." Without waiting for their response, she slipped through the door, headed for the stairway, and ran up to the attic room.

Sitting at the writing table, she pulled away the paper that had been folded around the package with neat, even edges. Inside, she found the poetry book James promised to bring her months ago, but had forgotten somehow. She placed the book on the table and paged through it.

Halfway along, she discovered an envelope containing several bills and a letter. Though the currency aroused her curiosity, she set it aside. The letter she now held in her hand captivated her, filling her with equal measures of trepidation and joy. Chills rushed through her being, while at the same time, her neck and ears grew warm. *He has not forgotten me.*

Unable to resist the letter another moment, she smoothed out the paper's many creases and began to read.

> *Forgive me, my dear Anne, for leaving without a goodbye. While working across the river, I met a fellow who was on his way to join an all-Irish regiment of the Union Army being formed in Ohio. After a brief reflection, I resolved to join him. I have two reasons for what may appear a rash action. My friend here feels an all-Irish legion will show this United States what the children of our homeland are made of. I have hopes I can help them succeed and bring this fighting spirit to the Irish workingman in St. Louis. The second, but most important intent, concerns you, Anne. I wish to put money ahead*

and have a stake when I offer myself to you.

I had Walter's horse with me when I left. I took her along as I will receive extra pay with a mount. Walter long urged Blacky on me in return for my help with his construction work, and I have written him to explain the situation.

The night before I departed St. Louis, I encountered Fortune headed toward his old home. I extracted the money in this envelope from his pockets before the coward escaped my grasp and ran. I pray it will relieve your mind some. I wish I could have recovered the entire sum.

Again, I apologize for leaving before I discussed this matter with you, but the choice was to go at once or not at all. I trust Martin told you I asked him to settle my account and retrieve my things from the boardinghouse. Please pray for me.

Yours always, James.

Anne rubbed the letter across her cheek. She had not allowed Martin an opportunity to explain, but she felt sure she could piece together what had occurred. At James' instruction, Martin retrieved the book from his boardinghouse, placed the envelope with the letter and money in the book, and wrapped it. The neat, precise package seemed so like Martin. The wrinkled, smudged, but dear note inside was more akin to James.

She paced in the attic room, wondering where Julia was, but at the same time, happy for some time alone. The matters raised by James' letter must be worked out in her own mind, before she discussed them with her sister. The money presented the greatest mystery. Had the altercation with Mr. Fortune been more serious than James described it? Did Martin know more details than he had revealed? And, the situation concerning the horse raised her interest. Surely, Walter discovered the horse missing some time ago? So many things puzzled her, but then much of it was her own doing. She had rushed from the dining room before either Martin or Walter could give her any explanations.

Anne received infrequent letters from James that fall and winter, often short notes, some written on paper scraps. These brief letters answered few of her questions, but she admitted to herself they were dear to her all the same. Always, he proclaimed his love for her. Always, he added a line about his plans for their future. She treasured each word. Each morning, she slipped the most recent letter in her pocket, along with her newest letter from home. She read each page so often they grew worn and fragile.

Her worries now turned to his safety. She set out to work hard and fill each moment of her day, occupying her mind with numbers, receipts, and such to hold her unease at bay.

"So many changes are occurring in the city," Mary said, as they worked together one morning shortly after James' departure. "Severe restrictions have been placed on travel, and few immigrants will be arriving in St. Louis, at least for a time."

"Bridget Rice told me yesterday that the mission is becoming a refuge for those displaced by the war," Anne said. "Indeed, the conflict has grown to be everyone's priority. In the bakery, news of victories and losses has supplanted talk of the folks left behind in Ireland.

"Ah, this dreadful war. It is creating strife everywhere. My family back home still suffers, and I continue to pray for them every day, but with postage becoming dear and mail deliveries unpredictable, I write to them only once a month now. I wonder if many of my letters home have even reached their destination.

"And then our quest to bring the children to America has been delayed. Though we have replaced the money Mr. Fortune took from us, and we have once again, saved enough for Kate's passage to America, her journey has now been postponed. It saddens me to think of it."

Julia brought work home most nights, and Anne sat beside her, laboring over her ledgers. She now kept two separate accounts, one for the shop and another for the army contract. Everyone at Dempsey's kept the same long hours. When supplies were available, the ovens operated night and day. Anne and Julia helped Walter and Mary in the oven room every moment they could.

Shortly before the Christmas holiday, flour and other goods became nearly impossible to obtain. This change was yet another difficult adjustment in their lives. "After weeks of working with little rest," Mary said, "we now have no flour or other baking ingredients available. Walter has been forced to close down the ovens and his deliveries to the Army camps have halted. He will be spending his days searching for supplies."

A week later, Walter's helper, Will, enlisted, and the Army assigned a young private named George Blake to help with the baking. He had sustained a wound in battle that caused him to walk with a slight limp. Though serious enough to interrupt his combat duty, the wound appeared a minor problem to him. There was nothing trifling, though, about the stir caused by the fact that he came from Great Britain.

"Aye, we've not a fiddler's chance of emerging from this war with any friends whatsoever." Walter confided his worries to Anne and Mary, while they worked out in the shop the morning after George arrived. "Our St. Vincent's congregation is divided. Our Confederate-leaning friends are condemning us. Word will soon spread around the neighborhood that we have employed a young Englishman. We'll be experiencing more turmoil than the folks down south."

"Why could Will not stay here as our army private?" Mary looked to Anne, and they both turned to Walter for the answer.

"That would have been grand, but war is seldom convenient or logical. George's superiors assigned him to Dempsey's with orders to help us provide bread for the Union Army. From what I've learned, he's not a tad happier about the situation than we are. He remains polite and respectful, though, in the face of the unfriendly reception he is receiving from all quarters here. Please extend every courtesy to him and implore the folks who come to the bakery to do the same."

Since Anne and Julia arrived in America, Colonel Scones, born in Massachusetts to English parents, was the closest they had come to a person from Great Britain. Moreover, as Martin's superior and Julia's employer, he commanded their respect. Anne wondered if they could accept working side by side with George Blake, though, fresh from the streets of London.

In the end, reason prevailed. In these days of worry and endless work, at times interrupted by unsettling days of idleness when all provisions had been depleted, Anne noticed that George's presence proved of little concern. Fruits and vegetables grew scarce as winter came upon them. Their diet consisted mainly of bread and tea, relieved on occasion with whatever else Mary could bargain for or obtain in trade. Walter threatened to learn to make noodles, but he never found the time.

Chapter Eighteen

March, 1863

"Are you far from home?" Anne questioned a young soldier, while Mary wrapped a large package of currant rolls for him.

"Yes ma'am, I'm from Michigan. My squad is headed to Jefferson Barracks. When my sergeant noted your shop, he sent me for fresh biscuits. They look mighty tasty."

"Would you like bread, too?"

"Oh no, ma'am. The aroma of fresh bread and the warmth of this cozy place could sway me, but I must take these biscuits the captain requested and hurry to catch the others."

A number of soldiers had patronized the shop in these past months. The sight of one or two at the counter, appearing strong and brave in their uniforms though scarcely old enough to be away from home, brought a sigh to Anne and Mary and their customers.

After the soldier paid for his purchases and headed out onto the cold city streets, Mary stood, looking out the window, shaking her head as she watched him hurry away. "Such a young lad to be marching off to war, it troubles my heart."

"He's no more than a child," Anne said. "Each time a soldier comes in the door, I am reminded that, in no time at all, my brothers will be old enough to serve."

"Sure, he must miss his family." A young woman standing beside the counter spoke up. "Torn from home ourselves, we all can sympathize." Anne placed biscuits in a sack for her, nodding her agreement.

"I never thought it would come to this." Another woman, cradling a baby in her arms, joined their talk. "The entire business is beyond me. Union, Rebs, who's who? My Kevin attempts to explain it, but all I see is poor injured boys everywhere you turn and desperate, homeless people pouring into the city. In truth, I doubt Kevin understands it himself. Well, it's sure I'm praying it will end soon."

When their customers had all gone, Mary turned to Anne with a quizzical look. "That young fellow, he did wear a Union uniform, did he not?"

"His coat was a bit faded, but I am certain it was blue, Anne said. Without a customer to serve for a moment, she moved to place a log on their fire. "A gray has not come to the shop since General Fremont surrounded the city with forts. I've heard they sometimes wear blue to disguise themselves, but I do not believe a few biscuits will make a difference in the war."

"Faith, I did add extras to his package, though." Mary's expression turned from questioning to sheepish, giving them both a bit of a laugh.

Anne and Mary and the entire Dempsey household were soon well acquainted with Union Army colors. In mid-March, through Martin, Colonel Scones requested the girls' assistance in sewing uniforms. They already worked long hours each day, but with the hope that their efforts might bring comfort to some poor young soldiers, they agreed.

"Oh my! It is all the same military blue," Anne cried out, when she helped Julia open a wooden crate filled with material the next Monday evening. Stacking the bolts of wool and flannel along the wall created a mountain of dark blue cloth.

Julia began clearing a side table and filling it with the thread and other sewing notions they would need. "Martin told me braid and brass buttons will be sewn on by other volunteers."

"Why must you girls sew uniforms?" Walter asked, as he and Eddie carried in an additional work table for their use. "I do not understand this entire project. I read a newspaper article last week about a fellow named William Browning who earns a fortune making military uniforms."

"According to Martin, Colonel Scones could not obtain a sufficient supply of uniforms," Julia said, "but he did receive this cloth."

"Perhaps you could use my sewing machine, Ellen." Mary brought in her own supply of pins, needles, and scissors for their use. "You became familiar with it while you nursed your poor leg. Sure, Walter insists I must have every new contrivance, but I never mastered the frightful thing."

Recovered from her injury now, Ellen had returned to her position at the factory. As Mary predicted, the diminishing number of immigrants arriving in the city since the war began and the resulting scarcity of workers forced her employer to reconsider and offer her a position. After declaring she would never work for the frightful man again, Ellen's desperate need for employment forced her to acquiesce and return to the factory she so despised.

"I encountered some difficulty with your machine, since it is different from the huge contraptions we use at the factory, but Kitty and I will practice. Our Kitty is so adept at the machines at work, I'm sure she will grow proficient with it in no time at all." Anne admired the way Ellen managed to find every opportunity to praise the shy, retiring girl, who blushed at the attention.

Many discussions arose over dividing the work, the cutting, pinning, sizing, and stitching. When they could not seem to make a beginning, Anne appealed to Ellen and Kitty. "You are our experts here. You must organize us in an efficient assembly system. While Julia and I received extensive training from our mother, much of her exertion was lost on us. Our sewing skills are average at most. Don't you agree, Julia?"

Her sister nodded a vigorous assent. "True, very true."

"I am sorry to say, the sewing machine has been shoved in a corner of the old oven room," Mary said. "Will you be able to work in there, Kitty?"

"Of course," Kitty said. "I am able to work anywhere." When she moved across the hall to look over Mary's machine, they all followed.

When she and Ellen offered to teach the others, Anne saw a great shaking of heads at the suggestion. "I've never seen a sewing machine before," Grace said. "I have no interest in learning to operate the thing."

"I would like to try," Julia said. Kitty spent a few minutes explaining the machine to her, but she soon lost interest.

"I suppose I will content myself with the monotonous hand work," she said to Anne when they finished for the evening and ran up the stairs to their attic room. "Is it not an incredible irony? Even after crossing the Atlantic, we did not escape the dreadful evening sewing chore."

All the next day, Anne could not erase from her mind the sight of poor Kitty left alone in the storage room while the other girls all worked together. She could not bear another evening of worry over Kitty, bent over the terrible, noisy machine with her face turned to the wall. As they prepared for their second night of sewing, an idea came to her.

"Could we pull the sewing machine up to the end of the table here?" she asked Mary, as the girls began to assemble their sewing equipment. Mary agreed with her idea, and they combined their strength and pushed and pulled the machine until they succeeded in drawing it away from its hiding place and moving it to a spot against the dining room table. Kitty would catch the best light from the gas lamps on the wall behind her, and for the long hours of sewing ahead, the others could gather on either side of her along the table.

Once settled into their work, Julia suggested they each take a turn at entertaining to alleviate the boredom. "Will you sing for us, Grace?" she asked. When they all joined in and pleaded with her, she relented.

Starting with an old tune from home, Grace sang "The Banks of My Lovely Lee." Soon they were all joining in. When she moved to "The Nightingale" even the men in the oven room, including George, could be heard singing along. Anne remembered that particular song well. It was an old English tune that had been adopted by the Irish.

While Anne enjoyed the singing, she was also pleased to observe the changes occurring around her. It was the first time she had even heard George speak, and now his rich baritone joined them in song. And then, turning to Grace, she observed the glow spread across her face. Anne marveled that these two poor souls, always so quiet and glum, seemed transformed by the music.

"I have no talent at all for entertaining," she said, when the music ended. "Whatever will I do when it comes to my turn?" She received a few suggestions from her sewing partners, none having anything to do with singing. They were only teasing, of course, and she joined in their sport. Pretending to pout over their lack of respect for her musical talent brought more laughter.

Julia joined the giggles around the table. Then, after reaching out to pull at a strand of Anne's hair, she offered a serious suggestion. "Why not read from one of Mary's books or James's poetry volume. We would all love the verse."

"I could not read and stitch at the same time," Anne said, "as Mother and Kate could." Julia reassured her, insisting the reading would help them all, easing the discomfort of weary shoulders and stiff fingers.

By the next evening, Anne had found her solution. "I believe I have solved the problem," she said to the girls, as she sat down at the table. "I've dusted off our Shakespeare book and brought it along with me. With occasional peeks inside, Julia and I will amaze you all and recite from Hamlet. Perhaps for a while, we will be able to entertain and sew all at once." The girls seated around the table seemed to enjoy the recitations. Several evenings of work flew by before Anne and Julia exhausted their Shakespeare repertoire.

Neither singing nor Shakespeare could compete with Julia's tales of home though. From her descriptions of her days at work for the parish priest in Blackwater to the antics of the younger Carty children, her stories always proved pleasant and positive.

Anne listened to one account she had heard many times about the little ones jumping in the creek and drenching their clothes and shoes with mud. Julia imitated their mother's stern warning to the lot of them to remain far from the house until they were scrubbed clean. Anne smiled when the girls' laughter rang throughout the bakery. Did Julia not possess the gift? Her sister could take a simple little tale, even such an old worn out yarn such as this, and use it to uplift them all.

She looked into the fire. For a moment, the story transported her back to her childhood home. So many recollections flooded into her mind. She turned to her sister. "Remember the scraps of material? Remember the nights we made the rag rug?"

"Oh my, yes." Julia put down her needle. The recollection was reflected in her expression. "You tell the story, Anne."

"Oh no, I cannot." Though it was she who first spoke of the rug, she now regretted it. "It embarrasses me, even now. Perhaps we should forget it."

"Please tell us." Ellen's attention focused on Anne now. "We all want to hear the story, especially if it is shameful enough to discompose the serene Anne Carty."

"Well then, I'll tell it. Sure, it happened many years ago, and we were all just young ones." She arranged a row of pins in front of her, hesitating a little, as she settled in to tell the tale. Even after so many years, she would not relish reliving it all again. "We were making a rag rug, meant for the floor space under our dining room table, don't you see. At Mother's insistence, Father suspended our lessons for the weeks that we worked on the rug. Instead, he read to us from the Bible.

"Mother gathered old clothing and rags, and the relatives and neighbors contributed goods in payment for her sewing work. She cut the strips and rolled them tightly so the edges were hidden. It was Julia's job and mine to braid the long pieces, attaching them to the rug as we went. Kate, a slip of a girl at the time, nine or ten and already an expert with sewing, knelt on the floor, practically underneath the rug. Following along after us, she tightened up our work with her needle."

Julia broke in, adding her praise for their little sister. "Though she worked in an uncomfortable position, Kate never grumbled. When it came to sewing, she never did complain."

"The rug expanded as we worked." Anne took up the story again. "After the first few weeks, it became a huge ungainly circle of a thing. Our hands grew tired. After so many nights of braiding, our fingers were numb."

Her sister interrupted again, offering excuses for the two of them for the misdeed that was about to be told. "We had already spent each long day working out in the field, after all." Seeming dissatisfied with her feeble attempt at an explanation, she sat back and waved to Anne to continue.

"Our little sisters, Lizzie and Maura, sat on the floor at our feet, catching any scraps and throwing them into the fire." Anne stopped working and rose from her chair. She looked to Julia, and after receiving her assenting nod, she continued. "The evenings were warm then, and as the rug grew larger, Julia and I were covered to our waists with the great, stifling thing. Poor little Kate became nearly buried beneath it.

"We did appreciate the beautiful rug that resulted from our work. When we finished each evening, we spread it out across the table and then stood back and admired the many shades and hues.

"And then one night, Mother began cutting strips from a coarse brown material. I held one piece up for Julia to examine.

"It reminded me of an old burlap sack." Anne wished them all to understand, but she could find no words strong enough to describe how dreadful those brown strips were. Finally she sat back down and continued with the story.

"We both grimaced at the ugliness of the cloth now being stacked in front of us. What an unsightly couple of rows they would add to our beautiful rug. The texture was so rough it bit into our sore fingers. We began to invent stories about where the unsightly cloth had come from. Kate, always ready with a gruesome idea, suggested an old beggar used it to clean up after his horse in the back of the cave where he lived.

"Mother ignored our protests. She only shook her head and went right on cutting. When she was not looking, I tossed a strip to Lizzie to pitch into the fire. We braided for a bit, and then I tossed another on the floor."

"I threw several strips into the fire too." Julia shook her head at the memory.

"In the evenings that followed, many coarse brown strips cut by our poor mother made their way into the fire." Anne's voice seemed to catch in her throat, and it was with difficulty that she moved to the conclusion of the story. "Well, one night, the little ones held several strips up for Mother to see before they tossed them into the fire. We were caught. I was mortified. I had never felt such shame, and there's the truth of it."

The girls around the table began to laugh. To her surprise, Anne discovered she could smile a little at the memory herself.

"Once we completed the rug, our punishment began. Our long days of working in the field were then followed by evenings of writing out Shakespeare passages. The sores we developed from braiding the strips, soon turned to dreadful blisters."

"The rug kept our cottage floor warm for years, but its charm had vanished." Here was a memory of home Anne would be happy to forget, but she squared her shoulders and finished the tale. "I could never enjoy it. I remember once Julia and I took it outdoors to clean, and we both enjoyed giving it a few extra whacks."

"Oh, that is a wonderful story. You could call it the incident of the rag rug. Or, the story of the missing burlap strips." Ellen leaned closer to Anne, wanting to hear every last detail. "Did your mother forgive you? It appears as though you girls have never pushed aside the guilt?"

"We were accustomed to our mother being vexed," Julia said. "She was often angry. But, when Father said we had disappointed him, Anne and I both suffered. We so wanted his approval. It took us many weeks to recover. My conscience nagged at me for a long time. As you can see, our Anne still bears some bad feelings.

"Oh Anne," Grace sat up straight, alert for once. "You were such a good girl. Did you really catch it from your father?" Grace began to laugh.

Grace laughed! Anne looked toward Julia. Her sister's head nodded and her expression told Anne she couldn't believe it either. This was the first time, the first unguarded moment of mirth to spring forth from the girl in all these many years. Anne's pain and embarrassment dissolved in the face of this near miracle. Grace Donahoo laughed, no giggle, no simper or smirk, but a healthy, hearty, rib-shaking explosion. The merriment over the rug story, mixed with wonder over Grace's good humor, spread to everyone seated around the table.

Gradually, their high spirits settled down, and for a while they worked quietly. Anne's thoughts turned back to the part of the story about their young seamstress sister.

"If only our Kate were here now," she said. "As you could tell from the story, our younger sister inherited our mother's talent with the needle. Both have the ability to design and complete garments from simple dresses and bonnets to tailored suits or coats. She would provide grand help to us here."

"Ah, a few years have passed since you've enjoyed Kate's company." Julia shook her head a little in disagreement. "Shall I tell you all about our Kate? It may be well to prepare you, since she will be here the moment the war ends."

She did not wait for encouragement. "Well, if she were here, she would work harder and accomplish more than anyone. She is a worker, that one. But, I am certain she despises this war and the delay it has caused her in coming to America. While she helped with this sewing task, she would condemn the entire Union Army and the Confederates alike.

"Kate would also disapprove of the style of these garments and insist on speaking to the person responsible and offering her suggestions," Julia continued. "When finished with the Army, Kate would turn her attention to us. In no time, she would provide each one of us with blueprints for improvements to our lives."

Anne chuckled at Julia's portrayal of Kate, causing laughter to erupt around the table once again. She felt such encouragement over the fact that Grace was laughing along with everyone. The sound of her mirth pleased Anne so her feelings of guilt over the rug incident dissolved.

"Now, Julia, do you really know Kate's opinions about the war?" Anne shook her head. "She has written nothing at all of it to us. Could you be embellishing a bit?" She wished to defend her little sister, but she must admit there was a grain of truth to Julia's story.

Ellen paused in her laughter long enough to agree with Anne's doubts about the description of Kate. "Sure anyone sweet and kind as our Anne—ah, and a storyteller as fine as yourself, Julia—must have a sister that is of a sterling character."

"Wait a bit, and you will see. I have not exaggerated an ounce." Julia's eyes twinkled.

Ellen's compliment brought a blush of pleasure to Anne, and those good feelings helped to soothe the mild concern that still lingered after hearing Julia's dire description of Kate. Her longing to have their little sister with them did not lessen at all. She missed everyone back home. She and Julia were working hard to save money for their passage. Surely, it would not be long until they were all here together.

She also missed James. Though she attempted to keep herself busy and occupy her thoughts every minute of the day, she could not keep memories of him from slipping into her mind. In truth, she daydreamed about him at many times while working in the shop during the day and a good portion of her often sleepless nights. She longed to resume their evening walks.

She missed their talks and wished to hold his warm hand once again. She reserved a special place in her heart for the memory of his sweet, brief kisses. Before she finally gave in to sleep each night, her last prayers were for him. *Please dear Father in heaven, keep James safe and bring an end to this dreadful war.*

Chapter Nineteen

Oct. 30th 1863

My Two Dear Children,

I received your letter on the 23rd of Oct, and we were happy to hear you are well which leaves us all here at present with the exception of Jimmy. He is getting worse every day.

Dear Anne, I went to Father Moran and got the certificate of both your ages and I sent it in this letter to you. Dear Anne, thank you for sending your likeness, the neighbors all came to see you.

Dear Anne, the times was never so bad in Ireland, the potatoes grew well until August and then the black set in and they are all gone. We had a half acre sowed and we had not one since the first of Oct. All clothing and material are dear, it is impossible for people to live.

My two dear children, if it is in your power to send anything, it never was so wanted, but we would not like you to pay a pound to send a pound. Lizzie and Maura ask you to send them the price of new dresses. Dear Anne, you speak of one getting a situation for Kate. It is hard to get a situation in town now.

Write as soon as you get this and do all you can to send us help. It is painful to ask for your hard earned, but these are hard times and the large family compelled me to do so. Only for the missed crop of potatoes, we would not be so bad.

So now I conclude and send you our love, your brothers and sisters join and send you their love. Uncle Martin and family, Joseph Read and family, Mrs. Dempsey, John Scanlan, and Margaret Scanlan send their love. No more from your affectionate parents,
John and Nell Carty

Dear Sister Anne you spoke of bringing me out with Kate. I am going to school every day and I will study hard and with God's help I will see you in St. Louis yet. Michael Carty

November, 1863

On a chilly, dreary fall morning, Julia awoke with a fever. Her limbs were so weak she could not stand without Anne's help. By afternoon, her discomfort had grown, and Mary sent Eddie for the doctor.

"I cannot determine the type of fever that has taken hold of Julia." The worry Anne observed in Dr. Gallagher's eyes betrayed his concern. His instructions were brief. "Keep close watch over her for new symptoms and administer this powder to bring the fever down. It is all the medicine I have, a mixture of my own making. Working with the wounded men at the military hospital depleted my supply, and you all know how unreliable the transport of any goods has been. Drug shipments are in particular danger of being hijacked. Those that do make it through are slow in coming."

After the doctor left, Anne sat beside Julia's bed, holding her hand. She remained there throughout the night, observing her closely, watching for any small change in her condition. As Julia rolled and thrashed in her fevered sleep, Anne felt helpless, wishing she could do something, anything, to ease her sister's distress. She began to pray, thanking God for bringing Julia here to America and pleading with Him to return her dear sister to her healthy, vigorous self.

Julia's arrival at Dempsey's changed Anne's life. Her sister's presence here, with her high spirits and joyful attitude, infused their little attic room with cheer and eased her dreadful, lonely nights. Her willingness to help save the passage money so relieved Anne's anxiety that in some fleeting moments she had begun to experience the lightheartedness of a young girl again.

Anne continued her vigil beside her sister's bed and watched for any sign of agitation. At any indication of her awakening, she jumped up to tend to her. At one point during the night, she removed the soiled sheets from the bed and replaced them with fresh linens. Even this disturbance did not rouse her.

Toward daybreak, Julia appeared to slip into a peaceful sleep. Anne settled back in her chair. After a few moments, she allowed her thoughts to drift to James. She remembered their many nighttime walks together. Her memories drifted to yearnings. She wished to feel again his strong arm at her waist. She longed to hear him speak, but though she searched her memory desperately, the sound of his voice eluded her. She could remember only his words. Turning again to prayer, she asked God for another blessing, pleading for his safe return.

She pulled his most recent letter from her pocket and strained her eyes in the dim candlelight to read through it once again. Finally, exhausted, easing back to rest on the soft arm of the chair, she nodded her head.

With the first rays of the sun peeking through the curtains, Anne jolted awake. She rushed to refresh herself and prepare a cup of tea before returning to Julia's bedside. Her sister rolled about restlessly now, but still, she did not rouse.

"How is she?" Ellen asked. She had come up to the attic room to sit beside Anne.

"She appears to be so sound asleep," Anne said.

Ellen patted her hand. "She will recover soon. I am sure of it."

Each of the Dempsey girls ran upstairs to visit with Anne and offer a prayer for Julia's recovery, before they rushed off to their own employments. They all worried about Julia's long, restless sleep.

When Mary came to the attic room to look in on Julia, she suggested Anne continue to sit with her for a time, while she took her place in the bakery. "'Tis a slow morning in the shop. With few provisions left in the oven room, there will be little on the shelves until supplies come in next week."

Late in the afternoon, she appeared again, this time to relieve Anne. "The girls and I will each take a turn, and we insist you sleep the full night." Anne protested, but Mary took a firm hold of her arm, and led her down to the second floor bedroom where she could rest undisturbed.

For the balance of the week, Anne divided her time. During the day, she worked in the bakery, rushing up the stairs to Julia when there were no customers at hand. Evenings, she sat at the desk in the attic, working over her books and jumping up to tend to her sister when needed.

Julia slept throughout most of the succeeding days and nights. She woke for brief, restless periods, appearing to know Anne, but calling any of the girls who came to help care for her, "Anne." She cried out in her sleep, and at times, seemed to believe she was in Ireland and called for her father and mother.

One morning late in the week, Mary talked to Anne about Martin's determination to visit Julia. "I felt I should alert you. He has come here every evening as soon as he could leave his post. He begs to see her. I told him the doctor will not allow it, but I must warn you, he will not be held back for long."

As Mary predicted, when Anne came downstairs to collect fresh water on Saturday afternoon, she encountered Martin at the bottom of the stairs. His resolute expression warned her he would not wait. He wasted no words in his declaration.

"I must see Julia."

"The doctor is concerned because of the influenza you suffered on your recent trip with the colonel. He said you could be susceptible to whatever has taken hold of Julia."

He placed a hand on her arm and looked into her eyes. "I hope you understand. I must go to her."

"Of course I understand." She was no match for Martin's determination. What could she do, but relent? "Allow me a few moments. I should gain the Dempseys' permission for you to go up to their attic, and I must prepare Julia for a visitor. Then you may come upstairs."

Anne ran to the oven room to talk the situation over with Walter and Mary. "I am in a quandary." She told them that, as Mary had already warned, Martin's insistence on seeing Julia was more that she could withstand. "I have grown fond of Martin, but I must do what is proper, as well as what is safe for him."

Walter held a huge sack of flour in his arms. He placed it on a shelf along the wall, and then walked over to Anne and Mary. "Martin is an adult. I believe his health is his own concern. Propriety presents another problem. Will it satisfy your concerns, if Mary sits with Julia while they visit?" When Anne nodded, he turned to his sister. "Will you act as chaperone, Mary?"

A short time later, Mary sat by the window in the attic room engrossed in her knitting. Martin settled himself at Julia's bedside, holding her hand. Anne stood beside the bed for a few moments, observing, as he touched her hair and her fevered cheek. Sensing she was not needed, she took the opportunity to go down to the Dempsey girls' room for a rest.

It seemed no more than a few minutes had gone by since she stretched out on the bed. Actually, when Mary awakened her, she discovered two hours had passed and Martin was preparing to return to his post. Anne straightened her clothing, brushed back her hair, and rushed out to walk to the door with him.

As they moved through the shop, Martin told her of his concerns. "Julia barely stirred from her sleep the entire time I sat beside her. When I spoke to her, she did not respond at all, or appear to know me." Martin looked distraught and Anne recognized the worry in his voice, but she had no answers to lighten his distress. Still, she tried to reassure him with the most positive words she could summon.

"Julia possesses a strong constitution." Could she sustain a confident tone and not betray her own anxiety? She resolved that she must try. "When we lived at home, she seldom fell ill. Then, when she made the trip to St. Louis, aside from fatigue, the journey had little effect on her. She needed but a week's rest before she could work a few hours at the rectory and help here at the bakery. Please do not worry, she will pull through this."

Anne returned from church the next morning and ran upstairs to check on her sister.

Julia stirred in the bed and tried to push herself up. "Could I have water, please?"

"I'll fetch it for you." Anne touched her sister's cheek. Julia's skin felt cool and her speech was coherent for the first time in a week. Waves of relief rushed through her. She went to retrieve a pitcher from the writing table. She poured water into a cup, and helped her raise her head and drink small sips. Julia could not hold her head up for long, but still, she appeared to be recovering. Anne could not subdue her smile, as she helped Julia settle back on the pillow.

Julia rewarded her with only the tiniest of grins before she drifted off to sleep again. As the day wore on, she continued to improve, awakening after short periods, each time remaining alert for longer intervals.

In mid-afternoon, Julia awoke again after an hour-long sleep, looking more responsive than she had in days. Anne hurried over to her bed. "Welcome back."

"How long have I been ill?"

Pleased at her sister's brightened countenance and strong voice, Anne could not suppress a chuckle as she added another pillow behind her head.

"A full week. I worried so. Martin has been frantic."

"Will he come to visit me?"

"He sat here with you yesterday afternoon." Anne smoothed the covers and fluffed the pillows. "He stayed beside you until he was required to return to duty."

"I must see him, please. Though I have no memory of it, I am certain his presence here hastened my recovery."

"Along with the prayers of everyone at Dempsey's, and St. Vincent's."

"Of course...the prayers." A touch of guilt, mixed with a measure of fatigue, edged into Julia's expression.

"I did not wish to upset you, dear. I suppose I am just giddy with relief that you are awake and talking to me. I only meant to tease you." Anne reached up to brush a stray strand of hair from Julia's forehead. "Allow me to redeem myself by helping you change to a clean bed jacket and brushing your hair. Martin indicated he would visit this afternoon, if he could secure time off. If he does come, I'll ask Mary to bring him up for another visit."

Julia began to slip her arms into the sleeves of the fresh wrap, but the simple effort tired her. Her attempt to tie the bow beneath her chin exhausted her so she sat back and allowed Anne to do it for her.

"Are you certain you are up to a visit with Martin?"

"Oh yes, I will be fine."

An hour later, Martin raced up the stairway. He sat beside the bed, with Mary once again installed in her chair at the window engrossed in her knitting project. He held Julia's hand and spoke to her in a soft voice.

Feeling an intruder in their private moment, Anne turned her thoughts to her own needs. In her excitement over her sister's recovery, she had missed breakfast. With time on her hands now, she decided to find a bit of nourishment.

As she descended the stairs, she offered a prayer for Julia and Martin. "Please God, return them both to full vigor." She also prayed that nothing more would keep them from the courtship that now seemed apparent. But health was not their only obstacle. Martin would surely be required to leave again on missions for the Colonel, and his journeys often placed him in dangerous battle areas.

As she had each day for the past two years, Anne prayed fervently for an end to the terrible turmoil. Surely, everyone in America on both sides of the conflict begged for this same thing. Still, the dreadful war droned on.

Throughout the next few weeks Anne worked hard to complete her own chores and keep close vigil over Julia. Mary set aside the best of the rations they could secure for their patient, and she could see her sister growing stronger each day. Still, she had not regained her full high spirits. The Dempsey girls tried to entertain her and bring back the familiar sparkle to her eyes they all insisted they so dearly missed.

"I am determined to make Julia smile," Ellen said. "I have developed a scheme for just that." Anne would later understand that Ellen held back some, letting her in on but a few of the details.

That evening, Ellen suggested to Mary that she would set the table. Anne volunteered to help, but before the setting was completed, she was called out to the kitchen and she returned to the dining room only a few moments before her sister arrived. Ellen, abetted by Kitty, had arranged plates, silverware, glasses, and candles all in proper order, and then they placed a clean linen tablecloth over the whole lot.

When Julia walked into dining room and noticed the bumpy tabletop, her hearty laugh brought smiles from everyone. They all giggled and clapped.

Their cheerful chatter dissolved quickly, when a small but insistent bounce began underneath the cloth. The weary bakers, Walter, Eddie, and George, were standing at their customary end of the table.

"I have no idea what that is," Walter said, when Mary glared at him. The girls all pretended innocence as they helped Anne and Ellen remove the extra cloth.

Mary, the calmest, gentlest person in the entire building, but no lover at all of small crawling creatures, turned pink with exasperation to find a turtle on her spotless table. She said nothing, and her silence subdued them all. Anne could not think of a thing to say that would sooth her, and apparently no one else could either. A few uncomfortable moments passed in the room, until Eddie disposed of the poor, squirming little turtle.

As they began to take their places at the table, they now discovered a large drawing of a member of the Dempsey group had been placed on each plate. The artists were amateurs, but Anne was amazed at how well each likeness had been done.

"Surely this cannot be me," Walter said. His sturdiness had been exaggerated to a full girth.

"My hair looks orange." Ellen was attempting to look stern, but she soon burst into laughter.

When Julia spotted her own portrait she dissolved in giggles. "That dress was a sight, for sure. I cannot believe I arrived in America wearing such a silly thing." By now, she was laughing so hard she was forced to sit a moment to compose herself. Anne decided the tricks and silliness had attained the evening's goal.

The room filled with merriment such as the folks at Dempsey's had not experienced in a long while. Anne had been assigned to create a portrait of Kitty. It was the one part of the evening's events the girls had informed her about. Not being an artist at all, she had experienced some moments of panic.

Finally, in desperation, she sought Mrs. Flynn's advice. Her dear friend had done a marvelous job. She sketched in Kitty's eyes, capturing her bright gaze to perfection. She lent Anne further advice, suggesting she emphasize Kitty's thick plaits and draw in bright pink bows at the ends of each braid. With Mrs. Flynn's help, the resulting portrait was a fair resemblance of the quiet, but lovely young girl.

"Oh, it's a fine thing," Kitty said. "Are you sure this pretty girl is me? Anne rejoiced to see her smile, as she continued to examine the drawing.

Mary's portrait had been carefully done. Anne recognized the skilled work of Kitty, the true artist in their group. She had accomplished a perfect depiction of Mary, capturing her soft, sparkling eyes and loving smile. Noticing the loaf of bread under one arm and ledger under the other, Mary's smile burst through the look of consternation that had been spread across her face these last few minutes.

"My, my," she shook her head. "Sure it is grand." It was plain to see, she appreciated the fine work. The turtle incident had been pushed aside for now, though Anne suspected Mary would not rest until she caught the culprit who brought the dreadful creature to her dining room.

Their good spirits and sense of hope were dashed the following day, when Anne learned of the death of Mrs. Flynn's youngest son, Barry.

The poor boy's funeral the following Saturday proved the saddest of the far too many they attended in these past months. Though Julia remained at home, still too weak to leave the bakery, Walter closed the shop for an hour and the remainder of the Dempsey group attended the service.

"His death is so senseless, so unnecessary," Anne said to Mary as they approached the church. "Mrs. Flynn told me Barry received a leg wound and he was transported to a hospital in Pennsylvania along with several other injured men. He survived the long, torturous ride in a hay wagon. Then, because the medical staff considered his condition less serious than many of the others, his litter was pushed back in the line outside of the surgery. While he waited, he fell ill with dysentery. Before he could be treated for either ailment, the poor young man, eighteen years old, succumbed to the terrible malady.

"If they had sent him home to recover instead of to that dreadful hospital, he would be with us today, it's sure," Anne said.

"Aye, 'tis beyond understanding. I pray their Andrew will survive and return home to bring the Flynns some relief from their terrible pain." Mary shook her head slowly and reached for her handkerchief.

"I tried to offer Mrs. Flynn consolation, but she seems beyond reach." Anne climbed to the top step of the church, and held the door for Mary. "If I could do something, anything, to ease her pain, I would rush to do it. Of course, it is impossible."

Sadness engulfed them all, and throughout the late fall and early winter evenings, everyone at Dempsey's worked hard to escape the melancholy. As the girls sewed uniforms one evening, Anne suggested they read from their family Bible. "When I left Blackwater, I wished to leave it with all of them," she told the girls. "My father insisted I bring the Bible here. He said each of the children would follow me to America and find a touch of home when they held the precious book."

Suddenly filled with longing for home, Anne turned to her sister. "Remember, Julia, on the long winter nights, we would begin with Genesis, and most years we read through much of the Old Testament before the seasons changed. In the spring, as we spent our daylight hours working out in the fields, Father would test us on what we remembered from our readings."

On many evenings after that, the sewing group turned to the Carty Bible for solace. At Anne's suggestion, they took turns reading favorite passages, while they sat in the dining room working over uniforms.

In the attic room each night, she allowed her thoughts to turn to James. Her reflections often focused on her memories of their times together. It had been a year and a half now since she had seen him, and though she still could not recapture the sound of his voice, she could summon a picture of his kind face before her. She longed for the day when they could walk the streets of St. Louis as they had before the war, and share conversations treasured by them alone. Those moments together had been like no other in her entire life, and she prayed she and James would experience these wonderful times together one day soon.

The death of Mrs. Flynn's son heightened her fear for James' well-being and threatened to overcome her at times. In her last prayer each night, she begged God to watch over him.

Chapter Twenty

Blackwater
Nov. 28th 1864

My Dear Children,
I received your welcome letter on the 23rd of Nov. We were happy to hear you were well with the exception of Julia. We were sorry to hear she is not getting her health. Write and let us know how she is. You know we will be in trouble about her. We also received a cheque of #4 for which we are thankful to you and Julia. May God bless you both and spare your life and health.

Dear Anne, Kate is at home yet. She would not like to go to a farmer. She is handy and good at the needle. I am on the lookout for a station for her in town. Jimmy's health is no better.

Dear Julia, we were sorry to hear you were sick but thank God you are recovered. Uncle Martin and family, Mrs. Dempsey, Margaret Scanlan, John Scanlan, Joseph Read and family are well and send their love to you. Your brothers and sisters send their love. No more from your father and mother,
John and Nell Carty

February, 1865

"We have stitched this blue material until our fingers will soon match the cloth," Bridget Rice said one blustery, winter night. "Will this war never end?" She stopped a moment, and then shook her head slowly. "Sure, I must not complain. You girls sew every evening but Sunday, while I come but one or two nights in the week."

"You contribute more to the war effort than anyone here." Anne sat beside Bridget. They were working together on a uniform jacket she prayed would be the last they must ever sew. "You help feed the refugees arriving at the mission, and you also tend to patients at the military hospitals. You remind me of our Aunt Elizabeth, you know."

"I agree," Julia said. "Elizabeth is bold and outspoken and never content to pursue what she calls ladylike occupations. As she does, you take on any necessary task regardless of the difficulty or unpleasantness."

As Anne worked buttonholes into the garment and Bridget hemmed the sleeves, she continued to voice her admiration for the work her friend had been doing. "Since you come from our own home village, Julia and I take great pride in your accomplishments." Bridget's family was well-fixed and hired in help for cleaning and other household chores. She could have remained at home with her mother, learning needlework and attending luncheons. She had chosen her own path, though, donating her time and all the vigor of her youth to the service of those less fortunate. "We would like to help minister to those poor wounded young men, if ever the day comes, when we finish this uniform sewing." Everyone around the table nodded their agreement.

Still, sitting in the warm, cozy dining room, wrapped in the friendship of the other Dempsey girls, Anne was ill prepared for the stark account she was about to hear. Bridget brushed her fingers through her soft, brown curls, and with her strong blue eyes looking sad, she began to tell of her experiences of the past few days.

"Officials at the hospital requested our help with the sick at the prison." Bridget put down her needle as she continued to speak. "I went in the company of a young doctor and two other volunteers. We encountered horrendous conditions there, dampness, putrid air, filth, and suffering such as I had not experienced in my life before. It was a pit of misery and despair."

"How could you even enter such a place? Sure, you must have been in danger?" Though Anne voiced the concern, the others nodded in agreement.

Bridget waved away their objections and went on. "On one floor of the building, we discovered women prisoners, pitiful creatures, suffering dreadful indignities. I understand nothing of this war, but what could they have done to earn this terrible imprisonment, lack of decent food, and separation from their families? And, I sit here in comfort. I cannot bear it."

For the next few moments, the girls around the table worked quietly. Anne heard nothing but the hum of the machine and the click of scissors, the silent work of each girl interrupted occasionally by a slow shake of a head or a slight bow as if in prayer.

Bridget pushed back a stray lock of hair, and acknowledged the dismay her story was causing around her. After a moment, she took up her work, and continued on. "Women of every age are housed there. Some appeared coarse and a few looked a bit wild and frightening, but most seemed ordinary people. We helped them clean their bodies and clothing, and the doctor tended to wounds and ailments. Many told of the children they had been forced to leave behind, often speaking of how they missed them. One young woman worried her baby was not receiving proper care.

"The doctor promised to write a letter of strong complaint to his superiors, with descriptions of the prison's terrible conditions and a list of demands for improvements. I mean to ask Walter and Mary to send bread to them. I know they will agree even the Confederates need basic food. Ah, this war is dreadful. Faith, it continues on and on, bringing about so much misery. I know there will be no true improvements until the conflict ends."

Anne fetched Walter from the oven room, and when he heard the account of Bridget's experiences, he offered to help.

"Aye, if our shipment of flour comes in this week, I'm sure Colonel Scones will agree to send the bread. But I may be able to do more. My friend Gus Mueller serves on the Western Sanitary Commission, the group responsible for the regulation of hospitals. They also work some with the prisons. I'll ask him to investigate the facilities, and with your doctor's letter of demands to back him, something will be done.

"I'll also ask the Colonel to investigate the circumstances surrounding the women's babies." Walter sighed. "Mothers separated from their children—*ah begorrah*—is this war not a terrible business?"

The following week, Anne opened two new crates to find not the usual military cloth but lovely muslin and silk material in wonderful shades of blues, greens, violets, and creams. With little cloth of any kind available now, this grand supply and the beautiful colors and textures brought a collection of sighs from the girls. She knew it was a mistake, but she could not resist the draw of such a treasure. None of them could. They lifted out the bolts, unfolding dress lengths, exclaiming over the beautiful colors, and holding them up for all to admire. Anne could not deny herself a moment's indulgence, a brief dream of the beautiful garments each yard of cloth would make.

After a time, she abandoned the daydream and returned to reality. She faced Julia, attempting to place a look of determination across her face more forceful than she actually felt. "You must explain this mistake to Martin and ask him to relay the message to Colonel Scones." It made her sad, of course, to return the stacks of lovely cloth to the crates. She could see the disappointment in each girl's eyes, but there was nothing that could be done.

Julia did as Anne requested. The next evening, she reported back to the girls. "The Colonel wishes us to keep the material. He told Martin he has no use for it."

"We cannot take something that is not ours." They all nodded in agreement with Anne. The crates were still standing open, but they had been left untouched throughout the day. She did not wish to pull out the beautiful cloth, and then be forced to fold it again and return it to the container. No one else wanted to do so either.

"I know you all agree with me. This material is not suitable for us." Anne looked around the table and gained a nod from each girl, before she continued. "The fine cloth and these rich colors will never do. Each one is more beautiful than the next. Each lovely bolt sets me off dreaming of fairy tales and grand waltzes."

Anne shook herself to chase away the visions of beautiful gowns that persisted in spite of her effort to dispel them. "We must return to our senses. It is fine to dream, but with everyone in the city wearing patched, threadbare clothing these days, we would appear foolish in bright, new garments."

Once again, Julia asked Martin to re-state their strong concerns to the Colonel. She returned from St. Vincent's with a note for Walter, and a few minutes later, he came into the dining room to read it to them.

> *Sir, explain to the Dempsey girls that I have*
> *no need for that cloth and beg them to accept it*
> *as our thanks for their work on the uniforms.*
> *Joseph Scones*

Walter returned to the oven room without further comment. Anne supposed the matter had been settled.

While they worked, they deliberated over how they would use the material. How could it be divided? How much would one dress require? Would dresses made from this grand cloth be any more suitable for the folks back home than they were here in St. Louis?

When they began putting their sewing away for the evening, Ellen turned to Anne. "We've made no progress here. You are our leader. You advise us, and we will abide by what you say." The others nodded.

"I am surely not anyone's leader." Anne walked to the table across the room and held up the uniform coat they had completed the night before. "After sewing men's tailored uniforms, it should be a simple task to create dresses. We've already devised an efficient system for cutting, assembling and finishing. It's as if we have become a miniature garment factory." Ellen and Kitty both shook their heads vehemently at her mention of the word "factory." Anne looked at them for reassurance, and when they both grinned, she went on with her proposal.

"I believe if we work a little longer each evening, using Ellen's basic pattern and adjusting it for size, we could complete several dresses a week. We could also cut additional ones for the next week. If our estimate is correct, each bolt of material should yield a dress for one of our group, another for a sister or relative at home, and of course, we cannot forget the poor folks at the mission and those desperate women prisoners Bridget visited.

"Do you have any suggestions about the vivid colors, Ellen?" Anne still worried over the bright, shiny fabric. "If we went about in this war weary city wearing dresses made from this cloth, we would draw unfavorable notice. And, though I do not believe we could be charged with abetting the enemy by giving those poor women at the prison a decent dress to wear, we may cause them to be ridiculed, or worse. Can you imagine a poor girl sitting in that filthy jail in a bright yellow frock? We do not wish them to look as if they've been invited to attend Her Majesty at Court."

Ellen shook her head. "You are right, of course, but I am not sure I have the answer. I've been thinking of aprons to cover a good portion of the dresses, but the only cloth suitable for that purpose is what we have already set aside to take to the hospital for bandages. I'm afraid there is nothing left that would do for aprons or overskirts."

Anne remained at the table with Ellen, while the others continued tidying up the dining room, preparing to retire for the evening. "There must be a way. With our clothing growing shabbier by the week, and not a stitch available anywhere in the city, we cannot allow this lovely cloth to sit here and rot. Perhaps we could use the more subdued colors."

Ellen moved to the crates where the bolts of bright material were stacked. "If we could salvage enough cloth from our old dresses to make aprons, we may be able to tone down the brightness a bit. I also wondered if we could use the reverse side of the material. See this violet." The girls walked over to take a closer look, as she held up the bolt at the top of the heap and then turned it over for them to examine. "The color on this side is dull." They all nodded their agreement.

"That is a grand suggestion." Anne had been concerned over the whole enterprise, but Ellen, who had declared her lack of ideas only a few minutes before, now provided some excellent ideas. The other girls, who had been preparing to leave, now gathered around the table. Their happy expressions gave testimony to the relief she could feel shining from her own eyes.

Anne stood beside the table now, discussing other possibilities with the girls. She was not aware her sister had come up behind her, until Julia dropped a length of cream silk around her shoulders.

"We have no wish to copy the look of her highness, when we have our own royalty right here." Seemingly out of nowhere, Ellen produced a long piece of white lace and covered Anne's hair. Grace added to her surprise by stepping forward and placing a small white flower in her hand.

Not satisfied with dressing Anne, Julia picked up Walter's hat from the rack by the door and placed it on her own head, as she approached the table. Then, her sister turned to Grace. "Please, sing for us."

Julia bowed low before Anne, took her arm, and they began walking. To the tune of an old Irish ballad, they made their way around the table. Warming to the show she was creating, Julia grew bolder, moving her theme from royalty to romance. "Sing a wedding song."

"A wedding song?" Anne blushed with embarrassment. She was not accustomed to such attention, and alluding to a wedding was surely not proper. She and James had no formal engagement, after all. If Julia noticed her discomfort, she ignored it and went on with her little drama.

Grace began an old favorite hymn, singing loud enough to be heard over all the commotion.

They had made a full circle around the table, when Walter, Eddie, George, and Mary came out from the oven room. Witnessing the charade, they all looked unsure, smiles beginning to appear but uncertain glances still darting every which way. After only a few minutes they recovered and joined in the fun, waving their arms, clapping and cheering.

"Ladies and gentlemen, may I present the soon to be Anne Carty Duff, on her way to the church to be married to the fine James Duff, himself just home from the war." Anne tried to forget her embarrassment and relax and laugh with the others. Seeing Julia looking bright and cheerful and appearing strong and healthy and back to her old enthusiastic self, warmed her spirit. And too, the always quiet, often glum Grace was singing without a note of caution or reserve. She couldn't help but give in to the silliness. Not one of them had taken a moment for anything but work in many months, and this small measure of cheerfulness was due them all.

When the fun was over, the bakers went back to the oven room and the sewing group took another few moments to decide what they must do. Agreeing to Anne's plan and applauding Ellen's suggestions, they resolved to begin work on the dresses the next evening.

One night a short time later, as the girls continued their work with the beautiful material, Ellen tapped her scissors on the table to gain their attention. "We must give a salute to Anne. You've guided us well, my dear." She looked all around the table. "Don't you all agree?"

"We've sewn a new everyday dress for each of us and one for Sunday," Julia said. "I've set mine aside for spring. Soon, others will be ready to ship to our families back home in Ireland."

"A few of my customers learned about our dresses and asked if they were available to purchase," Anne said. "Should we do that?"

Julia put forth an idea of her own. "It will be wonderful to store a supply of dresses at the mission for poor immigrant women. But when we've filled the cupboards there, could we not offer the rest to neighbors in return for a small donation to the mission?"

"Or, we could ask for a bit of white muslin that we could use for aprons," Ellen said.

"That is a grand idea." Anne still worried over the bright, colorful frocks, but she was forced to concede that the fresh, new material would bring a welcome change from the thin, patched clothing they all wore now. With the passage of only a few weeks, the many bolts of beautiful material began to disappear. The evenings ahead, sewing nothing but blue uniforms, would now creep along, drearier than they ever had been.

Chapter Twenty-One

Blackwater
April 8, 1865

My Two Dear Children,
We received your welcome letter on the 5ᵗʰ day of April and were glad to hear you were well which leaves us all here at present with the exception of Jimmy, he is very bad and he was not out of the door this two months. We did not expect him to be living at this time, but if he does not get better he will not be alive again May Day. He sends his best love to you and Julia.

My two dear children, your father and mother were thinking that if you would pay Kate's passage there perhaps she should sail out of Liverpool. If the money would not cost too much to send home it would be the best way to pay her passage to Mr. Hinton in Wexford. Besides, she may have a chance of some neighbors going with her, but if you pay her passage there she will have no chance of anyone from this county going with her. Julia knows what it cost from Gorey to St. Louis so now my dear children, do what you think is best. John and Nell Carty

Dear sister Anne, I suppose you are going to take me out and there shall be no disappointment again. I am glad to get the opportunity of going to you. I am afraid I will not have anyone going with me from this county. Perhaps there may be someone going again the first of August. Dear sister, Jimmy has been sick so long Father and Mother are not able to do anything for me. I will not leave my situation until I get your next letter. I must tell you I cannot get any clothes for myself. (Kate Carty)

Dear Sisters, after Kate is with you, I expect to be soon with you, with the help of God. I hope you won't forget me and Lizzie in your next letter. I remain your affectionate brother, write soon. Michael Carty

Dear Sisters,
I send this note hoping to find you in good health as this leaves me at present. I thank you for the ten shillings you sent me to buy a dress for my journey. I hope I will soon see you. I am living with Mr. Hogan. This is a lonesome place. All the neighbors are dead and gone. It is not like the place you left. I remain your affectionate sister,
Kate Carty

April, 1865

Anne gained the agreement of everyone at Dempsey's. The arrival of this particular spring brought blossoms more beautiful, with colors more striking, and fragrances more lovely than she could ever remember. Along with their rebirth came stories of the successes of General Sherman and General Grant and rumors of the imminent resolution of the war. Each scrap of news moved throughout the city like pollen spread from flower to flower.

"Everyone in St. Louis is talking about the newspaper stories predicting the end of the war and the changes that happy event would bring," Mary said, as she helped Anne serve customers. A large shipment of supplies had been delivered the day before, and business had been brisk ever since. It was as if the aroma of baked goods had drawn folks to the shop.

"My family back home must be reading these same stories. With the reports of the war nearing a close, Kate expects to be brought out and her pleas have become ever more insistent. Michael also asks to come."

"How old is your brother, then?"

"Well, I have lived here for six years, and he was seven when I left home," Anne said. "He would now be thirteen, or, if his birthday has already passed, fourteen. I cannot believe I have forgotten his birthday. Either way, he is too young to leave my parents and come to America."

"Don't the lads mature much earlier, though, with the harsh life of our homeland?"

"You are surely right. Before I left home, small though Michael was, he already contributed a day's work on the farm, even while attending school. I imagine he is full grown by now. Perhaps, we should consider bringing him out."

Reports of a truce continued to circulate throughout the city. People predicted the war would be over at every hour of every day. In fact, the end took a long time in coming. Just when the folks at Dempsey's felt sure it was done, and their hopes rose, they would hear an account of a new battle.

"Throughout these many months, I have dreaded the arrival of each crate of Army blue," Anne said, one evening in early May. "I shuddered each time we opened a new case. Now, with the war at last winding down, the need for uniforms will surely lessen." A few days later, the girls learned from Colonel Scones that this particular crate would be the last that would be delivered to Dempsey's. They couldn't help but sigh in relief.

"I know there are far more important reasons for jubilation than the conclusion of our small sewing project," Anne said, as they sat around the table working. "The end to the injuries and deaths, the beginning of recovery and rebuilding, and the relief from homelessness endured by the poor refugees pouring into the city are far more important matters. Still, I cannot help but rejoice that our miserable chore will soon be set aside" She added another point they could all agree upon. "This particular shade of blue we have cut and pinned and stitched for all these many evenings will never again be anyone's favorite."

"We all feel the same, Anne," Ellen said.

"Martin should be discharged soon," Julia said on another evening that same week, as Anne sat with her in their attic room. "Once he is released from his Army obligations, I feel confident he will propose marriage. I pray James will return soon, and then you two will be free to begin your lives together."

"I must not even think of it." Anne rose from her chair and walked to the window. Her tears had come without warning, and she did not wish Julia to see her cry. Without turning back to her sister, she continued to speak. "I cannot promise myself to James until I fulfill my obligation to the children back home. While I hope and pray for James' safe return, I also worry over his coming. My great fear is he will not wait until I am free to marry."

"My stars, Anne! For six years you have saved passage money, and at the same time, you've been sending something home each month. Can you not forget the family problems for once and think of yourself?"

Expecting soothing words, or at least a comforting smile, Julia's exasperation surprised and startled Anne. Her sister had almost shouted.

"That is the problem, Julia. I do sometimes forget." She bowed her head to hide the anguish that was surely spread across her face and the tears she could no longer push back. For a few moments, silence filled the room.

"I wish for naught but your happiness." Julia reached out to Anne, pulling her close beside her on the bed. "Please do not cry. I should not have used such a sharp tone. Forgive me."

For a few moments, Anne rested her head on her sister's shoulder and cried softly. "There is nothing to forgive. I know you want a good life for me." Anne tried to halt her tears. "I am so grateful for all you have done to help me accumulate the money we now hold in our immigration fund. After Mr. Fortune disappeared with our savings, I could never have managed to replace Uncle James' money and rebuild our savings on my own. Now, working together, we have put enough by to send for Kate and Michael.

"Still, I am so concerned. I care deeply for James. I want desperately to be his wife. Now it appears he will soon be returning to St. Louis, and I am sick with worry that he will not have the patience to wait for me."

"He does not write of his love?" Julia asked.

"Yes, he does. In each letter he proclaims his love for me. Each brief note is filled with plans for our future, but I've not allowed myself to dream it could all come true. Oh Julia, forgive me. My mind is in a whirl. I know I am not the only one with worries. I am truly ashamed for giving way to this foolish fit of tears."

"I am sorry I upset you." Julia pulled a handkerchief from her pocket and handed it to Anne. "We've both become overwrought, but a few sharp words could never divide us. We are a team, you and I. We will continue working together until we see this task through to completion."

"Thank you, dear."

"I'll not forget our obligations," Julia said. "I never would. I cannot halt my dreaming though. I see many visions of the future. In my favorite one, I imagine myself a married woman. In others, I picture our entire family together again right here in St. Louis." She took Anne's hand.

"Do you ever dream? Do you allow your thoughts to spin and fly? To a life together with James? To a home and family?"

"I do dream. I know I must fulfill my commitment first, but I do picture a home. My home. I do see James there—" Anne stopped herself.

"Excuse my poor humor, Julia. I build castles and indulge in fantasies the same as you. I suppose the difference is I attempt to bury these thoughts. I try to push my dreams so deep in my heart they cannot slip out into the light."

Harmony restored, Anne returned to the subject of home. Julia agreed without any hesitation on the course they would follow. They would send for Kate and hold the money for Michael's passage until after she arrived.

"Have you heard the gossip circulating in the neighborhood, claiming Mr. Fortune has returned to St. Louis?" Julia asked. "This morning, a man who came into St. Vincent's told the mission workers he recognized Fortune on a train, when he traveled from his Army post to St. Louis."

"I have heard the stories, as well," Anne said. "One customer in the bakery insisted he saw Mr. Fortune in the crowd at a church in New York City."

"I doubt that," Julia said.

At one time, Anne believed she would never find humor in anything connected with their lost money. It surprised her to discover she could speak of the matter without pain now, and she and Julia shared a good laugh. They agreed their concern over the dreadful Mr. Fortune had come to an end. Anne decided she would be happy to never see or hear of him again.

Chapter Twenty-Two

Blackwater
May 22nd 1865

My two dear Children,

We are sorry to tell you Jimmy departed this life the 12th day of May. He was very bad for four months. He often called for you and Julia. He suffered great agony before he died. My dear children, we were up night and day with him. He left us distressed at the present time. The poor fellow, he thought hard to die and his last words were to be remembered to you and Julia.

Dear Anne and Julia, Peter Breen is going to America. He is ready at the present time. He says he will wait for Kate if she will be ready in two months. She would be glad to have him going with her. He will be the same as a brother for her. He says he will go through St. Louis. May God send them both safe. Write immediately for it is good of him to wait for her and I do not like to delay him too long.

Grace Donahoo's father died six weeks ago. All friends desire to be remembered to you.

John and Nell Carty

June, 1865

"I knew when I left him I would not see him again," Anne bowed her head for a moment. She wiped at her tears and blew her nose. "Oh, I should have known, but I chose not to accept the truth. Now, his death is such a shock. I feel as if a fierce wind is pushing me over and I cannot regain my footing."

"From the day of his birth, he was so ill." Julia tried to describe Jimmy's difficult life to Mary, who had come to the attic room to console the girls. "I was eight years old, and Anne six when he was born, and we spent much of our time caring for him. His arms and legs were weak, you see, and throughout most of his life, he needed support from one of us to walk."

"The cough was the worst of it." Anne sat at the end of the bed, her arm around Julia's shoulder.

Mary pulled a chair close and sat facing them, her eyes filled with concern, listening as they shared memories of their brother.

"He coughed almost without relief," Anne said. "Since he showed some improvement if he remained in an upright position, he spent most nights sitting in his chair. When he attempted to speak, he could force out only a few words before he gasped for air."

Anne remained quiet for a time, remembering, but then she returned to their talk. "Sometimes, on fine days, we would place his chair in the garden, and with the strong rays of the sun shining down on him, he would be relieved of the coughing. Once the sun and warmth disappeared and the rain and chill returned, his coughs began anew."

Sorrow enveloped Anne. A cloud of grief hovered around her that she could not seem to escape. Her dear Jimmy, the wisest, kindest human being who ever lived, was gone. He had been freed from his pain and now rested in his heavenly home. Oh, how she ached for him, though. If only, she could talk to him and see his smile, just one more time.

She tried to picture her family gathered around the table or at work in the garden with Jimmy sitting in his chair beside them. She attempted to imagine them all attending church, with Father's strong arm bearing him up. Her visions of the folks back home must be altered now. A lump gathered in her throat. Could she bear to dream of home ever again?

"He never grew strong enough to attend school." Julia interrupted her thoughts. "Anne taught him to read. He knew every word of our Shakespeare studies and could quote endless passages from the Bible. Rather than complain, he sat and read his books and attempted to muffle his coughs."

"When I was ready to leave home, Father insisted I bring our family's Bible along with me." Anne had told this story before, but it soothed her somehow to relive it again. "'Carry it with you, as you lead the way for our family's escape from this tortured land,' he told me. I did not wish to take it from Jimmy, but they both insisted." No longer able to hold in her grief, she gave in to her tears.

Mary moved from her chair to sit between the girls. She attempted to console them, rubbing Anne's arm, then turning to Julia and stroking her hair. They sat in silence for a time.

"Our poor dear Jimmy, he will never struggle for breath again," Anne said, when she could speak again. "We have that small consolation."

"May he go with God." Julia bowed her head.

"Poor Father and Mother, they gave so much of their lives to his care." Anne rose from the bed and moved to the writing table. Retrieving the Bible, she held it close to her heart. "Difficult as it is for us to adjust to this loss, the grief our parents are bearing must be terrible. I have never felt at such a distance, so torn from those dear people. They are surely bent down with sorrow, and we not there to help them. Our written words will offer little solace. If we could but see them, even for a short while, perhaps we could provide some comfort." Even as she said the words, she knew it was impossible.

❀ ❀ ❀

On June 12, in observance of the customary Month's Mind, the girls attended a mass at St. Vincent's for the repose of Jimmy's soul. As she prayed, Anne held in her heart her last memory of her dear young brother who, with never a word spoken on his own behalf, had offered cheerful farewells when she left him behind and sailed for America. "Our precious Jimmy," she said to Julia on the walk home. "So many loved him. He will be missed by all who knew him."

Since Grace learned of her father's death well beyond the one month period, they included Mr. Donahoo in the prayers at Jimmy's service. Though filled with sorrow themselves, they attempted to console the poor girl. The news distressed her so, Anne worried Grace would fall back to her former sad state and Julia's efforts to cheer her would go for nothing.

Chapter Twenty-Three

Blackwater
June 6, 1865

My two dear children,
We received your letter on the third day of June. We were glad to hear that you were well which leaves all here at present.

Dear Anne, I went to the ship agent about Kate's passage, he told me passage from Cork to St. Louis is #8 and from Wexford to Cork 12 shillings. That leaves the whole route #8*12"0. If the passage would be cheaper by paying it there, you may pay it there, but if you pay it there she would have no one going with her. However go the best way you can for you know there is great expense to bring a passenger to America.

Dear Anne, we were expecting when the war was over you would be able to do something for us, but if Kate must go we could not expect anything for a long while. Kate is eager to go but we must look at the first want. Only for poor Jimmy's sickness and death we would not be in this way. I do not like to tell you the distress we are in, but I hope you will consider it. Send a little note to Kate. She is afraid you won't send for her anymore. Your affectionate parents,

John and Nell Carty

Dear Sisters,

Enclosed I send you this note that you may see by it how I am improving at school. I hope to see you in America yet and when I go there I will be able to write a letter home to my Mother. Maura and I are lonesome after poor Jimmy. Maura and I send our love to you,

Lizzie and Maura Carty

Dear Anne, we received a cheque of #2 for which we were thankful to you for this is a hard, dry summer here. Provisions never were as high.

John Carty

July, 1865

A wave of immigrants now began arriving in America from all corners of Ireland. One of the first to make his way to St. Louis was Martin Tobin's brother, Patrick. Having heard much about the young man from Martin, Anne had been anticipating his first visit to Dempsey's.

One morning, as they worked together in the bakery, Mary raised the subject of Patrick. "I know your brother was dear to you and Julia," Mary said, "and I do not wish to cause you a moment's additional sadness, but I believe we must go on with our lives. If you and Julia would not be troubled by a little company, I believe Patrick Tobin's coming provides the perfect opportunity to resume our Dempsey suppers. We must somehow move beyond the grief so many are suffering in these terrible times."

Anne had loved her dear Jimmy with all her heart. She could not even think about him without sorrow and tears, but Mary was right. Sorrow had filled her being since the day she and Julia received the word of their brother's death. She knew she could not continue on in this terrible state. She must move forward. She and Julia must find a way to push on with their lives.

"You are right, of course, Mary. Our brother, Michael, and our four young sisters remain at home, waiting with all confidence for their big sisters to bring them to America. I know Julia will agree that we must press on with our lives. Let us sit down together this evening and plan Patrick's special meal."

Anne and Julia worked with Mary over a menu, until she appeared satisfied. "I have another idea I have been considering," she said. "Mrs. Flynn's older son, Andrew, has been released from the Army. While I know it is too soon after their young Barry's death to invite the Flynn's for any social occasion, I thought, perhaps a small family supper, a simple meal and conversation with friends, would divert their thoughts from the loss and bring them some small measure of comfort." Mary appeared to be a little uncertain as she continued. "Our dear friend seems lost in her deep sorrow, and I so wish to help her."

Anne felt as uncertain as Mary, but she nodded in agreement. Since her son's death, Mrs. Flynn had been spending her days at home alone. "I believe we should pay her a visit. Even if the family decides they are not ready for a supper at Dempsey's, Mrs. Flynn will surely appreciate a little company."

"I agree," Julia said. "Let's walk to the Flynn's right now and extend the invitation."

When they settled in the parlor and Anne explained the reason for their call, she noticed a marked difference in the couple's responses. Mrs. Flynn's face held a tiny spark of a smile, but Mr. Flynn shook his head.

"Don't I have long days at the foundry, leaving little time for anything but rest and a bit of nourishment?"

Anne knew Mr. Flynn to be an amiable man. His grief over his young son must have prompted this refusal. A regular volunteer at St. Vincent's, he offered his services with home repairs for those in the neighborhood who were in need. She had observed his kind manner when he spoke with the people he helped. She admired his way of imparting a breath of gentleness and humor amid the poverty and hopelessness they were all working to relieve. She and Julia had enjoyed pleasant conversations with him on many an occasion. Perhaps, they had been too hasty with an invitation for a family gathering, after all.

Mrs. Flynn turned to her husband. "If you do not object, Tim, I know Andrew and the girls would be happy to be in company again. It is naught but a family supper after all. I will stay back with you, love, but we must go about soon. We need the friendship of other people to lift us from our sorrow.

"Have we not watched as these poor girls suffered the loss of their young brother, Grace Donahoo, the death of her father, and Bridget Rice, her grandfather?" Mrs. Flynn crossed the room to hug Anne and then Julia. "We would be hard pressed to find anyone in this city untouched by tragedy. We must carry on. We must try for the children."

"I know you are right, Delia. You go on to Dempsey's with the children. I will manage on my own, and I promise I will overcome this grief."

Mr. Flynn turned to Anne and Julia. "Please pay me no mind. And, beg the Dempseys to forgive my poor manners. God help me, but I cannot talk and be happy with people, not yet, not just yet."

In spite of the sympathy Anne held for the Flynns and her own sorrow over Jimmy's death, she determined she must make an effort to be cheerful on the evening of Mary's supper. As she worked in the bakery throughout the day, her emotions raced between anticipation over the pleasant evening ahead and a deep sadness. Her dear Jimmy was gone from her. He would never be arriving in America, nor would he experience the enjoyment of a meal at Dempsey's. In another moment, she reminded herself her little brother was surely resting in the presence of God. She drew comfort from this idea, until her emotions rolled about again. In another moment, her thoughts moved to her worries about James.

She pushed her concerns over his safety aside and resolved again that she would not allow her gloomy thoughts to spoil the evening. She must do her part to make the meal a pleasant one. After renewing her determination, her spirits rose. Later, as she helped Mary with the preparations, she even caught herself humming.

The dining room had been cleared of crates of material and sewing implements and cleaned and shined to perfection. The gas lamps glowed, and candles flickered along the table. The room had been returned to the pleasant, welcoming place Walter and Mary meant it to be. Anne read in the faces of them both the joy they derived from gathering their friends around them. As she gazed about the dining room, she once again vowed she would allow herself none but pleasant thoughts this evening. She would enjoy the meal and entertain their company with a smile on her face.

When the relieved and grateful group gathered around the table at last, they all seemed to have taken that same pledge, to cast off the gloom and move forward with their lives. Anne bowed her head and joined in the praise and thanksgiving, as Walter offered a prayer. She granted herself time for one brief silent plea—she could not ignore any opportunity. *Please dear God, send James home, safe and well.*

Martin's brother, Patrick, surprised them with the news that he had attended a service at their church in Blackwater before he left home and had visited with the Cartys. "Our conversation was brief," he said, "but I enjoyed speaking with them. Your brother Michael appeared to be hale and fit. Your mother and young sisters were a fair lot, one prettier than the next.

"Your father seemed a particularly kind man. He told me of the family's sorrow over the death of your brother." Patrick nodded to Anne and then Julia. "I am truly sorry for your loss."

"Patrick is the fine young man you assured us he would be," Anne whispered to Martin, who was seated between her and Julia.

"And, hasn't it become a rare treat to have you at Dempsey's for an evening visit?"

"Since the end of the war, I have been spending long hours working with Colonel Scones, recovering army supplies and equipment for storage at Jefferson Barracks. Julia remarked recently that I seem even busier than during the war."

"Martin will soon be leaving again with the Colonel." Julia shook her head. "The war is not over for them, it seems."

"Come back safe, Martin." Anne turned to Julia.

"And, you, young lady, eat every bite. Martin would be pleased to find you looking strong and healthy when he returns."

"Yes, I certainly would like to see your rosy cheeks once again." Martin looked at Julia, and they shared a grin.

Martin extended his smile to everyone at the table, and then he settled his gaze on Andrew Flynn. "I am sure you will agree that, with the hostilities ended, our travels are safer now than they have been these past years."

Anne observed Mrs. Flynn's son, as he responded in agreement with what Martin was saying. She was pleased to come to know Andrew. What a fine young man he was. He had left St. Louis, four years ago, only a lad. With the terrible war experiences he must have endured and the heartbreaking loss of his younger brother, he had emerged from the devastation and returned home a mature young man of twenty-two.

He surely gained Mary's favor by enjoying her supper and praising her cooking skills. "It is a marvelous meal, Mary," Andrew said. "After being away from home and eating army food, it has been a treat to come home and be served by the wonderful cooks of St. Louis."

Mr. Flynn had come after all, and as he spoke, Andrew looked across the table to his mother and winked. He spoke with ease to everyone at the table. By evening's end, the new arrival to St. Louis and the freshly-returned soldier were discussing their similar plans to head out west.

Anne observed Mrs. Flynn as they all talked and laughed. She listened to their conversation and expressed interest in the plans they were all beginning to make. Still, Anne could see the evening was difficult for her. She had not come with a book or other surprise hidden in her pocket for Anne. She wore a plain grey dress with no unusual ribbon or flower or other adornment, as Anne had come to expect. When she relaxed her smile, signs of her pain and the effort the conversation extracted from her were etched across her face.

At one point, she did succeed in making them all laugh. "I have been trying to persuade Andrew to wait, at least until the next Carty sister arrives, before he pursues his dream and moves on to Colorado."

"Now, Mrs. Flynn, you know Mary claims first rights on the Carty girls." Julia said. She turned to Patrick and Andrew to explain. "She's in search of a bride for Walter."

A groan escaped from Walter, and once again, everyone laughed.

Like Andrew Flynn, the majority of the young men of the neighborhood had been released from their military duties. The sense of relief that settled over the city at the end of the war had been tempered by the loss and heartbreak so many were suffering. Many men had received serious injuries. Others would never come home. These unhappy thoughts sobered Anne.

As she climbed the steps to the attic room at the end of the evening, she considered the many alterations occurring in her own life. With the uniform sewing over and her work on the accounts for the army ended, her hours of employment were shorter now. The time required to manage the bakery's bookkeeping and serve her customers in the shop left her free moments to wonder and worry.

As always happened, her thoughts moved to James. As the weeks passed and he did not return, her worries heightened. Had James been injured? Was he even alive? Did he still love her, as he had declared on so many evenings when they walked home from the mission? Did he hold to his intention to marry her, as he proclaimed in each letter she had carried in her pocket throughout these years? Of course, her faith in him had never wavered. She believed his love to be strong and true. But, what had become of him?

Once she had attempted to find satisfactory answers for these questions and convince herself he was alive and well, she turned to a new set of worries. How long would it be before her family obligations were discharged? And, when James did return to St. Louis, how long would he wait?

Chapter Twenty-Four

Blackwater
July 4th 1865

My two dear children,
    We received your welcome letter on the 3rd which gives us pleasure to hear you are well as this leaves us all here.
    Dear Anne, we posted a letter to you the 26th day of May about poor Jimmy's death. He departed this life the 12th day of May. He was four months sick. He often spoke of you and Julia and his last words were to be remembered to you. Dear Anne, in respect to Kate going out, your Mother and I were considering that if she would stay at home until next spring the money you send home would be great help to us. It would be a means of keeping us living here, besides Kate has a good place and a good master and mistress. If Kate goes now she leaves us in a bad way. Dear Anne, consider the children at home.
    Dear Anne, Kate is in her situation; still her wages are small, hardly able to keep clothes on her. Her clothes are not fit to bring with her and she has no means of getting better. If I had

it or could get it I would give it to her but I have not. We were expecting some money in your letter, for we never wanted it so. There was never more money came to Blackwater Post Office than came this year. It is a hard time on the poor and no sign of being better. Do all you can for us; it may be a long time until we trouble you again.

No more at present from your affectionate parents,
John and Nell Carty
All friends here are well. Write soon. M. Carty

August, 1865

With the end of the hostilities came a time for the country to recover and heal, and for the city to move forward. Since Anne and Julia sent money for Kate's passage in May, the time had also come for another Carty sister to sail for America. While working together in the shop, Anne and Mary often discussed the plans for Kate's arrival and for settling her in at Dempsey's. On one particular sunny morning, they spoke of the course the bakery would take.

"Will Walter work a little less now that the war is over?" Anne questioned Mary during a lull in the shop's business.

"And you, Mary Dempsey, will you do the same? You've both worked hard. You have earned some rest."

"We are developing a plan for that. When we learned Will intended to move on to California after his release from the army, Walter hired George Blake on a permanent basis to take his place. In spite of the criticism he will receive from some quarters, Walter believes George's wartime work has earned him a position."

"George is a fine man." Anne began sweeping the floor, while Mary collected empty trays and stacked them in neat rows. "And haven't I just stifled the temptation to add 'for a Brit?' It is a near impossible habit to overcome. When the army assigned George to work with us, I did not wish to like him anymore than he wanted to join in with all of us. We quickly learned what a good, kind man he is, and it became difficult not to enjoy his company. I must ever remind myself we are all Americans now."

"It's hard, sure it is," Mary said. "We feel disloyal to our dear ones back home if we befriend the British. Did Eddie not refuse to speak to the lad when he arrived here? Now, he and George have thrown aside the old hatreds and grown close as brothers. They gained a world of experience working together during the war years.

"Walter will rely on them to do the majority of baking, while he oversees, makes improvements to the building, and gains new contracts. Hundreds of folks come each week, setting up homes and businesses or gathering the supplies they need to head out west. With the city changing before our eyes, Walter has decided it is time to expand our large orders.

"We've asked Grace to stay on as our cook, since she has grown into an excellent chef." Mary gathered a stack of dust cloths and towels in her arms and turned back toward the oven room. "With Grace preparing meals, Cara keeping things clean, and you handling the shop and bookkeeping, I will don a fancy dress each day and preside over the place like a queen."

"Oh, Mary, you must. You deserve an even larger kingdom than this bakery—"

"I add my voice to that acclaim." Julia entered the shop in time to hear the last of their conversation. "You and Walter both merit a fine life."

"Thank you, Miss Julia." Mary bestowed a deep bow upon Anne's smiling sister. "'Tis a splendid compliment, coming from a grand lady such as yourself. But, what brings you back home in the middle of the day?"

Julia held up a long, official-looking envelope. "Colonel Scones is the cause of it. He planned to deliver these papers to

Walter himself, but I seized the opportunity for a brisk walk and volunteered for the task."

"After being forced to spend our time indoors these past years, it does feel grand to walk about freely now," Anne said.

"You are right." Mary nodded vigorously. "If the sun holds, let us plan our own escape this afternoon. If we prevail upon Grace to attend the shop for a bit, we could venture as far as the library."

"A walks sounds wonderful, but I could not leave Grace behind."

"Sure—what was I thinking? We may even persuade our Cara to join us as well." Mary took Julia's arm. "Come along, we'll take Walter his papers and perhaps we can persuade the master himself to preside over the shop, while we all take in some fresh air."

"See now, I've been successful in stirring up some mischief." With a grin, Julia turned to follow after Mary. "Have a nice outing for yourselves." She waved to Anne as she headed back to the oven room.

Anne was left on her own in the quiet shop. The floor had been swept, the shelves were freshly scrubbed, and her books were up-to-date. With no customers for the moment, she stood at the front of the shop for a time, gazing at the sunbeams streaming in through the window. The image of a perfect sunny morning back home slipped into her mind, and in an instant, her thoughts moved to her family.

The troubles in Ireland often pushed to the background through the war years now loomed large. She grimaced to recall her father's descriptions of the need back home. His sad accounts, however, paled in comparison with the reports of the country's desolation that shared space in the local papers, along with news of reconstruction here in America.

The recent communications in regard to Kate also concerned Anne. In their letters, her parents implied they still awaited money for her passage, while she had mailed the letter containing her fare weeks ago. In Kate's recent note, she seemed to believe her parents changed their minds about her coming. She and Julia examined the recent letters from home, reading them aloud, shaking their heads in puzzlement. She did not know what to think, and her sister shared her concern.

Even as she considered these matters, Margaret Scanlon, a granddaughter of the Cartys' neighbors in Blackwater, entered the shop. "My mother received a letter from home, and she found this page in the envelope." She held out a folded sheet. *Julia and Anne Carty* had been written across the outside in a bold hand.

"Thank you, Margaret. I pray it contains news our Kate is on her way. Oh dear, only a few minutes ago Julia walked out the back door to return to work. No matter, I will share the note with her as soon as she returns this evening."

The girls chatted for a few moments and then Margaret hurried out. As soon as the door closed behind her, Anne unfolded the paper and discovered a brief note that bore an altogether different message.

They have spent my money. Please take me out of this place. Kate

After walking to the library with the others, closing the shop, delivering bread to the mission, and sharing supper with everyone at Dempsey's, Anne's shock over Kate's note had lessened a little. At least, the pounding of her heart had returned to near normal. Her head still ached, though, and her thoughts still swirled with disbelief over Kate's words.

Lacking a private moment with Julia, she had been forced to keep the troubling message to herself until they climbed the stairs to the attic room. "Finally, we are alone," she said. They sat on their beds directly across from each other. "I cannot avoid this sad task any longer. I must share this message with you. It has been resting uneasily in my pocket for hours."

She handed the wrinkled paper to Julia. "I received it this afternoon." She watched her sister's expression turn grave as she read the few heartbreaking words.

"I realize conditions have worsened in Ireland," Anne said, "but—"

"I feel their suffering, and I long to care for them." Julia looked up from the sheet and faced Anne with a look of consternation. She began tapping her feet on the floor, shaking her head, and shifting her arms about. Finally, settling herself, she spoke again, her voice sounding sharp. "There is no excuse for taking the funds. They know about Mr. Fortune's disappearing with Uncle James' money and what we had originally saved for Kate's passage. They know how we suffered over Fortune's treachery and how hard we worked to replace the funds he took. I cannot believe they would do such a thing."

"In fairness to the folks back home, while the war occupied our attention, we did neglect them."

"Perhaps I was remiss, but you never were." Julia paced the floor now, stepping around the chairs, walking to the window, and then returning to stand before Anne. "Since you first arrived in St. Louis, you have been sending money to our parents each month, with no interruption during the war."

The pain and disappointment Anne struggled to overcome all through the afternoon paled in the face of Julia's indignation. Her sister's countenance grew bright red as the first of Mary's homegrown tomatoes. She resumed pacing about the little room as if being chased. Anne had never seen her smiling, affable sister in such a state.

"I did sometimes forget, you know. While I tried to think about our dear ones and offer prayers for them, the shop, the accounts, and the uniform sewing consumed me. Many times, when Sunday arrived and I sat down to write a letter, I realized a week had gone by, dissolved like a sugar treat melting away on my tongue. I had not given one thought to home since the previous week."

"Of course, Anne, but we worked hard and did our best. That's the truth of it. Now, a good portion of our earnings have disappeared forever." Julia continued her pacing, and her tears poured forth.

"Our poor Kate, waiting these many years, longing to be here with us, I cannot bear to think of her disappointment." She turned to Anne again. "Whatever shall we do?"

"We could send Michael's passage money for Kate."

"Your calmness in the midst of our turmoil is a blessing." Julia managed the tiniest of grins.

"Ah my dear, I was not so calm this afternoon. My walk to the library with Mary and the other girls was miserable. I'm afraid I spoiled the outing for them. I tried to talk and laugh, but my thoughts were spinning. It was difficult to concentrate on anything but the few words in that note from Kate. I must apologize to Mary tomorrow and explain the circumstances.

"I've had a few hours to absorb the blow of Kate's message, before passing the note on to you. I regained a little of my determination to push on. It will not be easy, but we must go forward. Somehow we must."

"That is all we can do. Bring Kate here now, and begin putting money aside again for Michael." While Julia agreed, tears continued to roll down her cheeks. "I am trying not to think ill of our parents, but we worked so hard to save that money. I cannot believe it is all gone." She repeated the words over and over.

At last, Julia's troubled spirit seemed to calm, and Anne decided it was time to move forward. "Well, the decision is made. I will ask Mary for a few minutes leave tomorrow. I'll rush to the bank to withdraw the money and once again post a voucher for Kate's passage. Perhaps we can recover and begin again."

As they prepared for bed, Anne noticed a few tears still visible on her sister's lashes. When she hugged her and wished her good night, she received a pat on the shoulder, but Julia's face still looked grim. The words she whispered sent a chill through Anne's being.

"I pray they will not spend Michael's money, too."

Chapter Twenty-Five

Blackwater
August 13th 1865

Dear Anne,

I wrote to you the 3rd and have received no answer yet. We were expecting a letter before this time. Kate is in great trouble because we are not getting a letter. Your Aunt Mary Kelly told us to write you she is thinking about going to America with Kate. She wishes we would all go together. There is nothing would give us more pleasure if we could go. Aunt Mary thinks if we were all in St. Louis and have a home we would live comfortably. We will do all we can to leave this place. If we all cannot go, Aunt Mary will pay Lizzie's passage. The passage is raised from five guinea to seven on account of the numbers going to America. There are a great deal of people preparing to go out of this parish. Lawrence Corrigan's sister has paid his passage. She is but three years out and has sent home 16 guinea.

Dear Anne, your Aunt Mary Kelly is not going there to earn her bread, she is bringing her fortune with her and if we all could go her

money would assist us to live there. I will adver-
tise now and if I make a sale of the place we will
all go together with the help of God.

No more at present from your father and
mother.

❀ ❀ ❀

September, 1865

With flour and other supplies slowly becoming available again in the city and baking for the army camps finished, the volume of goods on sale in the shop returned to nearly normal. The Dempseys' ability and willingness to share their abundance was welcome news for St. Vincent's. The need had grown dire at the mission. Refugees from the war poured into the city and immigrants came again in great numbers, many making their way to the church.

"I will be happy to take you to the mission in the carriage," Walter said, when Anne was preparing to deliver day-old goods for the first time in a long while. "There is a chill in the air this evening."

"No thank you, Walter," she said. "After the many wartime nights when we were forced to ride in the carriage or remain indoors, I look forward to a good, brisk walk." In truth, the freedom to go about on her own again thrilled her. The fresh air so raised her spirits she would pay little mind to the cold.

As she set out, Anne admitted to herself that it was an unusually chilly evening. She delivered her baked goods, and bundling herself against the wind, began to make her way home. While she went along, she attempted to concentrate her thoughts on the fine supper awaiting her back at Dempsey's.

Though she tried with all her might, she could not push aside her worries about James. Never a great correspondent, his letters had at times been no more than brief notes. Yet, how precious those few words were. Always loving, ever speaking of the future, he never failed to mention his plans for their life together.

She had not received a letter for several weeks, and as she trudged along the nearly deserted streets, she held him in her thoughts and her worries heightened. She would not allow herself to even consider the idea that he might have been killed. But, had he been injured? She recalled a recent discussion with Walter regarding James' whereabouts. Walter believed he was alive, and he provided her with good reasons for this assurance.

"The army notifies the family when a soldier is killed, and the Duffs would send us word," Walter had said. "Besides, there are a few men from the neighborhood who have not returned home as yet. Some may have headed out west, but James would not be among that group. Since I've known him, he has held firm in his determination to settle in St. Louis." Walter also informed Anne that he had enlisted Colonel Scones' help in inquiring among his contacts for any mention of James' whereabouts. He insisted they would learn something very soon. She clung to Walter's words.

She had read the newspaper reports of the missing soldiers, though, and heard the stories of hundreds buried in mass graves. She slowed her pace and reached inside her cloak to touch the worn pages of James' most recent letter. As she rubbed her fingers across the rough paper, optimism rose up within her. She imagined he would appear one evening, somewhere along her way, as he had on those many nights before the war.

As she rounded the corner into Park Street, the wind gained strength, grabbing at her cloak and blowing it all about. She lowered her head, reaching down to grasp both edges of the material and gather it close around her. When she raised her head again, a tall, broad-shouldered form was headed directly toward her. Her insides began to quiver. Could it be—?

"James!"

"Anne, my pretty mavoureen, I am so happy to see you." He enveloped her in his arms and lifted her from the ground. "If you are not the fairest girl in the entire world, I am done for. Sure to heaven, I love you so."

"I love you too." On many dark nights throughout the war years, she had fallen asleep with these precious words in her heart. With the shock and excitement of seeing him, she said them aloud now for the first time.

He set her back on the ground, and then he kissed her. When she kissed him back, she caught a glimpse of the dimple, low on his chilled cheek—ah, she had missed that dimple.

"Anne, do you mean it? Do you love me?"

She nodded.

"Will you marry me, when I secure proper employment?"

"I do wish to marry you. I have missed you so." She held his arm and they resumed their walk. "My situation has not changed, though. I still hold an obligation to my family." She could not discuss her family, not just yet. Too many questions remained unanswered.

She pulled her hand away from his arm with a brisk thrust. "I have not received a line from you in weeks. Where have you been? Why did you not write?"

"I was wounded in the leg and sent to a hospital—"

"Oh!" Remembering Barry Flynn's hospital experience, a gasp escaped her. But, she motioned for him to continue.

"The surgeon tended me without delay. But, worrying that, if I lost awareness, they would cut off my leg, I refused morphine and managed to remain alert. I demanded the doctor do what he could without the blade.

"Once they moved me from the surgeon's tent and a nurse convinced me the leg was sound, I lapsed into a semi-conscious state I lingered in for weeks. I incurred a fever that came near to claiming my life. After a time, I recovered from the fever and gained some strength. I had begun to move about, when the sickness overpowered me again. The doctor tended me when he could, but he was overwhelmed with wounded men.

"The nurses and volunteers, seeming like the saintly women right out of our old Bible stories, provided me with wonderful care. Their kind ministrations saved me, true enough."

They were stopped at the corner now, waiting for a carriage to pass in front of them. James took hold of her arm again.

She did not pull away. She could not. She had waited so long for this moment—*oh my word. And, him with an injury.* She turned to him with a slight nod, and he went on with his story.

"In the old barn where we stayed, row after row of sick and wounded men were stretched out on pallets and cots, their suffering unbearable to witness. After months of illness, recuperation, and then a new fever, I determined I must leave the place to free myself of the malady. The war had ended by then, and those still in need of care were being moved to hospitals, so I gained my release. I crafted a shillelagh to support my leg and set out.

"Walter's horse, Blacky, served me well for three years, but she sustained an injury at the same time I was hit, and I lost her. So, I rode in the back of wagons, or tramped along." James stopped a moment, and then after tightening his hold of her arm, he continued with his story.

"In Indiana, realizing I could go on no longer, a new fever taking hold of me, I accepted a ride from a farmer named Kevin Kavanaugh. When he offered me work, I stopped at his place for the summer. A peculiar, angry man, bitter for reasons he kept to himself, Kavanaugh spoke only when necessary. He treated his farm animals well, though. I stayed in a room he had built at the back of his barn. While caring for the animals, I rid myself of the fever and regained my strength."

"And still, you were unable to write a line?" Anne's emotions reeled. Joy to see him, sympathy for his wounds, love— oh my, how she loved him—all mingled with her exasperation because he had allowed her to worry. She felt a little dizzy with it all. Still, she clung to her anger.

"I carried your last letter with me all these many weeks." She reached inside her cloak and pulled it out for him to see. She wanted to tear herself from him, and yet, she could not bear to move away.

Her deep longing to be close to him and hear his voice won out over her exasperation. "Please go on."

"Well, if you're sure?" James looked at her, his expression hesitant.

She nodded, pushed the letter back in her pocket, and took a firm grip of his arm.

"Kavanaugh came out to the barn on occasion to hitch the horses. We rode to town together to sell the milk and eggs, but we never shared a meal or a true conversation. He seldom talked at all. I do not believe I heard ten words from him in the space of a week. I purchased what provisions I needed in town and prepared my own meals. I entered his home no more than five times all through the summer.

"He knew I had determined I would leave in the fall, and he did not appear surprised when I said I was preparing to go. He paid me a fair wage and drove me to the train station. When I thanked him and wished him well, his response was a mere grunt. He may have been the strangest, most close-mouthed man I will ever meet, but I am ever in his debt."

They stopped, and again James turned to face her. "I regret not sending you word. In my fevered state, I believed I could not come back to you an invalid. That is my reason for not writing. I see now the pain my foolish pride caused you. I am sorry for worrying you. Please forgive me."

Anne struggled to maintain her stern expression, but her anger had been slipping away. James stood before her, alive and looking strong and fit. She could not push aside the happiness that flooded through her. When she smiled up at him, he finished his tale.

"Because of Kavanaugh's fine horses, his sturdy cows and their milk, his pesky chickens and their eggs, I can offer myself to you, healthier than I ever have been in my life."

"You look grand to me." Anne took both of his hands in hers. "I thank that frightful farmer and I thank God. I prayed for you every day you were away. Now my prayers have been answered."

"Each day I survived, I felt your prayers." He kissed her again.

The brush of his lips and touch of his cheek sent a shiver through her, as quick and powerful as a flash of lightning. Together, at long last, Anne read in his eyes the love and trust that had endured through years of separation. She recognized the true joy in his smile and felt her own countenance glow with it.

She told him of her own experiences during the war years, keeping the books for the army work and sewing with the other girls in the evenings. She spoke of the death of her brother Jimmy, and James' expression of sorrow brought her great comfort. She talked of the imminent arrival of her sister Kate.

Now that she had allowed her anger to dissolve, she relished each moment of this walk and reveled in their conversation: her sharing of the private thoughts she had been saving for him; his words meant only for her. Oh, this exquisite happiness, lost for more than three years, returned to her once again.

Before her courage left her—and while a part of her remained a little put out with him—she must discuss her situation. "There are so many still at home. I do not know when I will be released from my responsibility to them. I prayed you would return eager to begin our life together. I also worried that once you were here you would not wait until I have honored the pledge I made to my father to bring the children to America." She hesitated to breathe, in fear of what his response might be.

"My wonderful girl, I longed for you all these many years. If I can but walk beside you and hear your voice, I will be patient. I give you my promise."

"James!" His name was all she could say.

He slipped his strong arm around her waist again and drew her close. "I must bring my own brothers out," he said, "and my father if he will come. We will accomplish this together. I must find a permanent position, and then we will discharge our obligations to our families and plan our future.

"I devoted my time during the war to the accumulation of a fund for us, never spending an unnecessary cent. When the fellows chided me for not walking to town for a pint or having a cigar with them, I laughed. By the war's end, they all knew of my goal. 'Annie's Fund', they called it.

"While I lingered in the hospital, my wages continued, and when I left, I collected my pay, a considerable sum. I also have the pay from Kavanaugh. I am sure I will soon accumulate enough to purchase a home for us. The two drafts are in my coat pocket and I am eager to secure the money in the bank, in case our old pal Fortune lurks about." They shared a laugh. Mention of that dreadful man could not dampen their joy tonight. "You are not to worry, my love, we will be together," he said. "I will care for you now."

Before joining the army, James had waited in hiring lines for hours, frequently being turned down at the last moment. He returned from the war, three years older to be sure, and secured a permanent position at the rail yard on his first day out.

It happened that he had been invited to dinner at Dempsey's on the evening he brought Anne the word of his success at finding work. She had been delighted to have him sitting beside her at the table. Now, his news of obtaining a position thrilled her even more.

When they all settled in and Walter's prayer began, she offered her own private thanksgiving for his safe return and added words of gratitude that he had gained employment. She listened with interest while James and Walter discussed his prospects and then moved on to talk of the city's recovery from the war.

"Your own business has prospered," James said. "Anne tells me you've acquired many new business accounts."

"Aye, our bakery fares well, but the city is not making the progress it should. The big money people back east associate us with that rag tag bunch of marauders and bushwhackers on the southern and western edges of Missouri who fought against the Union. Some of the blowhards are too narrow-minded to learn the truth."

As Walter spoke, his face turned red and his large frame appeared to grow with indignation over the injustices he described. "We remained loyal to our country throughout the war. We sent more men to serve the Union Army and raised more capital to support the war effort than almost all of the states with greater populations. In their ignorance, the foolish tycoons are reluctant to invest in new enterprises here. Then too, with each new business that opens, we lose that much or more trade as the Army closes forts and no longer needs our support."

"It will take time for the country to recover," James said. "St. Louis will be booming again. Why, on the way home, I heard a fellow say the nation's capital could be moved here."

"Nothing but talk. It will never happen." Walter's voice calmed a little. "You are fortunate to start out in the railroad business. There's one industry that will continue to grow."

"I'll not limit myself to the railroads," James set his fork down, and as he continued to talk, his eyes sought out Anne's. "My current position is not what I hoped for. It is naught but hauling logs and building railroad trestles and tracks, but the work is steady. Other opportunities will develop. I'm sure of it."

In the weeks that followed, Anne and James spent many evenings together, sitting on the porch at Dempsey's, discussing their hopes and plans for the future. Martin and Julia joined them, on occasion.

"We are so happy to learn of your marriage plans," Julia said on one such evening. "I assure you, I will help. I will put aside every possible penny for our immigration fund."

They sometimes went to the park or to the Flynns for a brief visit. The long, slow walk back to Dempsey's, with Julia and Martin in the lead and Anne and James following slowly along behind them, provided an opportunity to plan for the life together that would be theirs one day.

One evening, a week after James' return, Anne settled into her bed in the attic room, with Julia asleep in the bed beside her.

While sleep still eluded her, she recounted to herself the many blessings she had received. Her dear James had returned to her, with a leg injury, but otherwise intact. He declared his love for her each time they found a moment alone. He had already obtained steady employment, and he had vowed to help her bring her family out of Ireland. Would life not be complete, as soon as they were all here in America with her?

Chapter Twenty-Six

Blackwater
September 6th 1865

My two dear children,
*   We received your welcome letter on the 19th and a check of #12. Dear Anne, Kate will leave Cork on Thursday the 12th. John Doran and his wife will go with her to St. Louis. I hope you will do all you can for them. It is a great thing to have them going with her.*
*   Dear Anne, your aunt proposed going but she is now in failing health, we need say no more. Kate will let you know all about it when she lands. The passage is high now. We paid #10*18"0 from Wexford to St. Louis and the remainder was not near enough to fit her out.*
*   You need not answer this until Kate lands there. We remain your affectionate parents,*
*   John and Nell Carty*

October, 1865
   Walter learned the news from a farmer on his delivery route, and he relayed the message to Anne.

"'Tell your Miss Carty her sister left Cork in the company of my wife's brother and his family. We received a post this morning.'"

Martin heard additional word from a soldier at Jefferson Barracks. He passed the message to Julia, who shared it with Anne.

"'Kate Carty will board a train in Boston with my niece. God willing, they will arrive on Friday.'"

Once again, Anne left the bakery at noon. As she walked along toward the riverfront, she thought of the day some four years past, when Julia arrived in St. Louis. She had fretted over her sister settling in at Dempsey's and making friends with the others in the group. What a foolish worry that had been.

Kate was another matter altogether. This time, while she walked to the riverfront, her concerns were powerful and she felt certain they were justified. Six years had passed since she and Kate shared a home. She struggled to even bring an image of her sister to her mind.

Last evening, Julia reminded her Kate had reached her twentieth year. "I've not seen her myself for over three years. She was petite back then, with darker hair and deeper blue eyes than yours or mine, and so like our mother in appearance and manner. She possesses a grand smile, though I do not recall many of them. The years she waited to come must have been difficult for her. I imagine she has grown more serious and solemn than ever."

Anne had little time to wait and worry. The ferry arrived promptly. The first person to disembark—a young, slight version of her mother—walked toward her. Anne recognized Kate at once. She held herself with poise, her manner calm and serene. At first glance, her appearance showed no indication of a long journey. Hat, dress, cloak, and valise were all in blue, a lighter shade, Anne noted, than their dreaded military blue. Kate had surely created the entire ensemble herself.

"Kate, I am here." When her sister recognized her, her smile traveled all the way to her eyes, and warmed her face.

As she drew closer, Anne observed the slight cough she was attempting to conceal and the weariness behind her smile.

"Anne! I am relieved to see you. I did not know if anyone would be free to meet me." They hugged, then stepped back and gazed at one another for a moment. Kate sighed. "I cannot believe I am here at last."

Now that she stood beside her, Anne could see greater evidence of Kate's difficult journey. Her clothing bore the grime of the long weeks at sea, a miserable train ride, and the dampness from the foul smelling spray of a Mississippi River crossing. Realizing she had been staring, Anne pulled her gaze from the redness she observed around her sister's eyes and the grim set of her jaw.

"Was your trunk shipped on this ferry?"

Kate nodded. "It was removed ahead of me and is already on its way to Dempsey's."

Anne took Kate's valise and guided her through the throng of people. "I am pleased beyond words to have you with me." They left the riverfront and began to climb the hill. While they walked, she told her of the Dempseys' many kindnesses, which included allowing her to meet the ferry. Then, she turned to her own questions.

"What of your journey? Where are the Dorans? I assumed they would be with you."

"The Dorans decided to go to New York City instead of continuing westward. They invited me to join them, but of course, I would not alter my plan to proceed to St. Louis. They left me in Boston, but it was no mind. Many others traveled on, many families journeying together. They considered themselves my guardians and all were kind and solicitous of me. In truth, I find I manage quite well on my own." When they stopped at the corner, Kate changed the subject.

"Is Julia well? We all worried about her."

"She is fine. She caught a dreadful cold and experienced some weakness in the past weeks. We were concerned because of the illness she suffered during the war, and of course, cholera enters everyone's mind. Around the time we learned you had left Ireland, though, she experienced a turnaround and she is now her former exuberant self. Julia considers you her own sprite fresh from home and credits you with bringing her good fortune and good health." Anne took Kate's arm as they entered Park Street.

"Julia is excited about introducing you to her young man. Martin Tobin is a fine fellow. He has become a friend to us all. He serves in the Army still, but he gained leave to attend the supper Mary Dempsey has planned for you tonight."

"The Dempseys are preparing a supper for me? In my honor? I cannot believe it."

"It is true, and you will learn this is what Walter and Mary do for people. It took some time for me to adjust to this generosity that is a part of the Dempseys. But, you will see. You will love it here. You will also enjoy the wonderful meal."

"I look forward to it."

Julia and Kate were reunited just before Anne ushered the new arrival into the dining room that evening. After hugging Kate and swinging her all about, Julia insisted she must sit beside her at the table and introduce her to each member of the Dempsey group.

Anne had helped her sister change to a clean dress she pulled from her trunk. As she stood back and observed for a moment—Julia introducing their sister to everyone as they entered the room and Kate responding graciously—Anne relaxed. Kate looked refreshed and collected.

Her composure did fade a little, once she caught sight of the steaming dishes Mary and Grace brought to the table. She recovered enough to offer a kind word to Mary. "I compliment you on this fine meal. It is more food than I have ever seen on one table." A look of embarrassment crossed her face then, and she became quiet again.

Colonel Scones and his wife, Elizabeth, were in attendance. Elizabeth had been telling those seated near her of her long separation from her parents during the war and of how she looked forward to returning to their home in Massachusetts. Noticing Kate's discomfort, Elizabeth broke off from her own conversation and attempted to reassure her.

"I quite agree with you, Kate. Mary's meals are the most abundant and best tasting we've experienced here or in the East."

Anne smiled at Elizabeth. Aware that the British considered Irish food plain, she appreciated her attempt to bolster Kate's spirits. She recognized the same kindness and generosity in Elizabeth they had all admired in her husband, the Colonel.

Kate also turned to her with a smile. Then, taking a deep breath, she straightened her shoulders and gazed all about, studying each person seated around the table. Anne tensed when Martin interrupted Kate's contemplation to ask about her journey. She prayed her sister would pause a moment and collect herself before giving any sharp retorts. To her great relief, her response was brief but polite.

"It proved dreadful, far worse than I ever anticipated. In all my longing to come, I never could have imagined the horrors of it." Without further elaboration, she turned the conversation to her own questions. "I would much rather hear about you, Martin. Tell me about your Army duties."

Martin described the work he had been doing explaining to Kate that he served as the Colonel's assistant.

Colonel Scones broke into the talk with his compliments on Martin's excellent performance. "We are both spending long hours, inspecting and storing Army equipment as it arrives at Jefferson Barracks," he said.

When he and Martin had answered questions to everyone's satisfaction, Julia added a little about her own work for the Colonel, which had been gradually drawing to an end now that the war was over.

Anne had relaxed for only a few brief moments, when Kate moved her attention to James. "I am confused. I know your father and brothers, of course, but I do not remember ever encountering you in Blackwater or my sisters mentioning you in their letters. I memorized each line they wrote, wishing to discover any scrap of information I could about my future home."

Anne felt her color deepen when James responded.

"I will explain, Miss Kate Carty. After I completed my schooling and returned to Blackwater, I remained there for but a few short months before I left for America. You and I had little opportunity to make an acquaintance. Then, I lived here less than a year before I joined the Union Army. I was away for some three years, returning to St. Louis a few weeks ago. Now and again, I prevail upon Walter and Mary to invite me for supper."

Kate rewarded James with a brilliant smile.

Anne had relaxed her grip on her coffee cup, when her sister moved on to questioning Ellen and Kitty. "I am anxious to discuss your seamstress jobs," she said, and the three girls spent a few moments talking of dressmaking.

Then Kate turned to Mary. "I wish to learn all I can about the bakery. I am interested to know what it takes to operate a successful business such as yours."

Anne decided to place her cup safely on the table.

"Ah Kate, won't we give you every opportunity to learn, after you recover from your long journey?" Mary bestowed a grand smile on Kate and reached out to touch her hand. "Sure, what we are all waiting to hear, my dear, is news of our home and our families. Are your parents and your brother and sisters well? What can you tell us about Blackwater and Enniscorthy and the folks there?"

Anne silently pleaded with her sister to halt her inquiries for the moment and answer Mary's questions. She needn't have worried. Kate was all politeness and consideration in her answer.

"My family is well, thank you. The Dempseys also are fine. I spoke with them before I left, and they sent you a note."

She turned to Grace. "I also brought a letter for you from your brother."

"Thank you, Kate. I am relieved to have word from William. Since the notice of my father's death, I have not received a letter from home." Even with news from Blackwater, Grace's grim expression did not lighten. "With my father gone, I worried I would lose all contact with my family."

Kate looked up with a surprised expression across her face, when Walter's helpers excused themselves. She had eaten little. Anne supposed she had been intent on the conversation and did not realize the meal was over.

"Perhaps, they sensed they were next in line for questions?" Walter said.

Kate glanced at him, her look of astonishment now turning to concern. Walter's countenance displayed only kindness and humor, and after observing his kindly grin, she smiled along with him. The boys had prompted a general exodus, though, and the evening came to an end. Anne could not help but sigh in relief.

Later, in the attic room, Anne and Julia helped Kate prepare for bed. In spite of the rigors of her journey and her particularly long first day in St. Louis, she seemed wide awake. Her energy had not run out, nor did her store of questions. But, while she wished to learn everything about St. Louis, Anne was hungry for news of home.

Kate was in the midst of inquiring about the Dempseys' home and exclaiming over the wonders of it all, when Anne broke in to express her hope that the attic space would be suitable. "Mary thought we would like to be together on your first night, and she had one of the bulky chairs moved out and a cot installed in its place."

"I have never been in a more comfortable room," Kate said.

"You will need rest after your long journey," Anne said. "You will sleep in my bed, while I take the cot."

Kate protested, saying she was so exhausted she would be unaware of the difference between bed and cot, but Anne would not have it. She stood firm, and with the matter settled, she helped Kate change into her nightgown and ease back onto the bed.

"This home seems a grand manor to me." Nestling back against the pillows Julia placed all around her, Kate began to talk again. "In my ignorance, I imagined shops in America to be similar to those at home. I supposed Dempsey's would be like Hogan's Dry Goods Emporium, where I lived and worked for almost two years. I never envisioned you settled in comfort and surrounded by such pleasant companions."

Kate appeared not to notice when Anne covered her with the quilt they pulled from her trunk. She moved right on with the story of her years at home awaiting her turn to come out. "You have perhaps grown accustomed to the comfort here at Dempsey's. Surely, you've not forgotten the bleakness of our cottage in Blackwater or the dust and grime our constant scrubbing could never conquer.

"Even our sad little home is a fine palace compared to Hogan's. Perhaps I am overwrought from the rigorous journey and the excitement of my first evening here, but I must relieve my mind of this dreadful tale before I will ever rest." Kate pulled back the cover and sat up, swinging her legs over the edge of the bed.

"The shop and the family quarters at Hogan's were presentable, though not the clean home we maintained, but the workers' living conditions were frightful. We stayed in a wooden shack attached to the rear of the storage rooms. There were neither beds nor cots, just thin bundles of straw placed in the dirt. When it rained, the floor became a swamp and our pallets settled right into the mud.

"Six of us lived in that space. With male and female thrown together and no chance for privacy, we all experienced moments of embarrassment. I suffered the added shame of being the oldest of the lot. After months together in that squalid shack, needing all the energy we possessed to survive and having no strength to fret over trifling problems, little of that mattered. We tried to keep the place clean and ourselves respectable. With no warm water or soap, it proved impossible.

"The Hogans treated us like slaves. From early morning until late night, six days a week, we carried goods, loaded carts, cleaned, tended the fire, and fed the animals.

"They wished everyone to consider them kindly folks, caring for poor, sorry young people. They are the spawn of the devil, and that's the truth of it." Julia's gasp startled Anne, but Kate did not slow her story.

"They prepared substantial family meals for themselves each day, the aroma carrying throughout the place, making our stomachs ache for decent food. We were allotted a single crust of bread each morning, and we shared a common bowl of gruel for our evening meal."

The unbelievable tale had shocked Anne into silence, and she saw Julia shaking her head in disbelief at what they were hearing. Still, Kate continued on.

"On one particular afternoon while I swept the family dining room, a giant kettle of stew simmered on their hearth. My body craved nourishment, and in time my strength deserted me. Overcome by hunger, I fell to the floor. Mr. Hogan carried me to the shack, deposited me on the ground, and left. No one cared for me or inquired if I had recovered or died. The next morning, I rose with the others and returned to work." Kate sat back, tears filling her eyes.

"Mr. Hogan carried a stick he used to subdue anyone who rebelled against the cruel treatment. I, who could never control my impudent mouth, was bruised by that stick many times. He employed devious methods. He struck the most private parts of our bodies that we would never dream of exposing to our parents. He ground the stick into the skin until it bled. Mrs. Hogan was no better. Though he administered the beatings, she reported every offense to him and watched as he dealt the blows."

"Oh, Kate! This cannot have happened." Stunned, Anne looked away for a moment, attempting to hide her tears, searching her pockets for a handkerchief. She assured herself the dreadful account must be nothing but a frightful dream. It could not be true.

Anne could see her sister needed a soothing touch. Pushing aside her own distress and confusion, she moved to the bed and wrapped Kate in her arms. As she held her close, Kate relaxed gradually and accepted the comfort she offered. Still, the poor exhausted girl talked on.

"They took on children who lived a good way from their shop and whose parents possessed no means to travel that distance. Father came once. While he was there, the devious Hogans presented a good front. We wore smocks over our grimy work clothes, and they showed him the family quarters rather than the squalid shack.

"Some Sundays, we were allowed to clean ourselves and dress in our own clothing. We were driven to church, and after a day at home, Mr. Hogan collected us in front of St. Brigid's at eight o'clock. I dreaded that awful hour. I begged not to be sent back.

"Through it all, my thoughts focused on my sisters, working hard and saving their money for my fare. When Father spent the first passage money you sent, I thought I might die of the disappointment. Still, my faith in you endured, and that spark of hope kept me alive. Yet, in all my dreaming about America, I could never have imagined this fine home and such a wonderful life as you have made here."

The always lively, talkative Julia had remained quiet through Kate's telling of her terrible experiences at Hogan's. When Anne looked at her now, her head was bowed and her shoulders shook with sobs. Kate also seemed to sense Julia's misery and she moved close to her and placed an arm across her shoulders. Still, she could not seem to halt her words and her terrible recitation continued.

"Each Sunday I was allowed to go home, I told Father this story of the horrid Hogans and the frightful way they treated their workers. Before I left home, I again reiterated every bit of it. This time, while I bared my soul to him, I abandoned my modesty and showed him the scars from the force of Hogan's brutal stick. I did it for the children. I begged him not to send the other girls there. I am not sure he credited the full account of the appalling treatment, but he did witness my scars. I must tell you one final thing. I must confess that, if Father sends Lizzie or little Maura to that despicable place, I will not be able to forgive him."

Anne sat, dazed. Warmth crept along her back and her neck, and she began to tremble. She recalled the home she left six years ago—her father, strong, hard-working, and loving; her mother, often stern, always pre-occupied with sewing, but surely with her every thought for her children's welfare.

The story Kate told, she must now acknowledge, had surely been accurate. Father must not have realized the full extent of her ill treatment. Still, there was no excuse for his poor judgment. He should have investigated the place thoroughly. That he allowed Kate to be beaten and starved was unthinkable. What could have happened to her poor parents? What had caused them to abandon the diligent care and concern for their children who had once seemed the sole purpose in their lives?

Chapter Twenty-Seven

While Anne dressed for work the next morning, Kate attempted to rise from her bed, but she could barely lift her head from the pillow. She appeared more tired than she had been the evening before. Anne spoke softly to her, telling her she and Julia experienced the same exhaustion upon their arrival at Dempsey's, assuring her it would take some time to recuperate, and urging her to spend the day resting.

Before nine o'clock, though, her sister came down the stairs and entered the busy shop. With little instruction needed, she began to assist Anne and Mary, refilling bins and helping customers.

When Mrs. Rice, Bridget's mother, came into the shop, Anne rushed over to introduce them. While she welcomed Kate warmly, concern was evident in her eyes. "Faith, child, are you not exhausted from your long journey?"

"I am fine, thank you." Kate took Mrs. Rice's basket, removed the linen cloths, and began to wrap her bread with efficiency. She moved about as if she had been serving customers at Dempsey's for years.

"Ah, you are a sweet little girl like your sisters. It's grand to have you here. Still, you must be weary?"

"Mary and I have both urged Kate to rest. We will insist she go upstairs for a nap soon," Anne said, as Mrs. Rice took up her baskets and headed for the door.

"This is not work," Kate said, after Mrs. Rice had gone and they were without a customer for the moment. "It is a joy to be here, and I thank you, Mary, for the fine home you have provided for Anne and Julia, and now for me. I did wish to speak with you both, though, about an idea I am pondering." Kate kept her hands busy as she talked, rearranging trays, and cleaning the countertops.

"Hearing about your wartime sewing project and then speaking with Ellen and Kitty last evening, I formed a plan. I have the idea I could operate a seamstress shop. Since Kitty mentioned she intends to leave soon, I thought I would ask Ellen to work with me. Do you think she would agree?"

Anne turned in time to see Mary's gleeful reaction to Kate's words.

"I believe Ellen will shout for joy if you provide an opportunity for her to leave that desperate factory. For years, I searched for a way to free those two dear girls of their drudgery, Kate. Now, you've just come, and already you are working up a grand idea." Mary walked toward the door leading to the dining room, but she turned back. "Perhaps you could use some of the empty space across from the oven room for your shop?" At Kate's eager nod, she continued on through the doorway.

Though Mary was busy working in the oven room most of the day, she hurried back out to the shop from time to time. With each appearance, she brought along an idea, or recommendation, or offer of help.

"Ellen and Kitty could instruct you on the operation of my sewing machine, if you wish to use it," she said, while Anne poured tea for the three of them, later in the afternoon.

"While I worked at Hogan's, I discovered pictures of sewing machines in their catalogues," Kate said. "No one ever ordered such a thing, though, and I have never seen one."

Pride in the grand plan her sister proposed rose up in Anne. Her emotions spilled into her voice as she congratulated her. "The entire prospect is thrilling."

"I will speak to Ellen about it tonight." Kate's face glowed. The thrill of these new ideas and possibilities radiated from her dark blue eyes. "Your kindness overwhelms me, Mary. I will pay rent for the room, of course."

Anne felt her heart may burst with respect for the maturity of her sister. She turned to Mary, wishing mightily that she would allow Kate her desire for independence.

Mary must have read Anne's thoughts. "I understand," she said. "You'll want to make your own way. We will talk that over with Walter."

Anne's estimation of Ellen's interest fell far short of the outpouring of joy she expressed when Kate continued her talk of the seamstress shop at supper. In fact, Ellen's delight surpassed every outburst of energy and enthusiasm she had ever witnessed from the spirited girl.

"I'm thrilled you have included me in the scheme." Ellen left her place at the table and ran to embrace Kate, then also included Mary and then Kitty, who were seated closest to her, in the hugs. "Sure, I am impatient to begin. Did Kitty and I not slave in that desperate garment factory all these many long years? Each day I worked there, I prayed we could find better positions. Now the angels have brought us two miracles, and we will both be free of the place."

Ellen moved around the table to hug Anne and Julia. "Thank you for bringing your wonderful little sister here to Dempsey's. This is a grand day for me, to be sure."

Kitty joined in the exclamations. "Just when I prepare to leave, you discover a way out of the factory. Where is the justice?" Though Kitty spoke words of complaint, a smile crossed her face and her tone changed from chagrin to one of joy. "The truth of it is, I am pleased for you, Ellen. Now I may leave without worrying over you chained to that dreadful factory machine."

"Our Kitty will be married at Christmastime to a young man she met at a church social." Anne explained Kitty's leaving the city to Kate. "They intend to move out west."

"I'm sure Kitty has no idea at all what we are speaking about. Is her head not filled with her own wonderful dreams?" Mary reached out to tickle Kitty under her chin.

Kate went back to her plans. "It may be a sensible thing, Ellen, to continue at your position and work with me in the evenings, until we build a strong following." Ellen nodded, her expression wistful.

"I'll ask Elizabeth Scones to speak to the officers' wives about your new business, before she and the Colonel leave St. Louis." Mary rose from the table to fetch their desert.

"I will advertise the new enterprise with our customers in the bakery." Anne also rose, moving to the sideboard to retrieve the small plates and forks.

"A grand idea." Mary added her approval to Anne's suggestion, as she placed a magnificent white cake on the table.

Julia, too, offered a suggestion. "Perhaps, I could place a notice in the church vestibule, if Father Burns does not object."

"That's splendid." Ellen's face brightened. "With all your kind offers of help, I'm sure I will soon work full days in our new shop."

When the three girls prepared to climb the stairs to the attic room that evening, Mary asked to come with them to discuss the arrangement of their furniture. As they all settled themselves on chairs and beds, Mary offered her first suggestion. "Kate could sleep in the Dempsey girls' room."

The sisters resisted.

"I have been apart from you far too long." Anne's words were directed to Kate, but then she turned to Julia for her opinion.

"Oh yes, please, Mary, may we all stay together?" Julia asked.

"My sisters worked hard to bring me here," Kate said, "and I so love being with them. This cozy little room provides such comfort. I would happily hop over the beds if that would make staying here possible."

Hearing her young sister's words of appreciation for what she and Julia endured to bring her to America and her wish to stay close to them thrilled Anne. Her heart filled so with love and pride she thought it may burst.

Mary obliged. She called Eddie and George upstairs and asked them to move Anne's and Julia's trunks to the storage area just across the hallway. They would leave Kate's trunk in the room until she could unpack and arrange her things in the wardrobe. They removed the cot and one more of their comfortable chairs and used that space to place a spare bed retrieved from the Dempsey girls' room. Their attic space now held three beds, the massive wardrobe, the writing table and chair, Kate's trunk, and one remaining comfortable chair.

After receiving many words of thanks, Eddie and George returned to the oven room. Mary also left them, amid showers of hugs and expressions of appreciation, and retired to her own room.

The Carty sisters, with years of practice at fitting a large family and their belongings into a crowded space, now took over. Anne felt she had been transported to their little cottage back home, as they set to work and did some organizing. Amid much laughter, and a few missteps, they were finally satisfied. They had moved and shoved, until they arranged a path so they would not be forced to climb over furniture to settle in their beds.

Anne and Julia helped Kate unpack her trunk, stacking her belongings at the end of her bed. When they had emptied the trunk, they sat back to rest, Kate sitting atop the trunk and Anne and Julia at the end of the two beds across from her.

Something Kate said earlier in the day puzzled Anne, but she had been waiting until they were alone in their room before she questioned her. "What did you mean, dear, when you said your sewing venture would serve you for the present?"

"All the while I waited to come to America, I read everything I could find about the West. I dreamed of a new life there. I believe we must go. I am twenty. You are twenty-three, Anne, and you, Julia, twenty-five. This could be our one opportunity."

"I assure you, we have not forgotten Uncle James or Oregon. I understand your desire to go," Anne said, "but many things have occurred to delay our plans. I received a letter from Uncle James and a $100 check when I arrived six years ago. I have had no further word, though I have written to him every year since. I do not know what to think. I am not even certain he wants us to come."

"Father has not mentioned Uncle James in recent letters." Julia leaned closer to Kate. "Did you hear any word of him before you left home?"

"No, but I lived away from home for much of the last two years. I assumed you were in contact with Uncle James—

"Heaven's holy angels!" Kate jumped up from her perch on the trunk. "It has just occurred to me. They spent Uncle James' money too, and he is done with them."

"Julia and I held the idea that Uncle James sent additional money to Mr. Fortune for our journey to Oregon and he ran off with it," Anne said.

"I am certain it was our parents. While Father manages other people's accounts, he allows Mother to mishandle what little they have. You two know that well enough. Time and again, they have been forced to apply to you for help.

"This news of Uncle James alarms me, though." Kate walked back to the trunk and sat down again. "I suppose I've not planned this Oregon part of the journey well enough."

"There are other factors besides Uncle James," Anne said. "Though Julia and Martin have not announced their betrothal," Anne paused to send a grin Julia's way. "I am sure that, once he is released from the Army and obtains a position, we will be hearing wedding bells."

Julia blushed, but Anne pretended not to notice and continued on with a question for her. "Would you and Martin consider moving out west?"

"We have not even discussed it. Sure, it would be a grand adventure to travel on to Oregon."

Kate patted Julia's hand. "I am truly happy for you."

"Thank you, Kate. Anne is right, though. Martin often speaks of establishing himself in St. Louis." She raised her shoulders in a dramatic shrug, showing her uncertainty.

"One thing more remains." Julia now lowered her shoulders and folded her hands, but she could not suppress her grin. "Our Anne plans to marry James Duff."

"Oh Anne, what wonderful news. I should have guessed it. Caught up in my own affairs, I suppose I did not notice the attachment. I do that at times, you know. I concentrate on my own concerns to the exclusion of all else." A real chuckle escaped from Kate, and for the first time since she arrived in St. Louis, the three sisters sat and laughed together. "When are the weddings to be?"

Julia quickly responded that no formal engagement had been announced and she and Martin could not make definite arrangements until he had been discharged and obtained a position.

Anne reminded Kate of her responsibility to help the family in Ireland before she and James could proceed with their own plans. She explained about the money from Uncle James, once stolen by Dermot Fortune, now replaced and held safely at the bank. She told her of how she and Julia built the immigration fund to add to the $100. She added that they were now saving to bring Michael and Lizzie out. "Now that you are here, we have moved one step closer to our goal."

Kate's smile vanished. "They can all wait, just as I did. Once we are settled, we will tend to them. Right now, I am weary of blight and failed crops. I do not care to hear talk of home for a long time. I understand your hesitancy to leave St. Louis, but I will not abandon the idea of continuing on to Uncle James. When I earn enough, I intend to go on."

Anne sat back, stunned at Kate's harsh words. She thought of her time at home with Kate. She could picture her young sister breaking off portions of her own bread to share with the little ones. She remembered well how Kate, then only a child herself, cut up her own garments to make clothing for the younger girls. To hear the generous Kate speak of abandoning the children shocked Anne.

"And, what of Aunt Mary?" Julia drew Anne's thoughts back to the present. "Does she still talk of bringing everyone out?"

"Pah! You know Aunt Mary. Whenever an idea occurs to her, she is all enthusiasm and excitement. Overnight, her mind moves like a tornado, spinning to a new plan with no thought for the last. Father showed some spark of hope at first, but he soon realized it was another of her foolish schemes."

Kate stood again and raised the heavy lid of the trunk. "I brought you a gift from Father. He placed it here as I prepared to leave." She lifted a covering spread across the bottom of the trunk and pulled out a book and handed it to Anne. "Remembering how you both wrote of reciting Shakespeare passages during the war years, he decided to send you the second volume."

Holding *The Comedies of William Shakespeare*, Anne imagined she could grasp the scent of their beloved cottage. She pictured the children all seated around the table, waiting for Father to choose a volume from the shelf beside the hearth for their nightly reading. Only one book remained with him now.

She thought back to when she arrived in St. Louis and so dearly missed her home, her parents and the children she left behind. Kate seemed to hold no such longings, but then, she and Julia had not lived through the dreadful experiences their poor younger sister had. The thought of the vicious Mr. Hogan beating Kate with a stick and the idea of Father allowing it was more than Anne could bear. Still, she could not believe Kate would turn her back on the children.

One evening later that week, Anne, Julia, and Kate again sat in the attic room, enjoying their time together. Kate told them how Walter helped set up her new shop in a back room of the bakery building.

It pleased Anne to hear Kate's words of appreciation for the many kindnesses of the Dempseys. "They treat us, as if we are part of their own family," she said.

With a nod to Anne, Kate went on. "Walter and Eddie moved Mary's sewing machine into the room, along with two tables he said you girls used while sewing uniforms during the war. Mary contributed chairs for our use. They looked familiar. I believe one of them might be the chair Eddie carried out of here after I arrived. While we arranged things, I asked Walter what he planned for the huge empty space in back of the oven room."

Anne was discovering Kate was as accomplished a mimic as Julia. She rendered a perfect imitation of Walter's voice and manner. "'I originally intended to stable my horses there. When Mary suggested their fine fragrance would make its way into the oven room, the dining room, and the shop, I thought better of it. The horses and wagons remain boarded at the livery across the street, and we have a vast empty space back here. My ideas are not all great ones, I'm thinking.' His hearty laugh was contagious, and I could not help but join in with him."

Before she continued speaking, Kate walked over to look out the window. "There is nothing of 'the master' in Walter or 'mistress of the manor' in Mary, and yet you all work hard to please them. It is difficult to adjust to life here. I must ever remind myself I am at Dempsey's in St. Louis and not at Hogan's horrible establishment. I will do it, though." Kate moved back to the trunk and faced her sisters.

"Here we sit in this clean and pleasant room with no insects or rodents tormenting us throughout the night. At Hogan's, we covered the ground with any newspapers we could find and attempted to seal the openings in the walls with papers or twine, even cinders and dry leaves. Still the varmints came. We could not stop their attack. I also find it hard to comprehend that there will be no Mr. Hogan bursting in before dawn, prodding us with his torture stick."

"Please help me understand," Anne said. "Father worked hard to care for us, and Mother devoted her life to cleanliness. How could they allow the Hogans to mistreat you so? How could they allow you to live in such squalor?"

"You must realize little remains of the father you left all those years ago. He still spends long days in the field and labors over accounts at night, but he is bent down now and plods through the work. You remember when he was jovial and boisterous? Always ready with a laugh, or a song, or a story? Well no more. He ambles about and works in silence." Kate stood and walked a short way, imitating her father's shuffle, and then she dropped into the chair resting alongside the desk.

"One summer of rain and blight follows another. The meager crop Father manages to harvest goes for almost naught because no one in Ireland has money to purchase food or goods. He handles accounts for but a few businesses now. Some he works for cannot pay.

"The death of our Jimmy dealt the harshest blow." At the mention of their dear brother, all three girls stopped to bow their heads a moment. Then, Kate went on. "Though Jimmy's care created endless work for everyone, we all considered him our own special saint. He endeavored to raise our spirits. He encouraged us and tried to make us laugh. With Jimmy gone, all hope has slipped away from our little cottage back home. Our parents appear as silent, solemn ghosts. Mother now makes the decisions."

"Why did you never write a word of this to us?" Shock filled Anne's being. She knew it was reflected in her voice.

"I did try. Twice, I wrote the full story. Both times, Mother discovered the note and destroyed it. A true miracle brought the message to you in the Scanlons' letter.

"Jonas' whale!" Kate jumped up again. "I suppose you are right about the children. We must bring them out of that misery. Please forgive my tirade about the passage money. I try to repress it, but the bitterness overtakes me at times and I am helpless against its force. I just wished for a brief time to make a start for myself, but I will do what I can for them."

"Kate, where do these strange expressions come from?" Curiosity won out over Anne's shock. No one from home ever spoke this way. "Even with the saints and the angels included, your words sound blasphemous somehow."

"Well, on dark, rainy nights at Hogan's, the other workers and I would rest on our pallets, sinking into the mud, and we would think of the most vile, terrible names we could call those two devils who caused our misery. We could, none of us, invent of a term evil enough to describe them. Beth Murphy—you remember her, the Murphys' youngest daughter?—well, she worried the Hogans would hear us and increase the beatings.

"We agreed she was right. So, we devised a scheme to shout out the opposite of the curses we wished on them. Each night we spent hours creating the most elaborate and involved phrases." Kate smiled a little, as she remembered. "While we worked the next day, we called out a saint or angel or two, or the prophets. The holy name of God alone was held sacred. The game became a means of survival for us.

"The Hogans were confused. They hesitated to beat us, when we appeared to cry out in prayer. They became a bit frightened and demanded we work in silence."

This strange story still held Anne in a state of bewilderment. She felt as if she were tangled in a spider's web. "So then, when you say these holy phrases, you are, in fact, condemning us?"

"How clever you are." Kate chuckled. "You have caught on in an instant. Those stupid Hogans never figured it out. Do not worry. I'll keep my expressions to myself. My dears, your persistence in sending money for my fare saved my life. I believe that with all my heart. I would not have survived another winter of sleeping on the ground in that filthy shack. Never would I wish harm to rain down on you."

"'Tis beyond belief." Julia's face turned red, her hands and arms shook. She moved to stand beside Kate at the writing table. "Whatever has become of our family?" Julia began to cry, and Anne wished to soothe her. Torn between her two sisters in need, she patted Julia's arm for only a moment, and then turned to her younger sister.

"My poor dear, you are so brave. I cannot even think of the horrors you endured while we lived here in comfort at Dempsey's. Here you are, now, concerned over our little sisters. Of course, I agree with you. Father and Mother must not send one more child to that Hogan's place. What can we do?"

"I am at a loss," Kate said. "I cannot think of it with a clear mind."

"We must devise a plan," Julia said, "but for now, let us begin with a strong letter." She produced paper and pen from the drawer. She and Kate moved aside and motioned for Anne to sit at the desk. As she began to write, they contributed their suggestions.

Anne shuddered at the bold words she put down on the paper—their young sisters must not, under any circumstances, be sent to Hogan's. The letter addressed her parents with a tone of authority Anne had never before used. Kate and Julia assured her the gravity of the situation justified the strong language.

Julia softened a little. "Add our love and understanding."

"No," Kate said, "no messages of consideration or acceptance, no terms of affection. We must stand firm. They cannot be trusted to use good judgment. We could threaten to withhold money for passage or anything else, until we obtain their promise."

Anne forged ahead, making additions and changes, until the message satisfied them. "I know a single letter, coming from such a great distance, cannot hold much impact." She sighed. "I still pray it will give our parents pause and delay them from committing our little sisters to Hogan's."

❀ ❀ ❀

In the days that followed, Kate spent hours at work on the sewing machine. After a short time, Ellen pronounced to Anne that Kate had passed her in skill and would soon equal Kitty's proficiency. For her first sewing machine project, Kate stitched lovely coverings for the shop windows. Then, saying she wished to experiment with the lacy curtains so in vogue in the city, she convinced Mary to allow her to create a pair for the windows in her parlor.

"I am so proud of my fashionable windows," Mary said, "I have invited my friends to come to the parlor and see Kate's work. I have been receiving compliments from everyone who has had the privilege to inspect the curtains in the shop and in the parlor." She turned her attention to Kate. "You will be receiving orders from all over the city. Your business will flourish, I'm sure of it."

"I thank you, Mary," Kate said. "You and Walter have been most kind to me." Anne noticed that Kate persisted in seeking out ways to extend her appreciation in any small act or kind gesture she could perform. A small miracle, in the form of peace and calmness of spirit also seemed to have descending over Kate. And Mary's prediction rang true. In the next few days, she received several curtain orders from the good women of the neighborhood.

❀ ❀ ❀

As Christmastime drew near, Anne, Julia, and Kate helped with the preparations for Kitty's wedding, the first grand celebration at Dempsey's since the war. When Mary insisted she would contribute material for the dress, Kate offered to help.

"We have searched the shops of the city, but some goods remain scarce," Kate said. "There was not a bit of white cloth to be found. Mary did find a length of soft pink muslin tucked away in a cabinet, a leftover from your days of sewing dresses during the war. Ellen and I will work together to make the finest wedding gown in the city for Kitty."

"It is a lovely creation, indeed," Kitty said, when the dress was finished. "'Tis a dress fit for a princess."

The happy couple's families remained in Ireland, and Kitty and her groom knew few people outside of their workplaces, church, and the bakery. And so, they comprised a small assemblage at St. Vincent's that day. The Dempsey group gathered in the front pews, as their little princess in the pretty pink dress married Michael O'Brien, a carpenter by trade. The young man planned to seek his fortune out west, with Kitty at his side.

Following the ceremony, a joyous feast was held at Dempsey's. Many toasts were raised to the couple's health and happiness. Many wishes were shared for success in their new life. Not one mention was made of Simpson's Garment Factory, where Kitty spent her last moments at sewing piecework the day before.

"The celebration proved to be even finer than you said it would be," Kate said to Anne, later that evening.

"This hard-working, young girl we have all come to admire and love and her fine young husband deserve this grand farewell," Anne said. "How we will all miss her."

Chapter Twenty-Eight

Blackwater
September 8, 1865

My dear children

We received your kind letter yesterday and we were happy to hear you were well as this leaves us at present. Thanks be to God.

Dear Anne we are in great trouble about Kate and I want to know the reason neither you nor Julia spoke of her in your letter. We were expecting Kate would send us a little help these hard times. I hope she will not forget her father and mother. Nell Carty

Aunt Mary Kelly is married and in her own home. The wedding was held here and she stopped here for a week after she got married. Indeed she was happy to leave Ballynard for she was tired of them. Provisions of all kinds are dear and no sign of them coming down.

Dear sister, I expect to see you and Julia and Kate in St. Louis in short, the passage is low now. It is only about #5 from Queenstown to New York, Lizzie is eager to come out with me. She says if you three would join and bring her out with me in the fall, it is the best time to go, so we would be in for the winter. We could go in the spring and be in for the summer but would be in danger of sickness and also the passage is so low in the fall and then so many will be going in the spring which also makes it high. Lizzie told me to tell you she would pay you as soon as she would earn it. For me, I will do the same with the first I ever get if God leaves our life and health. I need not say more but I hope you will do what you can for me and Lizzie. We will not see you at a loss. I believe that is all at present. Michael Carty

Dear Anne, I hope you will do all in your power to bring me out in the spring. I am tired of this place, for this is a place of poverty. I remain your affectionate brother, Michael Carty

October, 1865

James appeared at Dempsey's one evening, a few weeks after Kate's arrival, and asked Anne to come along with him for a walk. His eyes glimmered, and she noticed a hint of a smile he was working hard to suppress. What could have excited him so? He surely had something of import he wished to tell her and he was bursting with it. Still, she could not resist a moment of sport.

"Shall we ask Julia and Kate to accompany us?" She wrapped her shawl around her head and shoulders, taking her time, moving with deliberation.

"I must speak with you alone, my dear." His voice sounded gruff, his impatience pushing through. "We must discuss some things and make some decisions. I know it is a chilly night, so I brought along an extra cloak to shield you from the fierce wind." He held up a heavy wool cloak that had been wrapped around his arm while they were speaking and arranged it across her shoulders. "Will you be warm enough?"

"Yes...but I do need to speak with my sisters." Sensing his great need to tell his story, she could not continue with her teasing. Her broad smile betrayed her.

"Ah my girl, don't I love you more than anyone on earth, and here you are bound to torment me." They laughed together, as he took her arm. When they started off into the dark night, his manner returned to seriousness.

"A friend at the rail yard is moving his family to Colorado Springs. His youngest son suffers from an illness of the lungs, and the doctors recommended the mountain air. Pat has become convinced that, with the war over, the time is right to make the journey.

"He must sell his place, and I pray it will be the home for us." James slowed his pace a bit. "With the money I saved during the war and what I have put by since, I believe I can manage the purchase."

Anne caught her breath. Hearing these thrilling, but unexpected, words caused her to shiver with excitement of her own. Never in her wildest imaginings could she have dreamed he wished to speak of acquiring a home for them.

"While my position remains less than I hoped for, I have not been a day without work since I returned to St. Louis. The fellows at the yard are all confident the bias against the Irish worker will lessen. Meanwhile, my wages are sufficient to maintain a home." They walked on a few blocks, and then James stopped.

"Here we are now. It's the grey frame house over there on the corner."

They moved slowly now, while Anne inspected what appeared to be fine looking homes along the street. Her smile faded when they came to stand before the last house. As they moved forward and crossed the road, she craned her neck to gain a better view of the place. Her good feelings plummeted.

"You can see, it needs massive repairs," James said, "but keep in mind Walter's bakery, built from two downtrodden warehouses. Try to picture the transformation I can bring to this place."

It was an unusual looking grey house, a large place that must have been stately at one time. Her first gaze went to the roof. Odd pieces of wood covered what must be an extensive hole. Her eyes moved to the tiny window below the roof that had been torn entirely from the wall and dangled precariously over the tall front entrance. Windows and boards were missing in several places, the front steps had collapsed, and the yard areas on either side of the house were filled with building materials mixed with trash. Oh, my word. The place brought to mind the shanties she and Walter had driven past on their ride downtown just after she arrived in St. Louis. Surely, the condition of the house would improve on closer inspection? She swallowed hard. Would it be possible to live amid this frightful disorder and debris?

James interrupted her thoughts. "Before we decide anything, you must inspect the inside. I thought, perhaps, we could ask Julia and Martin to walk through it with us on Sunday? You'll see what a fine home it can become. I beg you to hold your judgment until then."

"Of course, James. It is a grand place—well, a huge place. Much work needs to be done, but I know you will do a fine job of it." She attempted to mask her uncertainty and keep her reservations from showing on her face and in her voice. "I look forward to seeing the inside. In truth, I will be hard put to concentrate on anything else until I do."

When she returned to Dempsey's after her outing with James and climbed the stairs to the attic room, she was pleased to find both of her sisters there. She told them about the house James had taken her to see. "I must admit, I hold some misgivings, but James does seem determined to restore the place to respectability."

"Tell us every detail of the planned renovations," Julia said. "It sounds as if James has grand plans for the house."

Kate agreed with Julia, though she held a little more reserve in her words. "Give James an opportunity to make the improvements, before you set your mind against the place," she said.

"Why land sakes," Julia said, "a three story home. Will you not be the grand lady?" When Anne assured her there was nothing grand about the place right now, Julia would not hear it. "You wait. James will rebuild and rework until it is the palace you deserve."

With Julia's enthusiasm and Kate's reticent agreement, Anne's confidence began to grow. As she rested in her bed, waiting for sleep to come, she mulled over every moment of her outing with James. She had studied the house carefully. It stood in a sorry state now, that was sure, but she must trust James' judgment and have confidence in his skills at rebuilding. She attempted to picture the place as it would appear once he completed the work. She allowed herself to dream of living there, and in time, bringing her family from Ireland to join her.

Soon, she and her sisters would gather enough money to send for Michael and Lizzie, and with this home restored, she could provide a place for all of the younger children. Her reverie pushed a little beyond the house. With her commitment to her father fulfilled, she would be free to marry James. It was more than she had ever dared to hope until now. What a splendid gift James was offering her.

Martin and Julia did come on Sunday. Anne accompanied them through a side yard, stepping over boards and screens and all manner of refuse. They crossed a covered porch stretching along the rear of the house and then entered a roomy kitchen, both in total disrepair, both needing much work to make them presentable. As they went along through each of the rooms, James described his ideas for improvements.

The place surely would require many repairs. Holes dotted the walls everywhere they looked, paint peeled at each turn, and the floors were uneven with boards and nails ripped out in many places. The inside had proved to be in as sorry a state as the outside, and Anne stifled her disappointment and worked hard to move past its tumble down condition.

"There are six large rooms on each of the first two floors." James' plan unfolded as they walked. "There is also a third floor attic room. We can let four second floor rooms and set aside the rent from two for upkeep on the house. We'll save the money from the others for the immigration fund. I plan to move in right away, and when my brother Ned arrives, he'll stay with me in return for his help with the renovations.

"Once the place is respectable, we will hold the other rooms for members of our families. I do not know if my father or the Cartys will ever tear themselves from the roots of Ireland that seem so firmly embedded in their hearts. If they do, a home will await them."

"You know, Kate has already seen the place," Julia said. "After urging Anne to reserve judgment on the house, she observed it for herself the other day, and seemed to change her mind. She told me it looked a sight with the roof collapsed, windows broken, and who knows what inside. I beg to disagree."

Martin nodded. "Sure, it is a bit downtrodden, but I know you will transform it into a grand home. Your families will have a comfortable place to settle. Wouldn't your father and Mr. Carty wish to come right now and help with the work? I place myself and my limited skills at your service."

While James thanked them for their kind words and eagerly accepted Martin's generous offer of help, Anne took another look around. This time she began to see the place through the approving eyes of Martin and Julia.

Then Martin suggested it was time to go, and they made their way back out to the street.

Engrossed in their own conversation, Martin and Julia began walking toward Dempsey's.

Anne and James dawdled on the front walk, looking back at the house. "I've been talking all evening of my grand plans,"

James said, "but the scheme awaits your agreement and endorsement. I will not proceed without your approval. What say you, my love? Do you believe I can accomplish this task? Do you even wish me to try? I need your smile of encouragement before I carry on."

"Of course, I wish you to go forward." Caught up in James' grand proposal and bolstered by the enthusiastic endorsement of Martin and Julia, a seed of hope had begun to grow. Her thoughts swirled with anticipation and excitement. She could almost picture the completed restoration.

"Sure, I believe in you. The renovations are such an enormous undertaking, though, and it will require so much effort. If you are willing to take it on, I support you with all my heart and I love you dearly for it." Anne lowered her head, but she knew James caught the blush she tried to hold back.

"It is my fondest wish that, once the place is rebuilt and Michael and Lizzie are on their way to America, our obligations will be met and you will feel at liberty to marry me." James took Anne's hand, and this time she did not attempt to cover her feelings, but instead, gazed directly into his eyes and favored him with a grand smile.

"My sisters and I are gathering money now for passage for the children. We want them here as soon as possible after the first of the year. And, this house is so much more than I ever dreamed I could provide for them when they arrive."

Anne moved closer to James and took a firm hold of his arm. "I do not think there is any reason to wait. I believe we should speak with Father Burns and arrange a date for our wedding."

The three girls sat together in the attic room the evening after Anne and James talked of setting a date for their wedding. Anne spoke up as soon as they were all settled in. "Before James and I proceed, I must discuss our plans with you. You know all about the home James has offered for our family. With the children soon to be on their way and a home waiting, I believe I have fulfilled the promise I made to Father. I suppose, I am asking for your blessing."

"You and James must marry." Kate spoke as though her confident words settled the matter. "You have waited long enough."

"Yes, you must." Julia curtsied to Anne. "Once I serve as your attendant—and when Martin is finally discharged—my turn will come." Julia's expression grew serious. "I am being a little frivolous. Really, it is time for you and James to marry. Besides, you will want to be married and settled into James' house so the children can move in when they arrive. I am sure Walter and Mary would allow them to stay in the attic room for a time, but a permanent home with you and James would serve them best.

"I have a small sum I've saved for my own wedding, but I will have time to set money aside again. Please include it with our fund. I am so sorry it is only two dollars. While I am attempting to become more proficient at saving, I have not yet mastered the practice. Perhaps, my small contribution will provide them with a little extra for new clothing."

Kate pulled a cloth sack from her pocket and unfolded a thin stack of bills. "I have a few dollars, too."

Anne could not keep from smiling. "I have sixteen dollars I planned to deposit next week. With what you are both offering me and the money we hold in the account already, we should have enough to bring both children here without disturbing Uncle James' $100. I thank you my dear sisters. We have all grown proficient at saving, have we not?"

"We are learning from the master. Well, Kate is a quicker study than I." Julia moved behind Anne and tickled her neck.

"If the money is not spent by our parents, once again." Kate stamped her foot. It seemed, she did not share her sisters' optimism.

Anne tried to offer Kate encouragement. "With the latest news of the home being made ready for them all, our parents would not think of spending the passage money again." Julia echoed her sentiments, and their high spirits appeared to lift Kate out of her gloom. They agreed to move forward with this new plan.

She sent the money for Michael and Lizzie the next day. She had already informed her parents of her plans for marriage to James. In her letter accompanying the money, she told them they would be setting a date for the wedding. She also described the home that would be ready for the children when they came. She assured them of her continued pledge to save the fare for the rest of their family and reaffirmed Julia's and Kate's plans to continue their help.

Kate added a line to the sheet in her own hand. In bold words she insisted their parents must use the money to send both children together and they must come right after the beginning of the year.

Anne shivered at Kate's stern words, but she had to admit she agreed with the message.

One evening, a few weeks after they sent the letter, she mentioned to Kate their parents' lack of response to the news of her coming marriage. "Thanks to you and Julia, we sent off the passage money for Michael and Lizzie. With the fine work James is doing on the house, I will provide a home for them once we are married. By the time Maura and Maggie are old enough to come, we will have accumulated passage for all of them. Surely, this will satisfy the promise I made to Father."

"The house is coming along well, Anne," Kate said. "I once doubted James could make it livable, and I must say, in just this short time, he has accomplished a remarkable improvement to the roof and windows and turned the house into a respectable place. I intend to offer him my apologies for my lack of faith.

"For heaven's sake, Father and Mother should trust your judgment. You've lived in America on your own these many years, caring for all of us, and at the same time, sending them money. Sure, our mother can no longer cling to her foolish notion the Duffs are of a class beneath her because they once owned a pub. Such snobbery appalls me.

"Mother deems herself a fine lady, sewing for everyone in the county from the goodness of her heart. She is, in fact, paid for her work with food, material, or what other goods our neighbors have. I do not hold with such pretense.

"After all her talk about her daughters never being in service, she convinced Father to commit me to slavery at Hogan's. Now we learn our demands went unheard and they sent our sweet Lizzie there. What right does she have to pass judgment on anyone, much less a good man like James Duff?

"I cannot imagine Father holds with such foolishness, but if Mother disapproves and he allows it that is unforgivable. And, if I read one more greeting from the Hogans in their letters, I will rip them to pieces."

Anne shared some of Kate's misgivings about her parents' handling of the money they had been sending and about her mother's disregard for James' family. This was a happy time, though. The house James was preparing, the children surely on their way soon, and her engagement about to be made official made it impossible for her to remain discouraged for long.

Throughout their conversation, Anne had been fingering an envelope, postmarked Blackwater, Ireland. The message would only rile Kate. She shoved it deep into her pocket.

Chapter Twenty-Nine

Blackwater
November 9, 1865

Dear Anne,

I am afraid the passage will be high in the spring on account of many going. A great deal of the people must go on account of the bad crops, there was not so bad a crop this many years. It is the opinion of the ship agents that it will be a great deal higher in the spring.

Dear Anne, if the passage was entered before Christmas it would save a great deal. I am sure there will be many going in March for there is no one in this country has half a crop of anything they sowed. It is a happy news for Michael and Lizzie to be leaving this unfortunate country and all I can do is to pray for you all for your kindness to them and I hope when they are there that they will not forget you a day, or a year.

Dear Anne, Michael has no clothes that are fit to go there, nor is it in my power to get any for him, on account of the hard summer and bad crops. The winter is likely to be worse with the poor. Flour is 4 shillings a stone, oaten meal

2..6, india meal 1..10, so you may judge how the poor are circumstanced here at present.

Dear Anne, write as soon as you get this and let me know what kind of clothes he will need to bring with him. Let me know if he will want flannel.

I hope we will see the day when we will all meet once more. Tell Kate that Mr. Hogan desired us to tell her if she knew if Mr. Ryne of Castlehill, Enniscorthy was in St. Louis.

So, I believe that is all I have to say. No more from your affectionate parents,
John and Nell Carty

I am going to return you the most sincere thanks and if God leaves me my life and health it will not be a loss to either of you with the help of God. We wish you a Merry Christmas and a Happy New Year. I remain your loving brother,
Michael Carty

I believe that is all we have to say at present. We remain your loving parents,
John and Nell Carty

December, 1865

With the renovations to the house well underway and the children expected to leave Blackwater shortly after the beginning of the New Year, Anne decided it was time to set the date for the wedding. She and James visited Father Burns on a Sunday morning just at the beginning of winter. James had arranged the meeting in advance, and when they appeared at the rectory door, the housekeeper ushered them right in, saying the priest was waiting in the parlor. With her tea tray all prepared,

Kathleen seemed to have been anticipating their visit. With great ceremony, and a sly smile across her face, she poured tea for the three of them and then slipped quietly out of the room.

They settled in the comfortable chairs across from Father, and he listened attentively while James related the story of their courtship and outlined the plans they had made. Of course, Father Burns knew them both well and his expression showed no surprise as James told him of their wish to marry.

Anne squirmed and shuffled her feet. While she felt comfortable with James speaking for them, she did experience a bit of unease to have the feelings she had been holding private for all these many years now spoken aloud.

Father Burns permitted her little time for musing and worrying. He looked directly into her eyes and addressed his words to her. "In these past years, I've heard many stories from Julia about your promise to bring your family to America and your efforts to fulfill that pledge."

He then moved to James. "I've also been observing the progress of the renovations you are making to that tumble-down house. You are doing a fine job of it."

He turned back to Anne. "Now, I'll be asking only a few questions.

"How is your family's health? Will they be capable of making the journey? And, will they be content to live in the home James prepared for them?"

She tried to answer Father's, questions. She told him about her family back home and of their apparent good health. She assured him they would be thrilled to settle in James' grand house. While she talked, his attention appeared distracted.

He had pulled a small, worn date book from the desk drawer and now began shifting through it. Nodding toward them absentmindedly, he continued paging. "I wish you every happiness."

Anne and James exchanged quizzical looks. Apparently his telling of their story and her answers to the questions Father posed had been sufficient. When, at last, he came to April 28, they watched proudly as he printed their names neatly across the page.

Giving them both a grand smile, he extended his hand to James, and then to Anne, and once again, wished them well.

"Hold our dear Lord Jesus at the center of your marriage and you will be blessed indeed. As a new, young couple, you will assume a strong role in our church family. Go forth with your plans. You have my blessing."

After leaving Father Burns, she and James walked to Dempsey's and related the story of their meeting to Walter and Mary. When she learned their wedding date had been officially set in Father Burn's schedule book, Mary showered them with hugs and wishes for good health and a long, happy life. She followed her exclamations of happiness over their engagement with ideas for the wedding.

"Congratulations!" Walter said. "I heartily agree with what Mary is proposing. The wedding supper must be held here at Dempsey's."

"I am sorry, Mary, Walter," Anne said. "I do appreciate your splendid offer, but we have not spent a moment talking about the wedding. Allow us to discuss it some, and then we can begin to plan."

Mary seemed satisfied for a bit, but as soon as James left for the evening, she had one question she could not seem to hold back. "Surely we can begin a search for cloth for a wedding dress?" After the words were out, she appeared unsure, a little timid. When Anne smiled at the mention of a dress, though, her words grew more confident. "With the difficulties we experienced in obtaining material for Kitty's dress, we must begin right away. I will apply to Kate for help."

"Kate exhausted all of her sources, and we had about given up," Mary reported to Anne a week later. "Then I remembered the fabric stored at the bottom of my own trunk. It will be perfect."

"Oh, it is too fine." Anne examined the ivory muslin Mary spread out for her inspection. "I cannot possibly use your material."

"Of course you will," Mary said. "I'll hear no arguments. This cloth will make a beautiful dress. After your wedding, we will pack the gown away carefully. Perhaps I will wear it my-self one day...and my daughter...and yours."

When they finished their chores that evening, the Dempsey girls gathered in the attic room to examine the beautiful cloth. Giggles and sighs filled the little room, as they inspected the material and exclaimed over its splendor.

"We will combine our efforts and create a splendid dress for you," Ellen said.

"With two such grand seamstresses as you and Kate," Julia said, "Anne's dress will be magnificent."

Kate entered into the joyous mood of the evening. She sat right down at the table and began sketching a design for the dress. She also volunteered to make the few necessary items Anne would need for a trousseau.

Anne trembled with happiness at the kindness that was being bestowed upon her by these wonderful girls. Kate's offer was particularly generous. Her orders in the shop were grow-ing, and the sewing she did for Anne would take her away from her business.

"Will we use the sewing machine to construct at least part of the gown?" Ellen applied to each one for their agreement. Kate nodded, but the others resisted.

"A dress this important must be hand sewn," Grace said.

"I must agree with Grace." Anne spoke softly, not wishing to offend anyone, uncertainty creeping into her voice. "I can-not imagine a wedding gown sewn by a machine."

"The expert sits right here beside you," Ellen said. "With Kate's skill on the machine, not even an experienced seam-stress would guess it was not handwork. And this marvelous soft material will not require the double seams we needed for that coarse uniform cloth." After a look around at their sad fac-es, she relented a little.

"Perhaps, we could use the machine on the long seams of the skirt and train, and you fussy ladies could finish the rest by hand. It will be splendid, you will see. I must tease you a little about your out-of-date ideas, is all."

From that evening on, they gathered in Kate's shop in the evenings to work on the dress. With each night that passed, the bolt of cloth, along with some delicate, hand-tatted lace contributed by the sisters at St. Vincent's, developed into an exquisite wedding gown. An elegant veil, trailing to the floor, completed the ensemble. Though she and Julia and Grace sat back and allowed the experts to do the majority of the work, Anne sensed the girls all took delight in the dress, each considering herself a part of the coming celebration. While they worked one evening, they questioned her about the wedding plans.

"The wedding will be simple." Anne turned her attention to Mary, who had just come in to join them. "James and I talked it over, and we will sit down with you and Walter, one evening soon, to settle the details. With so many in the city mourning the loss of loved ones, wouldn't it be proper our wedding be solemn and subdued? Of course, I will wear this lovely dress you all are working hard to create for me and our friends will be welcome to attend the ceremony, but afterward, there will be no party."

"Surely, Walter and I could arrange a small family supper for you?" Mary sought support from Julia and Kate. "That should be appropriate. Don't you agree?"

Julia and Kate glanced toward Anne before they responded. After seeing her smile, Julia answered. "I think that would be grand." Kate nodded her agreement.

"A family meal would be wonderful." Anne said. "Thank you, Mary. But it must be family and our dear Dempsey friends only."

Grace surprised her by asking to sing at the wedding. Anne marveled at her generosity. With her own plans destroyed, Anne's marriage would no doubt prove a difficult occasion for Grace, a sad reminder of what her own life might have been.

"That is the nicest gift you could give me, Grace." Anne hugged her. Then she included them all in her words of gratitude. "You are so kind."

With the all-important matter of the dress resolved and the plans for the wedding coming together, Mary now turned her thoughts to a betrothal supper. "It is time to invite our friends to come together, Anne. We must have an opportunity to honor our favorite couple. We will all rejoice in your good news and share in your happiness.

"Since the holiday season is at hand, why don't we set the date for the supper for the first week of the new year? I will need some help from you in planning a menu."

Anne soon discovered the selection of dishes for the meal would be the only thing Mary would allow her to do in preparation for the occasion.

After the many suppers Anne attended at Dempsey's in these past years, it was difficult to comprehend that all the anticipation and excitement centered on James and her. It proved to be true, though.

With certain foods still scarce around the city, Anne observed the trades involved in securing enough for the meal. Once again, the benevolence of the Dempseys overwhelmed her. Their kind actions also gave her inspiration. She prayed she would one day be capable of imitating their selfless, admirable lives.

On a blustery Friday evening in early January, their preparations completed, the Dempsey group and the priests from St. Vincent's gathered in the dining room.

It was a treat for Anne to have James with her. He now spent every spare moment working on the house, and his appearances at supper were rare. On this special occasion, he brought along his brother Ned, who had arrived in St. Louis a month earlier and already secured a position at the rail yard. They all agreed with James' earlier assertion that his brother, a quiet, pleasant young man, did indeed resemble Martin Tobin.

"What a grand party for a fine, deserving couple." Kate greeted them as she came into the dining room from her shop.

Julia arrived from her work day at St. Vincent's, at almost the same moment, with Martin and his brother Patrick, who had escorted her home. While Grace and Cara placed platters of steaming meat, potatoes, and vegetables on the table, they each took a moment to add their own congratulations.

Ellen came in through the bakery. With Kitty married and living in Kansas City, she now returned home from the dress factory each evening on her own. After supper then, Ellen worked long evenings in the dressmaking shop with Kate. "I am delighted for you both," she said to Anne and James. "I wish you a happy life."

"My partner and I have an announcement of our own," Kate said. "With our business growing steadily, Ellen's days at the factory and her solitary walks home will soon come to an end." Anne led everyone in applauding the two girls and wishing them well.

In the next moment, Eddie and George arrived and extended their warm wishes to Anne and James, and they turned back to the reasons for this happy celebration.

"God bless all here." Father Burns' hearty voice rang out as he entered the room.

"God keep us all." Father Daly came in right behind him and led them in the familiar response.

They had all settled in at their places at the table when a brisk knock sounded at the front of the building. Walking out through the shop and opening the door, Anne was pleased to find Pat Dwire, an old friend from Blackwater.

"I am headed west," he said, "but I stopped in St. Louis for a few days. I have a communication for you and your sisters from your father."

Mary graciously invited Pat to stay for dinner and rushed to make a place for him at the crowded table. Anne introduced him to everyone, and a great round of greetings burst forth from all those from Blackwater who were seated at the table.

Surprise registered across Pat's face, when he discovered not only the three Carty girls, but also James and Ned Duff, Grace Donahoo, and Bridget Rice, all from his former home. Anne further astonished him when she explained the connections with Blackwater that Walter and Mary Dempsey and Martin and Patrick Tobin held. When it had all been sorted out, they settled in for prayer.

"Father, we thank you for the fine meal," Father Burns began, "And we ask your blessing upon Anne and James. We pray they will have a happy and blessed life together. Amen."

"Amen! Amen!" The responses came from all around the table.

"Let us raise our glasses in salute to Anne and James," Walter said. "We wish them a world of happiness." Though he drank only water himself, Walter had offered wine to all those who wished it.

"*Slainte!*" Best wishes filled the room. She had never tasted wine before and she could not be sure she would enjoy it, but Anne felt honored that Walter considered her betrothal to James such a special occasion. Wine had never been served at the Dempsey's' table, since she had been living here.

While Anne began taking the first tastes of the special dishes Mary prepared for the evening, she thrilled at this new happiness. Mixed with the joy came concern about Pat Dwire's visit, but she held her peace throughout dinner. As the meal drew to a close, curiosity gained the better of her, and at a lull in the conversation, she questioned him.

"What word do you bring from home?"

"I will begin with what I am sure you already know." The talk stilled, as Pat's expression turned grim and his voice held a quiver he seemed unable to control. "In this past year, the need back home has grown worse than it has been in a long time. With that said, the message is that the hard times forced your father to spend the money you sent for the children's passage. He asked me to tell you he held no recourse. The rent had come due on the hired land, and the family neared starvation." Pat apologized for interrupting their celebration with such a sad message. Rising from the table and thanking the Dempseys for the fine meal, he took his leave.

"We do appreciate your coming." Anne hastened to reassure Pat, as she and Julia accompanied him to the door. "I only wish Father had written a letter rather than burdening you with this task."

Julia added her thanks and good wishes for a pleasant journey and a happy life in America. They watched together for a few moments as he walked away from Dempsey's. Anne, still in shock over the message from her father, shook her head and sighed softly.

When they returned to the dining room, they were greeted with silence, and after a few moments, with murmured goodnights. The priests were the first to take their leave. "Please tell us if there is anything we can do to help you," Father Burns said, as he went through the door.

"You have only to ask, and I will be at your service," Father Daly said, before he followed the Pastor out.

Walter and Mary, Walter's helpers, and the Dempsey girls all said their farewells and left the room.

Anne could find no words, her mind had grown blank. She could not sort her thoughts or take hold of her emotions.

Kate suffered no such loss. "How could they have done such a thing? James has been working long into the nights to prepare a home for the children. Those poor dears, waiting to come out, they must be heartbroken. I know what that disappointment is. And, the passage money was not Father's to spend. It came from the three of us. We saved every penny. Now it is all for naught."

"They must have suffered over this," Julia said. "We know they wished Michael and Lizzie to enjoy the opportunities we have had. We must try to understand."

"Please remain calm, Kate." Anne spoke quietly, not sure if she could even force the words out. "We must absorb this news and try to comprehend how desperate they are."

"I am finished with the business. I cannot discuss it any longer." Kate rose from the table. With the silence in the room, Anne could hear the stomp of each foot as she climbed to the third floor.

"We will do anything to help you." Julia patted Anne's shoulder, and then she left the room to walk Martin and his brother out. James' brother, Ned, left with them, and Anne and James were alone.

James held Anne before him, grasping her arms, drawing her close. "We must be together, my love. I will find a way."

"I want to be with you too." Now that they were alone, Anne could no longer hold in her grief. She rested her head on his shoulder and sobbed. When she composed herself enough to speak, she did not pretend any understanding or soften her words. "I am sorry for taking on so. Right at this moment, I cannot move beyond the disappointment. I do not believe we should go on any longer."

"You cannot mean that." James released his hold on her and stepped back. "I love you so, and I know you love me. I feel your love."

"I do love you with all my being, but I can see no end to this misery. We sent my parents more than enough for the children's passage. With what we have sent home in the past few years, all of the children could be here right now, or on their way at least. My family endured the pain of the death of one son from the misery that has befallen Ireland. We sent them the means to save the others. They should be gathering money right now to come themselves. They know a home has been made ready for them. I cannot imagine what their thinking can be.

"No matter what my parents have done though, I cannot break my pledge to my Father. While I still breathe, I must work to bring those poor children to America."

"You are distraught. Sure, and I do understand it. I am in a sorry state myself. I will not give up our plans, though. I will not abandon our dream. Please let us take some time to work through this terrible shocking revelation that has thrown our lives into such a spin.

"Give me your promise, Anne. Will you think this through before ending our dream?"

"I see no other way, but I will think it through." Anne held James' hand, drawing comfort from the touch of his warm skin.

Then, without a hug or a smile, he dropped her hand, turned and left the room. When he shut the shop door behind him, the thud pounded through Anne as if she had been dealt a physical blow.

As she headed for the stairway to the attic room, her thoughts were in a dreadful state of disarray. It would not be the last she would ever see of James. She would not allow her mind to imagine such a foolish or unrealistic thing. He lived in her neighborhood, attended the same church, and shared the same friends. The home he purchased and had been working tirelessly to restore just for her stood on the corner, three blocks away. Was this, though, the end of the vision they shared for so many years?

She walked slowly up the stairs, each step seeming an impossible, steep mountain to attain. A tremendous weight appeared to bear down upon her, impeding her progress. Her shoulders shook with the emotions she willed herself to keep in control. Reaching the top step and entering the attic room, she lowered herself to her bed.

Burying her face in her pillow, she surrendered to her sisters' ministrations. Kate brushed her hair away from her face, while Julia offered a warm cloth and soothing words. When she recovered her senses, she would thank them for their care, but at this moment, she could not speak. They remained together, in this manner, until she felt herself drifting into sleep.

The day immediately following the spoiled engagement party seemed an endless one. After enduring hours of cheerful conversation with her customers, and a miserable supper, her

Dempsey friends all attempting to pretend nothing had gone amiss, Anne was finally free to retire to the attic room.

One glance at her sisters revealed they had been waiting for her. Kate sat at the desk holding a small paper, tapping the rows of numbers on the sheet with a pencil. Julia, who perched on the bed nearest Kate, reached out to pull Anne down beside her.

Kate spoke first. "We have worked out all the details—"

Anne interrupted. "It may be too late. I told James we must halt our wedding."

"Oh no, Anne." Julia began to cry. "Surely, James did not agree. We will not permit this to happen."

"Of course not. We will not allow anything to stop your wedding." Kate was all business. "Just listen to our plan."

She nodded for Kate to go on. Still, she could not be sure what James was thinking right now. She had seen the hurt and disappointment in his eyes, when she told him they could not proceed with their plans. Though he pleaded with her to reconsider before making any rash decisions, his own injured feelings may have prompted him to cancel the wedding already.

Kate broke into her thoughts. "We will remove Uncle James' money from the bank and send it home for passage for Michael and Lizzie."

"We replaced that $100 once before." Julia elaborated on their plan. "We three will work together and accomplish the task one more time." They sat around the desk, Kate explaining the details, figuring where money could be saved and how quickly the money could be returned to their account.

Finally, satisfied the scheme was solid, Anne agreed. Still, she worried their parents would spend the money again. Since her sisters held the same concern, the decision brought no peace of mind or feelings of confidence that they had solved the problem. There were no cheers or jubilation.

Kate stood up and moved about the room for a bit. Then, she ceased her pacing. She stood before Anne. "I see you are still doubtful. You still believe you have not fulfilled your promise to Father." At Anne's nod, she went on.

"Let us settle this matter now and forever. Though I was still a young girl, I remember well the night you made that vow to Father. You agreed to two things: one, to make a home for the children; and two, to help bring them to America." Kate waited for Anne's nod, and then she went on.

"You have more than met the first promise. Three blocks from here stands a home more magnificent than Father could have imagined. Do you agree this part of your pledge is fulfilled?"

Anne could only nod her head again. Kate's forcefulness and the clarity of her argument had rendered her dumb.

"Now, on the matter of fare money," Kate moved on. "For the second time, we are sending money for Michael and Lizzie. Once they arrive, we will begin to save for Maura and Maggie. There are only two alterations to your fulfilling of this part of the pledge. First, you will still be saving the money, the only difference is you will have some help from Julia and I. Finally, our parents will have one benefit that did not even occur to them. They will have no need to worry about the children being cared for. They are still young ones, after all. You and James will provide a wonderful home for them.

"Now, are you ready to marry James?"

While she and Julia stared at Kate in wonder, Anne's heart and mind began to fill with peace and joy.

"Thank you, Kate. Your words are like a magic balm to me. I have not felt such peace since James first arrived here in St. Louis and began speaking of joining our lives together. I am confident now that our marriage is the right thing."

Anne nodded her head to both sisters. "I will remove the money from our account and post it to Father." She still could not feel any spark of hope about her parents sending the children, but since hearing Kate's impassioned speech, she had begun to feel secure in the belief that she was following the right path.

"Have you spoken with James since the engagement supper?" Julia asked.

Anne shook her head. "I have not seen him. Of course, it was all my doing. In a moment of disappointment and anguish,

I was the one to lose faith in our plans. After all of James' hard work on the home he has been preparing for me, I dashed our hopes for a future together. It is no wonder he has been avoiding me.

"I know he is still hard at work on the house. Walter went over to help out last evening. I experienced a bit of disappointment when James did not send a message to me by way of Walter. I do miss him. A word of greeting from him would have soothed my troubled soul."

Even this unhappy situation did not discourage her. She felt confident she and James would make their way back to one another. She would not even allow herself to worry because he had not come by on his way home from the rail yard on any evening the past week, as he sometimes did, or come by the mission to walk her home. She did long to see him again. She must have an opportunity to apologize for her lack of confidence in him.

The week seemed to stretch on forever. When Sunday came at last, Anne walked to church with Walter and Mary. She attempted to converse, but the Dempseys were quiet. They appeared to be searching for the right thing to say to her. Finally, she gave it up, and few words were spoken the rest of the way. The folks at Dempsey's had been subdued since the evening of the disastrous betrothal dinner. She knew they worried about her, but she could not convince anyone of her confidence that all would be well.

They climbed the steps to the entrance of the church, and Walter held the door open for them. To Anne's surprise and delight, James waited inside the door.

The congregation had already begun singing the first hymn, so they could take no time to talk. Before they moved down the aisle, though, James whispered. "I have arranged a meeting with Father Burns after mass."

The sound of his fine voice was the thing she had longed for all during the week. His message caused her heart to thump. With a nod, she agreed.

After church they followed behind Father Burns as he returned to the rectory.

"I am sorry I stormed out the other night." James whispered in her ear, as they slowed their steps and fell a little behind the priest.

"I am sorry I lost faith in our plans." If Father Burns heard their words, he pretended not to.

"I love you more than my words can tell you."

"I love you too." She could say no more. Father Burns had opened the door, and he was ushering them into his office.

He had been with them at Dempsey's the night Pat Dwire brought the fateful message, and so without any discussion, he began immediately to share his thoughts. "You two are of an age and sensible enough you need no guidance from me." He sat back and smiled. "Since you have come, though, what sort of an old Irish priest would I be if I had no opinion?" He turned to face Anne.

"My dear, we have already spoken about the pledge you made to your father. We've been over that promise before. I admire the manner in which you lived by that word for all these years, but with the passage of time, your situation has changed. When he placed this obligation on you, your father could not have known you would lose contact with your uncle in Oregon. He could never have foreseen he would be forced to take the passage money you sent, and instead, use it for food and taxes."

Anne shifted uncomfortably in her chair, but she could not entirely subdue her smile. This was the same message Kate had presented to her in such a clear and forceful manner. Thanks to her sister, she was ready to accept Father's advice. The priest appeared not to notice her strange mood, and he went on.

"Another development presented itself. James Duff, here, has been working to provide a mansion of a home for you. The place is large enough to house your entire family, is it not?" Anne nodded. "And, fine though the Dempsey's home is, you could not bring them all to your attic room?" She shook her head.

"For months, this fellow worked through the nights to re-build the tumbling down place, until now it looks for the entire world like a fine manor. Will they not all be well situated in that great comfortable house, the children, and your parents, too, if they gather themselves enough to come?" Anne smiled her agreement. James squirmed.

"My word, young lady, your father, himself would be dumbstruck, if he could see James' grand home. You certainly have exceeded all his expectations in that quarter." Anne nod-ded her head. "And have you and your sisters not already sent additional passage money for the two children? And will you not want to be married to James before they come to live in his house?" She nodded again.

"James, have you not promised to scrape and save until Anne's family and yours are here in America?"

"Yes Father, I have given Anne my word," James said.

"Now, my dear girl, will you give me one good reason why you should not marry this big omodon and take his sad face out of my house?"

They left Father Burns' office, their faces aglow with hap-piness, their arms locked together, their wedding still planned for April. Oh, what perfect bliss. Anne nearly skipped along. Her dreams had come true.

At Sunday dinner, Anne shared with everyone around the table the outcome of their meeting with Father Burns. "We will go on with our plans and the wedding will take place in April."

An atmosphere of excitement once again filled the air at Dempsey's. "We will tend to the dishes without you today, Anne," Kate said. "You and James must sit with Walter and Mary to sort out all the particulars of the wedding."

With the table cleared, Mary was ready to discuss their ideas. "Now, you have already arranged with Father Burns that the wedding will take place on the last Saturday in April. And we have already discussed having a celebratory supper here at Dempsey's following the ceremony. Will that still be agreeable?

"Of course, Mary. You are so kind and generous, and with the many suppers and celebrations I have attended here at Dempsey's, I know everything will be splendid." Anne knew she was blushing with excitement. "I only ask that the party be small, with only family and a few dear friends." She looked to James for support.

"I do agree with Anne. A quiet celebration is all we will need." James held his hand out to Walter. "We owe you a great deal. Thank you so much."

He walked around the table to hug Mary. "You have made Anne and me very happy. We will never forget your kindness."

"Aw, it is a pleasure to me," Mary said. "You two are my favorite people. Well, after Walter, of course." She offered her brother a wily smile.

"Why don't we extend this grand afternoon, by walking to the new house to inspect what Ned and I and our helpers have accomplished?" James asked.

Anne, James, Walter, and Mary spent a happy hour together, examining and admiring the latest refurbishments to the place. James wished her to see each improvement as it was completed, but Anne's visits were limited. She could not go to the house unescorted, and with everyone busy with their own occupations, she hesitated to impose on anyone by asking them to accompany her.

Now, she and Mary sat in what soon would be her own grand kitchen and planned for the arrival of Michael and Lizzie. Walter and James moved off to inspect the parlor and discuss the next steps in the renovations.

"The work James has already finished is grand," Mary said, as they looked all about and inspected every part of the room. "The lovely, soft cream walls are wonderful, but these brilliant shiny floors may just be my favorite thing."

"I did not realize James had already installed Mrs. Flynn's rug on the floor under the table. It is beautiful. What a wonderful wedding gift. I will never be able to thank her enough."

Anne's thoughts soon floated off to a time, one day soon, when she would preside here, mistress of her own grand place, preparing dinner at the massive, and a bit intimidating, oven. James would return home after a long day of work and sit down to a meal—my husband, our own kitchen—oh, this is more happiness than I ever could have dreamed would be possible.

She drew herself back to the present and realized Walter and Mary were gathering coats and hats in preparation for setting out into the early evening cold. She and James, wishing to prolong their time together, decided on a short walk before going home.

They started off arm-in-arm, talking of their home, their wedding, and their many blessings. She enjoyed the stillness of the night and this precious time in each other's company. They had surmounted so many obstacles. Surely nothing more could delay their being together.

Chapter Thirty

February 2, 1866

My Dear Children

We received your welcome letter on the 28th. We were happy to hear you were all well, and we are all well here, with the exception of Maura. She is poorly in health these three months. She has fallen into consumption. Dr. Sheridan told us she would not do any good. She is short on her breathing. I have to be up with her sometimes by night. She is reduced very much. We also received a cheque of #4.0.0 for which we were thankful to you.

Dear Julia, you wanted to know if there were any letters from Bessy Furlong. There was one last week. She said she had letters from you and she also said you were sick for a month. We were in great trouble till we got your letter.

Dear Anne, we were happy Kate is well. I suppose she will never write us a letter. I thought she would not forget her mother.

Remember us to Grace Donahoo and tell her all friends here are well.

No more at present from your loving parents, John and Nell Carty

March, 1866

With the wedding day drawing near, Anne's happiness was tempered by her concern that, though her brother and sister were scheduled to leave Ireland soon, her parents failed to mention anything about their departure in recent letters. She attempted to push back her ever-present fear that her parents had spent the fare money elsewhere.

Leaving her position at Dempsey's also concerned her more than she thought it would. Mary tried to reassure her about the bakery. "With Julia's work for Colonel Scones coming to an end, she will be able to devote some time to helping in the shop and Grace has also volunteered to step in when needed.

"And, of course, when your sister Lizzie arrives, Walter and I have already agreed she will be your replacement. We would love to have another Carty sister in the shop. You will see, Anne, it will all come together."

Now, if only Lizzie arrives before too much time passes, she thought.

Anne's longing to have her parents and the two youngest children with her remained, but along with the advice she had received from Kate, she also held in her heart the gentle suggestion Mary offered.

"Be grateful for the blessings you have received and accept the gifts God provides." Mary's words stayed with her as she went along throughout her days. Sure, it was difficult not to allow some joy to slip into her heart. She and James must, indeed, be the most fortunate people in all America. They would live together in their own home, with Michael and Lizzie settled in with them, and Julia and Kate nearby.

While she made the vow to indulge herself in this happiness, a young man, whose face looked familiar to her, entered the bakery. Kate walked through the doorway from the dining room in time to see him remove his hat and close the front door.

"John Ryan." She passed through the shop, moving toward him quickly, eagerness evident on her face. "Have I not just left you in Ireland? Sure, it is good to see you again—"

"What is it?" Anne noticed Kate's abrupt halt in the center of the room. Her eyes moved to John in time to recognize the troubled expression her sister had observed.

"I am the bearer of terrible tidings." He stopped speaking for a moment and lowered his head. He raised it slowly, and began again. "Before I left home, your dear sister Maura died." Perhaps overpowered by the weight of the message he delivered or worried about the outpouring of emotions that would follow his words, he pushed his hat back on his head, turned, and without another word, walked out the door.

Anne started out to overtake him, to thank him for bringing them the message, even this sad word. Then, Kate collapsed onto a chair, and she ran back to her sister. The usually composed Kate rocked back and forth, crying softly, her cheeks turned to pink.

After a moment, she calmed herself enough to speak. "I should never have left her. I should have insisted the girls all come out with me. It is my fault. I concerned myself with gathering the proper clothing for the trip. My thoughts should have been focused on the others."

Walter came out to the shop, as she brushed away her tears. "Aye, what is troubling Kate? What will I do for her?"

"We received word from home of our little sister Maura's death," Anne said. "Please send Eddie to St. Vincent's to fetch Julia."

Walter offered them his sympathy, his expression filled with sadness and concern. Then, he called to Eddie and sent him after Julia. He knelt before Kate and offered to carry her upstairs to her room.

Anne's strong, determined sister managed to overcome her shock and sorrow. She pulled herself up and straightened her shoulders." I will be fine," she said. "I will not need any help." She trudged up the stairs with Anne close behind.

Walter followed as far as the second floor landing. "Kate has safely reached the chair in the attic room," Anne called to him. With her promise to fetch him if he was needed, Walter headed back toward the oven room.

While Anne tended to Kate and attempted to console her, she could hear Julia rushing up the stairs. She hurried down to the second floor landing to meet her, wishing to warn her of the outpouring of bitterness and the surprising lack of control Kate was displaying.

"The word of Maura's death has brought on a state of extreme agitation." Anne placed her hand on her sister's arm as they climbed to the third floor. "I tried to comfort her, but nothing I do or say seems to sooth her."

After a few minutes of sharing tears and prayers, Anne helped Kate to her bed while Julia propped pillows behind her head, trying to make her comfortable. After a time, she seemed to recover. Growing calmer now, she began to reminisce about their young sister.

"Surely, our little Maura is a saint," she said. "She encouraged us when we became sad or disheartened. She set an example of goodness and kindness.

"Father and Mother will miss her so, and Lizzie, Michael and Maggie will be lost without her. They must persevere somehow. Our Maura rests with the angels now."

"You remember Maura as a young girl, Kate," Anne said. "She was a wee baby when Julia and I lived in Blackwater. And then, your separation from her is so recent, the wound of your parting has been reopened. I am sure this word of her passing is overwhelming for you."

Kate nodded. "Father's recent letter is the first I knew of her being ill. She appeared quite healthy when I left home. What a sweet girl Maura was," she said again and again, while Anne and Julia tried to comfort her."

They sat with Kate a long time, listening to her talk of Maura and weathering the storm when her agitation returned and her anger and outrage spilled forth.

Throughout the afternoon and early evening, Kate continued to need her sisters' comfort and strength. She would calm herself at times, talking of Maura, and then, her indignation rose up again. She began placing the blame, her emotions gaining force. At once, it was the sad conditions of Ireland. "The dampness of the cottage and the lack of decent food caused our little Maura's death," Kate cried out.

While Julia rushed out to fetch warm towels to bathe Kate's face and arms, she lashed out again. "The British are to blame, it's sure. They stand by and watch the Irish people suffer and make no attempt to aid them."

Anne ran down to the kitchen to make tea, and when she returned and began pouring a cup for each of them, Kate's grief seemed to have gained strength. "Our parents should have allowed the little ones to come out," she said, "and I should have insisted. It is my doing. It is my selfishness that killed her."

They sat with Kate, as close by as she would allow, and mustered their own strength against the force of her wrath. They could only listen. It seemed nothing would soothe her sister.

Anne could find little to dispute in Kate's words, but the bitterness of her outcry and her apparent state of unreasoned thought shocked her. It seemed the peace of mind Kate demonstrated since the opening of her shop had now slipped away. The distress she displayed when she arrived in St. Louis had returned.

After what seemed like hours, her anger and passion at last appeared to dissipate. Kate drew herself up with renewed energy, turning her focus on Anne.

"You must not allow this terrible tragedy to delay your wedding," she said. "For too many years, you placed everyone else's concerns ahead of your own plans. It is time for you and James to move on with your lives." Kate would not be appeased until Anne promised she would consider her words.

Anne had been attempting to push back her thoughts of the wedding. Hearing Kate's demands caused her to tremble. She realized the enormity of the decision that would soon be forced upon her. It was too soon to make any such rash judgments, but to appease Kate, Anne nodded her agreement. At last, her sister gave in to her exhaustion and fell into a deep sleep.

❀ ❀ ❀

Anne and James took some time and walked together along the streets of the city. She wished to be alone with him for the conversation they must have, and a walk was their lone opportunity to talk in private.

She began by sharing with him her sorrow over little Maura's death and the turmoil she now experienced. "When I left Blackwater, I pined for the children. Each night alone in the attic room, I pictured the little ones and longed for them. I worried over Maura. She seemed frail, clinging to my skirts more than the others. As the years passed, I continued to think of them and offer prayers for their well-being each night, but I sometimes could not picture their faces. Maura must have grown and changed, and I wondered if I would even know her. While I look forward to the arrival of Lizzie and Michael in St. Louis, I worry that they, too, will be like strangers to me. Ah, it is a sad thing.

"Kate is insisting we go on with the wedding. I must confess, she is not alone in her thoughts. Once I absorbed the shock of Maura's death, I too considered the effect the sad event would have on us."

"I understand, my dear. I am torn, myself." James placed his strong arm around her and drew her close. "I am sorry indeed for your grief. At the same time, though I know it is callous of me, I believe we must marry now. We cannot wait. I cannot pace each empty room, or climb the stairs from one vacant, hollow floor to another, or live in our silent home without you any longer."

Anne's emotions were so troubled and confused she could not halt her words. She relaxed her reserve and poured out her heart to James. "I have experienced this same torment. Each night, when we are forced to part at Dempsey's, with but a touch of hands or brush of cheeks, and go off alone, I feel I am being pulled to pieces. I long to bid goodnight to you...as your wife...in our own home."

"In our own bedroom." James took her hand.

She looked up at him. For a moment, the world stilled. Anne stepped back a little, and looking into James eyes, she nodded. They stood together for a time, not speaking. Then, the magical moment slipped away and the world with its hardships and grief returned. They began to walk again, heading back toward Dempsey's.

"I am the dreadful one, James." Anne's words continued to pour out. "It shames me to even tell you of my selfishness, but I cannot allow you to think you are uncaring. While the news of my little sister's death saddened me, sure, after a short time of sorrow, I turned to a count of how many remain at home to bring out. And, this is not the first time I harbored such thoughts. I reacted in the same manner when we learned of Jimmy's death." Her cheeks had grown warm with her admission. She turned to James to ascertain his reaction. "What must you think of me?"

"Anne, my love, you are the most generous girl the world over. For so many years, you saved your every coin and filled your heart and mind with plans for bringing each member of your family here. It is a natural progression of thought to contemplate how many are now left at home. Do not be too harsh with yourself." James gazed down at her. "I must say, if but a small measure of your thoughts are now focused on me and our future, I am well pleased."

"Your kind words help to allay my guilt, but my mind is in a whirl. I am filled with questions and doubts. Could I have made greater economies, sent passage money sooner? Could I have saved Maura's life, if I provided the means to bring her here? Is her death a message or sign? Is our marriage contrary to the promise I made to my father to bring them all out before I pursued a life of my own?

"I sound irrational. I know I do. I am in such turmoil. So many people must be considered, so many matters must be attended to. I am aware of the many reasons we should proceed with the wedding, the preparations Walter and Mary have already made, and the home you are preparing for me and for our families. And, don't I love you more than life itself and long to be with you? I cannot imagine I can go ahead and be happy, though, when I have failed in my mission.

"I must also consider Kate. It has been but a short time since she lived at home with Maura, and she is distraught over her death. Though she insists we go on with the wedding, her thinking may change in the next few days as the reality of Maura's passing settles in. I cannot inflict additional pain on her. Please bear with me. I must resolve this in my own mind."

"Take some time to absorb this tragic news and allow your sisters to counsel you. Whatever you decide, my girl, you will forever remain my dear love."

"Please continue with the preparations." As the girls dressed for work the next morning, Kate stood before Anne, a determined expression spread across her face. "This matter of your wedding is important to me. You must not change your plans. You said yourself that you did not know Maura as I did. A dearer person never lived. Her heart was filled with generosity and concern for everyone. With the memories of Maura that I hold deep within me, I believe she would wish you to proceed."

Julia contributed her own thoughts. "I prayed about your situation last night. I asked the Holy Spirit to help you make the right decision. I also asked our Heavenly Father to care for us all. I am at peace now, and I pray you will both receive this same measure of serenity."

Anne hugged Kate, and then she turned to Julia. "Your prayers are sending a world of calm over me already." Anne bowed to her sister. "I will strive to be more like you. I must resist the notion that I can decide all things for myself and remember to place my trust in God."

"Sometimes, I even forget to pray," Kate said. "I, too, needed the reminder that I cannot battle my way through life without God's help and His love."

"Bless you, both for the kind assurances." Anne placed a hand on each of her sisters' shoulders. "The decision is made. The matter is settled. I stand here with you, at ease and without any uncertainty. We will arrange for a memorial mass for our dear little Maura. Though we are left with little time now, we must take out a small portion to mourn her. Then, the preparations for the wedding will move forward."

Anne stood in the shop with Kate, Mary, and Mrs. Flynn, a week after they learned of Maura's death. They had been discussing last minute wedding details, but their attention was diverted by a few of her customers offering superstitious sayings and words of warning concerning her marriage.

"You will want a sunny day." Mrs. Roach, a regular morning customer in the shop for many years, called out a last bit of counsel as she headed for the door. "You must all pray for sunshine, and pray hard. I'll add my own petitions for you." The dear lady meant to be kind. Many of Anne's friends and neighbors had already offered her their opinions and advice. Though wishing to be helpful, they could easily have upset the bride. Anne decided that, between the deep sorrow she and her sisters bore and the dire forebodings of her customers, everyone at Dempsey's needed a good dose of humor.

"I am receiving suggestions from everyone I encounter these days," she confided. "It seems certain clothing will bring good luck. Special teas and fruits will increase my husband's love. The wedding day, itself, is of particular concern, with Tuesday's brides blessed with sturdy children, and the offspring of Wednesday's brides leaving home before they are grown. The predictions grow more foreboding as the week continues. Sure, I do not know what to make of it."

"Ah, that is shocking," Mrs. Flynn said. "These foolish women should not speak of such things to you. It is naught but lunacy."

"Anne, you are the most sensible girl here at Dempsey's," Mary said. "I cannot believe you would even listen to such foolishness."

"And their advice lacks any sense at all." Mrs. Flynn placed her basket on the counter with enough force to make them all jump. "Do not listen to a word of it."

"Of course, I do not believe any of it. It's just that we girls have all heard stories aplenty from our Grandmother Carty, tales of rainbows and moonbeams and such. Sure, it's enough to unsettle a person." Finally, Anne began to laugh at the memory of the anecdotes they heard as youngsters back home in Ireland.

Kate joined in with her. "And fairies and banshees don't forget those little fellows." Kate giggled and Anne was thrilled to see it. This was the first smile she had seen from Kate, since they learned the news of their little sister's death.

Mary laughed, too. "Aw, you girls are teasing."

Mrs. Flynn, still bent on renouncing the customers' foolishness, ignored their frivolity and continued to rail against the superstitions. "Instead of frightening you with their tittle-tattle, they should forget this silliness and spend time on their knees, praying for God's mercy." She addressed her next thoughts to Anne.

"Since James is able to gain a few hours away from his work on Saturday, hold to your plans," Mrs. Flynn said. "There are no two finer people in the city, and you will soon enjoy a wonderful life together. There's the truth!"

She started for the door, but she turned back. Her face had grown more serious. "I would dearly love to be with you at church on your blessed day. With my Tim overwhelmed with sorrow, though, I cannot prevail upon him to attend the wedding and I cannot bring myself to come without him. Our young ones will be there, that's sure, and I will watch over your meal while everyone attends the wedding."

"I do understand, dear, and I appreciate your kind offer of help." Anne embraced Mrs. Flynn.

Kate and Mary nodded their agreement. Coming to the special supper Mary held immediately after the end of the war, had taken a great toll on Mrs. Flynn. She confided to Anne that she would not go off again, until her husband recovered from his deep sadness. Anne suspected Mrs. Flynn still suffered herself. She seldom shopped at the bakery now. Sure, she had only come in today to renew her offer of help with the wedding supper.

Anne missed her cherished friend. She had come to depend on her fine humor and her good counsel. She prayed Mrs. Flynn would soon recover from her terrible grief over the death of her young son.

As she opened the door, Anne caught a flash of white lace cascading along her skirt. "Mrs. Flynn," she rushed to her side before she could slip out the door. "Is this a wedding veil? Your veil?"

When Mrs. Flynn turned back, Anne could see it clearly now. Mrs. Flynn still wore her same grey mourning dress, but draped at the waist, anchored with a thin brown belt, hung a delicate lace veil, billowing out around her skirt and covering most of the back of her dress.

"It belonged to my mam. With your wedding approaching, I am thinking of her, but it's you I'm praying for. I wish you to be a happy bride, my girl."

Anne hugged Mrs. Flynn, her heart pounding with joy. Her friend would always carry sorrow over her son's death. With her visit today, her mother's wedding veil wrapped around her grey dress, it was sure to Anne she had turned a step or two away from her deep mourning.

Chapter Thirty-One

April, 1866

On the Thursday and Friday before the wedding, the wet and gloomy weather tempered everyone's spirits. Still, the rain removed the mud from the streets and doorsteps and washed the neighborhood clean. To Anne it signaled a new beginning and a bright, hopeful future at hand for the city and for James and her. When the great day arrived at last, a brilliant sunshine appeared, as if proclaiming it was time to push aside the gloomy days and deep sorrows. In the end, Saturday proved an excellent choice for a wedding.

"I will relieve you of your laundry chore on your wedding day," Grace said to Anne. "It is only fitting you spend your final time at Dempsey's working in the shop."

Anne spent the morning accepting good wishes for health and happiness from her customers. A few could not resist adding teasing remarks about the day being her last as a young maid.

Mary came out from the oven room early in the afternoon to close the shop. "The majority of our regular customers managed to purchase their baked goods this morning," she said. "Of course, they have all had advance notice, but we would never leave our customers without. I will place a covered hamper filled with bread on the doorstep for any who find themselves in need.

"Hurry on upstairs, young lady," she said to Anne, "you must have some time now to prepare yourself for your wedding."

Grateful for a little time to herself, Anne rushed up the steps. She would not be alone for long.

In a few moments, Julia hurried in from the rectory. Following close behind, came Kate. "I closed my shop for the rest of day," she said.

"I am so thrilled to have you both here to help me dress."

Anne did not wish to allow this joyous mood to pass away, but she could see that Kate, still pained over her their little Maura's death and angry over what she perceived as their parent's betrayal, struggled to hold on to her smile. As their talk continued, her sister's questions and complaints began to pour forth, more blunt today than ever.

"I do not understand why Father and Mother never mentioned James while I was at home or wrote a word about him in their letters since I came here? James is a fine man. He will make a grand husband for you, but I knew nothing of your attachment until I arrived in St. Louis. Did you write to them about James? Well, I'm sure you did. Mother must have destroyed the letters."

"At first, I mentioned him casually." Anne attempted to explain, even to herself. "I did not wish Father and Mother to believe I sought a release from my obligation to bring the children to America. Our parents must know I will never abandon my duty there.

"When we finally made the arrangements for our wedding, I wrote to inform them. I described the home James made ready for our entire family. Still, his name has not been mentioned by Father or Mother, though I questioned the matter in each letter since. James also wrote to ask Father's consent to our marriage. I received no response, and he received no reply.

"I remember Mother's prejudice against the Duff family because Mr. Duff owned a pub." Sadness flooded over Anne, even as her sisters prepared to slip her lovely wedding dress over her head. "I do wish Mother could forget all such nonsense and be happy for me. And, just a few words from Father—his approval of our marriage—would mean the world to me, but I waited in vain for his blessing." The dress was set aside for a moment, while Anne's sisters tried to reassure her.

While they talked, Mary entered the room with a tray and set out teapot, cups, and biscuits. Hearing their conversation and seeing Anne's distress, she took time to pour a cup of tea for each of them and then she sat down beside her. After they passed a quiet moment together, she offered her opinion.

"We cannot assume what your parents are thinking. Surely, they would wish you to hold pleasant thoughts on this blessed occasion. Say a prayer for them and keep them in your hearts. We must be thankful and rejoice in the blessings we have received. We've had few happy moments these past years."

Mary took Anne's hand. "We must remember what circumstances transpired to cause your mother to grow so stern. You know, I would offer all I hold dear to have my own mam with me. I often speculate, though, about what her life would have become if she had lived on in Enniscorthy. Would she remain the saint I now hold in my memory, if she lived through the terrible hardships your poor mother has? I also wonder if the lack of food, clothing, or proper medicines for her children would have marked her as it surely affected your poor mam?" She stopped, and then said in a quiet voice, "I've no right to speak out so. My tongue flies away from me at times."

"You speak the truth, Mary," Anne said. "Julia, Kate, and I appreciate your reminder of the great sacrifices our mother made to send us to America. We will think of the good things she has done, will we not?"

Kate bowed her head and said nothing, but Julia spoke up, agreeing with Mary, insisting they must be cheerful today. "Now I order happy faces for all of us. The Lord blessed Anne with the handsome James Duff for her husband, and we will set aside all sorrows and concerns and declare this a day to celebrate. Besides, Michael and Lizzie could be on the way right now. With poor Maura's death, our parents may not be thinking clearly enough to send us word. It could be the case?" Anne nodded, but Kate looked doubtful.

Julia persisted with her attempt to cheer them. When Mary rose to leave, she blocked the stairway and would not allow her to pass.

"You must smile before you will be allowed to go forward, girleen." They all laughed together, and even Kate joined in when Mary escaped Julia's barricade and hurried off to finish dressing.

"Joyful thoughts are ordered for you, too, dear sister." Julia turned her attention to Anne. "It will help no one if you are gloomy on your wedding day, and it will please James if you are happy."

Finally, her sisters slipped the dress over Anne's head, and Kate fastened the many covered buttons at the back. Both sisters stood back and exclaimed how beautiful she looked. Kate retrieved the delicate lace veil spread across the bed, and with Julia's help, secured it in Anne's hair and arranged it to her satisfaction.

"I've just heard the carriage roll up outside of the bakery," Julia said. "You must set aside all cares for this one day. Think of your soon-to-be-husband and no one else. Do you promise?"

"I promise." Touched by the growing maturity and wisdom of Julia, Anne agreed. Her dear sister was right, and she meant to keep her pledge.

They began descending the stairs, attempting to guard the dress from soiling or ripping. Julia walked before her, lifting the front hem. Anne moved carefully down each step, and Kate followed behind, holding up the train. As she made her way to the carriage with her sisters, all grim thoughts of home flew from Anne's mind, replaced with excitement and joy and prayers of thanksgiving.

Anne, Julia, and Kate rode in the carriage with Walter and Mary. The Dempsey girls and Walter's helpers followed behind them. Walter had offered them the bakery wagon, but it was a fine day, and they all preferred the walk. As they proceeded along, friends approached from all streets leading to St. Vincent's. By the time the carriage drew up at church, a crowd had formed, and when Walter helped Anne down, they gathered around her, waving and cheering. Were her eyes deceiving her?

"Praise God. I believe I am back at home," she said. "This little procession brings to mind a village wedding in Blackwater. How grand."

The moment she entered St. Vincent's, the crowd was forgotten. When her eyes adjusted to the candlelight, she could see James standing at the altar with his brother, Ned, Father Burns, and Father Daly. She met his gaze, and she felt their hearts join together as well. At that moment, perfect, blissful joy filled her being.

Finally, everyone settled in the pews on either side of the aisle. Holding Walter's arm, she began to walk toward the front of the church, drawing closer to James with each step. She offered a silent prayer that God would care for this kind and patient man He had chosen for her husband and keep him safe for a long while. She renewed her determination that, for the rest of the day, she would honor her promise to Julia and think only of her dear James.

Anne could hear Mary's sigh of approval, as she walked past her, moving down the long aisle. The Dempsey girls were all smiling, as well. Anne could only think of the beautiful wedding gown as their family dress. It was the combination of Mary's lovely cloth, Kate's design, and everyone's fine handiwork.

The ceremony proceeded, solemn and beautiful. Anne looked into James' eyes, and the elation she experienced seemed to raise her up on wings. As they recited their vows, she felt she may float on her own. When he took her hand and placed his mother's gold ring on her finger, her heart soared. Anne and James promised, before God and the entire congregation of family and friends, to love and honor one another throughout their lives. Standing at the altar, her hand on James' arm, she prayed this perfect, precious happiness she now experienced would spread out to everyone around her.

Organ music filled the church. Anne felt sure it could be heard all the way to the riverfront. For a moment, she allowed herself to wish it could be heard in Blackwater—*no*—she remembered her promise and forced herself to turn her thoughts to her new husband.

Grace's magnificent singing did succeed in drawing Anne's attention. The dear girl's voice sounded more beautiful than she could ever remember. Perhaps everything appeared more striking today.

"She should always sing." Anne heard the not-so-soft whisper of Mary, sitting right behind her. "The music transforms her."

After the ceremony, she and James turned and started down the long aisle together. The wonder of resting her hand on the arm of her husband caused Anne's breath to catch for a moment. She looked out over the faces of her many dear friends who had come to wish her and James well.

After leaving the church, the crowd spilled into the churchyard. Anne and James made their way to the Dempseys' carriage with their friends surrounding them, cheering and clapping and offering good wishes.

Her sisters insisted they would walk beside the carriage with the other girls, while Anne and James rode with the Dempseys. Julia, Kate, and Bridget fell in step with Grace, who was receiving compliments from everyone around her for her fine singing.

"Have you noticed we all look alike?" Anne heard Julia ask as they moved along. The ladies all wore their best dresses, many sewn by the Dempsey girls.

"I have been saving my dress for almost a year," Julia said, "and it still feels out of place. It has certainly taken the city a long time to move away from the gloom of the war years."

The carriage turned into Park Street, and the horse halted, held up momentarily by traffic. "It was my doing," Anne called out to the girls, who were stopped alongside of them. "How foolish I was to suggest we work together on the dresses. Each frock is nearly identical. I should have advised that we divide the cloth and leave everyone to sew on their own."

"We look like dreadful tinker's girls, dressed all the same and dancing around a caravan," Bridget said.

Anne couldn't help but chuckle. "Do you think anyone noticed?"

"Sure, everyone has noticed." Bridget gestured to the crowds hurrying along the streets. "This bright, shiny material stands out against the worn, drab clothing we're accustomed to wearing. Once your wedding day has passed, we may want to hide our finery away until the city regains its footing."

Anne turned to James and they both began to laugh. No problems or worries could touch their happy hearts. Nothing could disturb them today. He placed his arm around her for the entire world to see and drew her attention away from the girls. The traffic moved again, and the carriage rolled ahead. New dresses and old, war and recovery all slipped away for these few moments. She was surely the happiest person in the world. When she placed her hand in his, James smiled at her and gave her a quick hug.

"Now you are my wife, and I will never release you," he whispered.

"A crowd seems to be waiting for us," Anne said, as they approached Dempsey's. People were gathered in the garden, on the porch, and in the street. This wonderful spring day and the long-awaited wedding brought a promise for the future that would not be contained. With everyone emerging from the gloom of the war years and recovering from the long, cold winter, they seemed unable to allow these happy moments to go by.

"It looks as if we will have a wedding party after all," James said.

Eddie and George, still in their wedding clothes, served cider they pulled out from the cellar. After a consultation with Anne, Mary asked Bridget and Grace to slice and serve the huge wedding cake they had all combined their talents to bake.

When the cake had all but disappeared, Mary and Cara moved inside to assist Mrs. Flynn with their supper,

"You and James remain outside and enjoy yourselves," Mary said. They moved among their friends, James holding her arm. They accepted everyone's good wishes and thanked them for staying for the impromptu celebration.

Amid shouts of "health and happiness!" and "long life!" from the crowd surrounding them, Anne also heard "Thanks be to God, the war is over at last!" and "Praise God, peace has finally come!"

By dusk, only the Dempsey regulars and their special guests remained. Anne and James had invited Father Burns, Father Daly, Bridget Rice, and Colonel Scones and his wife, Elizabeth. They had also asked Gus and Tilda, but Gus declined, saying it was a family party. No matter how Anne coaxed him, he would not relent.

"Oh, the dining room has been transformed," Anne said, when they entered the room together. "Mary and the girls would not allow me even a peek until now. With the white linen tablecloths, Mary's best china, and these lovely fresh flowers, it is beautiful!

The meal surpassed any Anne remembered since the beginning of the war. With the wedding cake already consumed, she sent silent thanks to Gus and Tilda for the delicious desserts they had insisted they would contribute.

Throughout the joyous evening, James never did move away from Anne. His hand rested on her waist or her shoulder or her arm when they drank a toast and even while they ate the elaborate wedding meal.

After dinner, another surprise awaited. "I know how you enjoy dancing, Anne," Walter said. He had cleared the old oven room and a tiny ballroom was waiting for her.

"I recognize the musicians, your friends from St. Vincent's," she said to him.

As she and James came through the doorway, the fiddlers struck up a lively tune. James bowed to Anne and she moved into his outstretched arms. As she lifted the hem of her skirt and they stepped out to keep pace with the lively music, everyone gathered around to watch the bride and groom dance together for the first time as husband and wife. She had no chance to catch her breath. The music slowed to the strains of a lovely ballad, and James pulled her close, and they swayed to the melody together.

Then, it came time to go. "Come with us," Julia said.

"But I have given my word," Anne said. "I must concentrate on my husband. I cannot leave him." It took some doing for Julia and Kate to separate Anne from James. She had given her promise, after all. Amid much laughter and juggling, they drew her away from James and they all ran up to the attic room.

She thought her heart could not possibly hold any more joy, but she was mistaken. Her sisters had one more surprise. A new dress and bonnet Kate made for her were spread out carefully on top of the quilt. They giggled when Julia pointed out the freshly sewn undergarments discretely folded at the end of the bed.

"Some lovely lacey-lacey for my pretty sister," Julia sang to her.

"Now do not tease her," Kate pushed her elbow into Julia's side. "It's her wedding day, remember."

"Thank you both. I have never owned anything so pretty. It has been a grand day, and this last surprise is wonderful," she said, as they helped her change into the precious new clothing. What wonderful sisters they were.

Walking from the room and making her way down the steps, Anne became aware that this was the last time she would run the stairs as one of the Dempsey girls. She had little time for sentiment. When she entered the dining room, the fiddlers struck up a grand fanfare and Julia and Kate presented her to her new husband.

She and James joined hands, thanked their hosts and each of their guests, and said one last good-bye. As they moved toward the door, Anne looked back for a moment to see her younger sister dancing with Walter. How tired Kate looks.

Then she remembered her promise and turned her attention to James. Together at last, their arms entwined, they walked the few blocks to their new home.

Chapter Thirty-Two

May, 1866

"Aye, Julia, if you had seen this place six months ago, you would know the marvelous transformation James accomplished here." A week after the wedding, Walter escorted Julia, followed by James and Mary, on an inspection of the house. Anne fell a little behind them. She still could not resist trailing her fingers across the smooth wood of the kitchen table, patting the walls, rubbing out each imaginary spot.

"I did see it," Julia said. "Martin and I came to view it shortly after James found the place. Ah, it sat here in a sorry condition that day. And, I agree with you, Walter, the renovations are grand."

"Even Kate approves," Walter said. "She told me at the wedding she never thought it could be made livable, and she now believes it is beautiful. You can depend on the truth from our Kate, that's sure."

"She apologized to me at the wedding." James led them through the parlor and into the front hallway. "She assured me Anne's fine home made her proud. Since she admitted to her mistake, we must invite her along next time to inspect the inside."

"We did invite her," Walter said. "The poor girl decided to take this free afternoon to rest. She is working to build her business strong enough to support two seamstresses. Since Ellen left the factory and now works with her full time, Kate shoulders the responsibility for them both. Though she seems to find fulfillment in the sewing, she works too hard."

"Kate delights in the growing success of her shop." Mary turned a concerned look toward Anne and Julia. "Still, I worry. She has a slight cold."

"Perhaps, this afternoon of rest will cure her cold," Anne said.

"I'll bring her here to Anne, one day this week," Julia said. "Together, we will convince her to take some time to recover."

"She would surely approve of the work you've done." Walter continued with his narrative. "Notice these floors James refinished, the walls he plastered and then painted this nice shade of green, and the wood trim, restored to a fine dark oak. 'Tis magnificent."

"I myself have not seen this most recent work. I could make no time to come by and help, while we prepared for the wedding." Walter gave the walls in the entryway a careful inspection. "You and Ned have done an excellent job.

"You must come and take a close look at these chandeliers." He called out to Mary and Julia, gesturing toward the fixtures in the parlor and the entryway. "A few weeks ago, grime filled every crevice, and now they have been cleaned and polished and the windows shined to perfection. This once gloomy house now stands bright and cheerful."

"That is Anne's work, James said. "She has been putting a shine to the place since she arrived here."

As they moved on up the stairs, Anne could not push back the pride she felt in James' renovations. Every word of description from Walter, and each bit of praise from the others brought her a thrill. And her esteem for her husband's work continued to grow, as Walter indicated where ceilings and floors had been replaced because of the water damage from the leaky roof. He pointed toward the window James installed in the attic to replace the one that dangled along the outside wall and earned the house Kate's disapproval.

"Your friend could have saved himself a long journey, by patching the roof and repairing the windows." They paused in the second floor hallway, and Walter bent down for a closer inspection of the refinished floors.

"I agree with you," James said, "but Pat determined he must make the move. I pray his boy benefits from the change in climate."

"And, are we not the fortunate ones, to be left with this grand home?" Anne spread her arms wide to take in each bedroom and the long, lovely hallway.

"'Tis the most wonderful house I've ever seen, James," Julia said. "Your renovations are splendid. Even with the bedrooms down the hall as yet unfinished, it all looks magnificent."

Anne felt the warm glow on her face. The work had all been done for her. In her mind, the place represented James' love.

"Do you think it will suit your family, if they deem to come to us?" James turned his question to Julia.

"I believe one of these marvelous blue bedrooms will suit the discerning Cartys of Blackwater."

"What will you do with the attic room?" Walter began to climb the narrow steps that reminded Anne of her former stairway at Dempsey's.

"Father Daly asked us to open the room to a young Irish girl at the mission with no family here and little money. Peggy is thrilled at the prospect of coming to us. She will arrive next week to help Anne with the household chores in exchange for her room and meals and a small sum."

When their company had gone, James carried their new tea tray, a wedding gift from Bridget and her family, out to the porch. Once they settled in together and Anne poured their tea, she retrieved a folded paper from her pocket and handed it to James.

She allowed him a few minutes to read, before she spoke out. "Have I captured the marvel of this place? I tried to describe the wonders of our home so well my family will long to come. I also wish them to know how much you have given me."

"Ah, you've done a fine job of it." He folded the letter and returned it to Anne. "I thank you for your kind words."

She never tired of talking with him about the house. She wished him to know how much she appreciated the magnificent gift he had bestowed upon her. "Our beautiful home will always sparkle." With a grand, wide smile she could not subdue, she had set out each day to clean, dust, and polish with all her might. "I love keeping our beautiful home spotless. I intend to see that it remains as perfect as it was when I arrived here as a bride."

"Take some time to enjoy it. I will never be happy here alone, if you work yourself to the bone and must be carted away to your final rest."

"You know I will not die from the cleaning. I just love this house so, and I am grateful for the work you have done to rebuild it for me. I still cannot believe this place is ours."

"Anne—"

"Please bear with me. You lived here all these many months and worked to create this wonderful home, while I was able to see it on but a few rare occasions." As she talked, Anne looked directly at James. She shivered with joy at the love she found in his eyes. "Once I clean each room, polish each corner, and arrange each small adornment to my satisfaction, I will feel it has become my own."

"I do understand, but I wish you would slow down."

"I will ease my pace."

"I am sure Peggy will be happy to hear it."

James pulled Anne close. "You know, my love, I do believe our years of waiting have been well worth this one week we've spent alone in our own home. With the meals we've taken together and our evenings here on the porch, just the two of us, our sacrifices have been repaid tenfold. When we retire to the bedroom each evening and spend the nights close together in our own fine bed, the years of parting at Dempsey's door have melted from my memory."

"I must confess," Anne looked up at James, "I am grateful for this interval. Being here alone, just you and I, for the few days before Ned returns next week and Peggy arrives, has been wonderful. I've learned more about you in this past week than in all our lives before. I knew you were strong, but I did not realize the comfort and security having your strong arms about me would bring." Though Anne willed herself not to, she blushed.

"I learned how soft you are, my Anne." A few tears escaped and trickled down her cheeks, and he brushed them away. "Since this is the last Sunday we'll have to ourselves," James brought his face down to hers, until their foreheads touched. "Can we not sit here and rest our thoughts on one another for this little while?"

They sat on the porch, their hands touching, and their heads bent close. They talked of their wedding, his position, their plans, and then came back to the house. She would never tire of talking with James, listening to his voice, sharing her thoughts with him. *Thank you, Father in heaven, for this great blessing.*

When the sun disappeared and the mosquitoes joined them on the porch, James put his arm around Anne. A soft smile formed on her lips. Surely the peace and happiness she felt must be shining from her eyes. She wrapped her arms around his waist, and keeping their firm hold on one another, they eased themselves up from the chair. Together, they moved inside to prepare for their early start the next morning.